The Legacy

JANE E. WOOD

GRIGSONPUBLISHING.COM

ISBN: 978-1-7638344-0-8

Published by

Grigson Publishing

Cover design & interior formatting
Mark Thomas / Coverness.com

For my family.

CHAPTER 1

DAY 1 FRIDAY, EARLY OCTOBER

"In one hundred metres, turn left."

Emma slowed her new sedan to turn off the highway and drove up the narrow, well-maintained gravel lane.

"In two hundred metres, you will reach your destination," intoned the car's navigation system.

"New life destination, we hope," Emma said to the black-and-white dog beside her in the passenger seat. She continued driving up the hill, focusing on finding the house. About a hundred metres further on, she saw it.

Emma stopped the car to survey her new home. It was rectangular in shape and made of well-worn weatherboards, showing little evidence of paint. Three chimneys poked out of the rusting corrugated iron roof, and she could see a veranda running across the near side and front of the house. The front windows, facing out over the valley, appeared to be rather unsuccessful attempts at bay windows. The whole house seemed to shout out for attention; it certainly looked unloved. In front of the house and further downhill, she could see what might have once been an orchard. Old, grey-barked trees, with spring blossoms still clinging to their misshapen straggly branches, stood in rows, long, still-green grass banked up around their trunks.

"Looks like we'll have plenty to do, Maxie." Emma happily anticipated painting and renovating the house until it was back in mint condition and whipping the trees back into shape. She needed this, this distraction from the past. Emma sighed and continued up the laneway, turning right into the driveway and stopping the car at the back of the house. They had left Melbourne two hours earlier, and both dog and human were ready to end their journey.

With the engine turned off, she closed her eyes and listened to the quiet. Only the distant sound of a moving tractor penetrated the soft sounds of animals and the light spring breeze moving through the trees.

"We're here, Maxie." She leaned into the passenger seat to release the dog's seat belt.

The dog, on full alert, barked a warning as someone rapped on the driver's window. Heart thumping, Emma turned sharply. A man was standing there, making a winding motion with his hand; she cracked the window.

"Who are you?" she demanded.

Emma looked at him carefully. He was dressed in a navy suit and wore a white open-neck shirt. His sandy-coloured hair and beard were carefully contoured, and the smell of his cologne hit her nostrils even through the barely open window. Obviously someone who spent time and money on his appearance.

"I'm Carson Richardson, we spoke on the phone."

Emma's shoulders relaxed. "Sorry, I didn't expect you to be here." Carson had spoken to her on the phone; he was the solicitor handling her late great-uncle's estate.

"You didn't give me much notice of your arrival, so I was trying to do a bit of clearing and cleaning for you. I've switched the fridge on and bought you some basics as well. I hope that was okay."

"Oh, thank you, that was kind of you. But now I just need to let the dog out of the car and sort out where my furniture is going because the moving van is only about half an hour behind me. Please give me the keys, and you can get on your way."

"Can I help?" queried Carson.

"No, thank you. Maybe in a couple of days when I've got my head around what needs doing…. But I appreciate the offer." Emma didn't want to appear ungrateful.

"I hope you won't be too upset by the state of the house, but like I said, you didn't give me much warning." He held up the keys and then posted them awkwardly through the small opening in the window before walking further along the driveway. He disappeared around the corner of the shed, reappearing in his late model four-wheel drive, and waved as he passed Emma on his way back to the laneway.

Emma pushed her door open and climbed out, stretching the tiredness from her limbs, briefly wondering what else was around the corner of the shed. In her mid-thirties, Emma could have passed for a teenager; her skin was flawless, her figure slim in shorts and a tee shirt. Her chestnut hair, pulled back into a ponytail, added to her youthful appearance. More than once, she'd had to provide her licence to be served alcohol in a hotel, even at age thirty-four. Circling her vehicle, she opened the passenger door to a very grateful dog. Maxie leapt from the car and ran in circles, sniffing everything and investigating her new territory before relieving herself in a spot she deemed suitable.

Emma grabbed the dog's water bowl and bed from the car and headed towards the back door.

"Here goes!" She opened the house's shabby but solid back door and walked into an enclosed veranda, the dog following close behind. Emma was immediately hit by the smell- a mixture of the mustiness that older people seem to carry and sourness from stale or rotting food.

"Carson didn't mention the smell," Emma muttered, pressing her hand to her nose. To her left, she could see what she thought might be the laundry, judging by the sizeable concrete tub sitting hard against the wall. The veranda was mostly empty apart from a kitchen chair and a pair of well-worn gumboots lined up next to the door she had just come through.

"This doesn't look too bad!" she thought, looking around the space. "Needs a good airing, that's for sure, and a sweep, but that's about all."

Emma stepped through the next door and found herself in the kitchen. The polish on her optimism began to slip. The room was decidedly dirty. Heaven knew what it would have looked like if this was the 'after' shot, after Carson's cleaning. Everywhere she looked, surfaces were covered in newspapers, boxes of all sizes, saucepans, empty tins of food and oddments like string and nails. And it was definitely NOT CLEAN! On the sink were dirty plates covered in ants. Possibly left over from her great uncle's last meal here, she pondered. No wonder the house smelt.

"Oh, Maxie, this isn't looking good."

Emma opened the fridge, and true to his word, Carson had filled the shelves with milk, cheese, butter, ham, tomatoes, and apples. But the fridge smelt, and mould was growing on the shelves. Her own fridge was arriving with the removal van, so this wasn't too big a problem, except she wasn't sure she'd be able to bring herself to eat anything that had spent time in the old fridge. Carson's cleaning obviously hadn't extended this far.

Closing her mind and the door on the fridge's contents, Emma headed down the central passageway that led to the front door and the rest of the rooms in the house. She could see two doors on either side of the passage. She opened the first door on her right. Emma stopped short and looked around in horror. How could anyone have actually slept in this room? She could see that there was a bed, a wardrobe and a chest of drawers but everything was covered. There was clothing, shoes and slippers strewn around the floor. Boxes of various sizes and piles of papers covered every surface, including half of the bed.

Emma shut the door, her heart beating faster and her mind struggling to come to terms with the hours of cleaning and sorting that lay ahead of her.

Filled with trepidation, she crossed the passage and opened the door opposite. Her mouth fell open. The mess in this room was incomprehensible; she backed into the passage and slammed the door shut.

"Where on earth am I going to put my furniture when it arrives?" Emma wondered as tears formed in her eyes.

There were two more rooms, and she approached fearfully, the dog at her heels.

Emma stood in front of the next door on the right, took a deep breath and thrust it open.

"Maxie, look at this." She let go of the breath she'd been holding. This room contained only an old wardrobe and, apart from thick layers of dust, little else. Emma crossed the floor to the wardrobe, opened the doors and was pleased to find it empty. She sniffed; there was nothing unpleasant about its smell either.

"I can probably use this," she thought. "It'll save me buying one, for now." Emma crossed the room to look out the grimy windows. There were three windows arranged in a sort of bay shape. Emma wiped her hand over the glass's surface and looked through the hole she had made in the dirt. When these windows were clean, she would have a fabulous view of the valley and the forests climbing the hills on the other side.

"We'll sleep in here, Maxie. This will be our bedroom!" She reached out and stroked the head of the unsettled animal. Maxie was anxious in these unfamiliar surroundings but was soothed by Emma's nearness.

Crossing her fingers, Emma crossed the passageway to view the last room. Another surprise. It, too, held very little in the way of rubbish. An old sofa sat in front of a bay-shaped window, and a TV from the last century stood on the small coffee table. Her breathing had slowed a little after seeing these last two rooms, but she was still reeling from what she had seen earlier.

"Well, Maxie, we'll make this the lounge room." Feeling a little more cheerful, Emma headed back into the passageway. Maxie looked at her expectantly.

"What's up? It's not food time yet!"

Emma groaned. "Oh, you poor thing. I've forgotten to give you any water. I am sorry, Maxie. This has just been so much worse than I'd expected. I didn't think."

Emma headed off to rectify the problem, wondering how bad the place had looked before Carson had done some cleaning.

"And," she asked herself, "what did he actually do?"

Emma filled the dog's water bowl from the sink in the kitchen, relieved to find that the water ran clear. She placed the bowl on the back veranda floor, much to the dog's relief.

"Maxie, we have to find the bathroom. I hope the toilet isn't outside!"

Emma returned to the kitchen and was decidedly pleased to find the bathroom, including a toilet, was in the small room that led off the kitchen. Her relief was short-lived when she realised how dirty every element of the bathroom was.

"We might have to start in here, Maxie. I am going to need a bath after tackling the dirt in this place. So, Maxie, first the toilet. I reckon that's the most important for me, then the bath and basin. My bedroom after that. Everything else can wait."

Emma was about to head out to the car to collect her cleaning products when she heard the sound of a truck lumbering up the hill, so she went out the back door to meet it.

The van was preceded by a grey four-wheel drive. The vehicle slowed as it passed the end of her driveway, and the occupants waved a greeting. Emma thought she could make out a man and woman in the front seats and two children in the back. Her neighbours, she wondered.

The large truck turned into the driveway and pulled up beside her. Maxie hid behind Emma's legs as the moving men alighted the truck, waved a greeting and asked where she wanted the furniture. She pointed at the back door, and they headed inside the house. The men had been very cheerful when loading her furniture back in Melbourne. However, after one trip inside, their eyes were full of sympathy, and their noses wrinkled against the smell.

"Are you sure you want us to unload your stuff? This place is a disgrace!" the older man's voice was full of concern.

"It's certainly worse than I had expected, but I am sure a good clean is all it needs," Emma tried to engender her voice with confidence. The man looked at her sceptically.

"Where do you want to put your things, then? You can't want us to leave anything in that kitchen," the older man shook his head in disbelief.

"Please put the things marked bedroom in the front right room, that includes the suitcases and the bed. The armchairs, coffee table, TV unit, and TV go into the front room on the left, and everything else can go on the enclosed veranda here at the back. Oh, and if it's not too much trouble, please bring the old fridge outside and put mine in its place." Emma hesitated before continuing. "And one last request, if you could possibly drag out the old sofa and TV from the front room on the left, I would be extremely grateful."

The men were very efficient in their unloading, following Emma's instructions, and it didn't take long to bring out the requested items to leave them outside the backdoor. With one last look of sympathy, they were soon on their way. Emma waved them off and trudged dispiritedly back into the veranda. Overwhelmed by the mess, Emma slumped onto one of her own chairs. She held her head in her hands and wept. This had seemed like the perfect solution to her problems. Now, she was anything but sure. Maxie padded over, pushing her dark, wet nose into Emma's hands. Emma stroked the dog's soft head and felt herself calming. It had been love at first sight at the animal shelter when Emma decided the time was right for a dog. The foster carer had told her that Maxie had been poorly treated by her former owner and that Emma would need to be patient with her. She had been prepared to do that, but the two of them had bonded right from that first meeting, and Emma could not imagine her life without Maxie. She was a very intelligent dog, was house-trained within a day and had learnt to obey many commands. But best of all was her devotion to Emma.

"Thanks, Maxie, I'll be okay now." Emma stood up. "The situation is not going to be improved by me feeling sorry for myself, so let's make a start. First off, let's open some windows to let in some fresh air." She went from room to room, opening a window in every one. All of the rooms had sash windows apart from the back veranda, which had louvres. Some were a little stiff when pushing up, but eventually, a fresh breeze flowed through the house.

"Now, Maxie, if I bag up anything with food scraps on it, that should help, too."

Emma went out to her car and rummaged through the boxes until she found scented candles, cleaning products, rubbish bags, gloves, and a vacuum cleaner. There was no point bringing anything else inside until she had dealt with the source of the smell.

Emma donned her rubber gloves and threw everything that had even a hint of food on it into rubbish bags. With the bags outside and the windows open, the odours in the house were becoming more acceptable. The scented candles also helped. She had decided that the bathroom and her bedroom were the two most important projects, so she went into the bathroom and sprayed the bath, basin and toilet with the most potent cleaning solution in her possession. She then dragged the vacuum cleaner to the room she'd nominated as her bedroom.

Entering the room, Emma was both delighted and touched to discover that the very kind, moving men had obviously taken pity on her and assembled her queen-sized bed before leaving. It took her an hour to vacuum every nook and cranny in that room, including reaching up to remove spider webs. Emma found her mop and bucket, washed the floor and wiped any surface that needed it, which was all of them. Leaving the floor to dry, Emma then returned to the bathroom. Donning her rubber gloves again, she first tackled the toilet. She scrubbed and disinfected and scrubbed again. An hour later, the toilet looked like it could be used without risking exposure to some vile disease. Emma then tackled the bath and basin with as much energy as she could still muster and eventually sat back on her haunches to survey the work.

"Now that looks better, doesn't it, Maxie?"

The dog had been keeping her distance, staying well clear of the smell of the bleach, but her tail wagged in agreement. While the bath and basin didn't exactly gleam, they were now a respectable shade of off-white. Washing the floor required Emma to be on her hands and knees, scrubbing away the built-up grime with detergent, a strong brush, and many changes of water. Finally, Emma was happy with what she had achieved. She rested momentarily while waiting for the floor to dry and then went out to the back veranda to find the box labelled 'bathroom', which she carried in and set on the floor. The cupboard there was yet to be cleaned, but Emma couldn't bring herself to tackle that tonight.

"That's enough for today, Maxie, I've had it." It was growing dark, and Emma's rumbling stomach told her it must be time for food. She knew she couldn't face any more cleaning today anyway.

Maxie looked at Emma with an anticipatory wag of her tail.

"Yes, I haven't forgotten, I'll feed you now."

It took Emma a little while to locate the dog food and dinner bowl, but the dog just sat patiently, her tongue lolling in her open mouth.

While the dog ate, Emma located the Esky she had brought with her, stocked with supplies, and retrieved a bottle of wine.

Emma found a tumbler in a box, not a wine glass, but was too tired to care. She slumped back on her chair and relaxed for the first time in months despite the many challenges that now awaited her.

"Cheese and biscuits for dinner tonight, I think, Maxie. I'm too tired to bother with anything else, and I couldn't possibly cook in this filthy kitchen."

Emma carried her scratch meal out the front door to the veranda and was struck immediately by the beauty of the evening; the sun was setting behind the hills opposite, turning the sky all shades from orange to pink to purple. Despite her tiredness, Emma felt at peace. She had dragged one of the old kitchen chairs out with her and now sat on it, enjoying the cheese and biscuits and sipping from her tumbler of wine, with the dog lying at her feet. The quiet of the country was all around her, broken only by the occasional sound of sheep and distant vehicles.

By the time she had eaten, it was dark in the house and, Emma realised, now that she had stopped working, quite cool. She experienced a moment of panic, unsure whether or not the electricity was connected until she remembered that the fridge was working and she had used the vacuum. Switching on her phone light app, Emma re-entered the house, calling for Maxie to follow. She closed and locked the front door behind them and returned to the kitchen. Using the light from her phone, Emma located the switch on the kitchen wall and was relieved when the room flooded with light when she flicked it to the 'on' position.

"Come on, Maxie, let's find all of the light switches."

She walked down the passageway, entering every room to turn on the lights and close out the cool air drifting through the wide-open windows. Neither room on the left had light bulbs.

"I need to start a shopping list, Maxie."

Emma entered the room that she had dubbed her bedroom and groaned. The bed was still not made. She headed to the back veranda and checked the labels on several boxes before she found the one marked 'Bedding'. Back in her room, Emma quickly made up the bed.

"Now for you, Maxie." Emma returned to the kitchen, grabbed Maxie's bed from where she'd left it when she first arrived and carried it to her room.

"What do you reckon, Maxie? Toilet then bed? Come on, I'll take you outside." Emma walked to the back door, looking for a light switch. She opened the door and was pleasantly surprised to see that the area beyond the house was well-lit. The dog raced outside to relieve herself and then scampered back inside.

After a quick wash and brush of her teeth in her now mostly clean bathroom basin, Emma crawled into bed and snuggled under her doona. Moments later, thirty-five kilograms of dog leapt onto the bed and lay down hard against Emma's body.

"Just for tonight, buddy."

CHAPTER 2

DAY 2 SATURDAY

Emma woke early, thanks to the filtered light coming through the dirty but uncovered windows. The dog was still tucked up against her. She lay there contemplating the enormity of what lay ahead to make the place habitable before she got anywhere near renovating. She had expected old; she had expected neglect, but Emma hadn't expected to have to deal with the incredible mess of rubbish and papers that had confronted her. Yes, yesterday's efforts had rendered the bathroom and her bedroom useable, but the kitchen was not. Emma didn't really know where to even start. And those other two rooms! Emma felt tears trickling down her face. Could she do this? Or should she just head back to Melbourne? No, that wasn't an option. All the reasons why she had left the city still existed. There was nothing for her there. She could always head up to Queensland to join her parents in their retirement unit, but she hadn't lived at home since she was eighteen and going home to them seemed like a backward step. There was nothing else for it. She needed to make this house her home.

Her phone rang. It was her mother, Meredith. Emma swallowed hard, trying to force the tears from her voice.

"Hi, Mum."

"Hi Emma, how was the drive? Have you unpacked everything yet? What's the house like? Will you send us some photos?" Emma's mother had no idea of the enormity of what she was asking.

Emma didn't see any point in revealing the actual state of the house.

"No time for photos yet, Mum. I'm too busy. Everything's okay, though. Gotta go now. Ring you soon." And with that, she hung up and let the tears fall. Maxie pushed her face up against Emma's hand, offering comfort the only way she knew how.

"I can do this, Maxie. I know I can." Emma stroked the dog and felt herself calming. "Come on, time to get up." As she made to get out of bed, pain shot across her back, no doubt the result of her previous day's cleaning efforts. She managed to stand and slowly made her way down the passage to the kitchen, Maxie close behind. The dog raced to the back door, and Emma shuffled over to let her out. She wasn't gone long and was back inside looking for her breakfast before Emma had time to fill the kettle for her morning coffee. Maxie fed and her coffee made, she pulled a kitchen chair across the floor to the doorway to the back veranda and sat down, her hands wrapped around the mug. Facing into the kitchen, Emma surveyed the scene. Perhaps she wouldn't feel so overwhelmed if the tasks were broken down. She retrieved a notebook and pen from her handbag and started listing what needed doing by looking around. The stove, sink and fridge all fitted along the wall to her left. The fridge was hers, so that was okay, although she would need to arrange to get rid of the old one. The sink would need scrubbing like the basin in the bathroom, and the stove…. Emma stood up and cast an eye over it. Surprisingly, it wasn't that bad. Perhaps Clive had used the microwave for cooking. It sat on the bench near the stove, and when Emma pressed the button to open its door, she was hit in the face by the smell of a thousand meals. Trying not to dry retch, Emma unplugged the device, grabbed it with both hands and took it outside to join the old fridge.

Back on her chair, Emma turned her attention to the old wood-fired range. Its appearance suggested a prolonged lack of use. Still, she thought it could be a future project to help keep the house warm in winter, which, fortunately, was many months away. On the wall opposite was a large dresser covered in papers, crockery and tools. To her right, and sitting in the middle of the room, was a table surrounded by the other five chairs, and beyond that, under the window, was another storage cabinet. All of them had stuff sitting on them. Emma listed the jobs she would need to do and wondered about hiring a skip as there seemed to be so much rubbish, given that she hadn't even started on the other two rooms. She could ask Carson about that.

Coffee drank, Emma checked the cupboards in the dressers. What a surprise! The one opposite her contained a dinner set. Emma carefully took hold of a plate. The pattern was beautiful… a peacock spread its tail in the middle of the plate, and small pink roses, gloriously entwined with emerald green leaves, formed the border. Emma counted the plates and bowls. There appeared to be a full complement. "This must have been the 'good' set," she told Maxie, who was watching her every move. "It's really beautiful and probably very old."

Emma moved on to the other cabinet, which contained crockery and cutlery. Still, its less-than-spectacular appearance said this was for everyday use. This was where she would store her own crockery, she decided. Uncle Clive's things would be sorted into a 'keep' pile, a 'rubbish' pile and a 'donate' pile.

Very relieved neither dresser contained actual rubbish to sort through, Emma felt less panicked by what lay ahead to make the kitchen useable.

"I need to eat first," she told the dog. Emma had emptied the contents of the Esky into her fridge before bed the previous night. Hence, the milk for her cereal was refreshingly cold.

Hunger assuaged, work clothes donned, Emma began. Reasoning that the sink and stove were the most important, she got to work. Two hours later, both utilities were in clean, working order. Another hour was spent in the cupboards under the sink. She found chemicals under there that she was sure had been banned many years previously, so she very carefully stacked these into a box for safe disposal.

By four o'clock, the kitchen looked a different beast than in the morning. Emma had sorted the various items that had covered the floor, table and dressers into recyclables, keep and rubbish. Mixed up in the newspapers and farming magazines were documents that appeared connected to running the farm. Many dated back over ten years, but Emma thought she should check with Carson before adding them to the recycling pile. The separate piles still sat in the kitchen, but Emma reasoned it was fine until she found out where to put it all.

"I think I've earned a glass of wine," she told the dog. Emma was just about to pour her reward when a vehicle could be heard coming down the driveway.

Emma stepped outside in time to see the same grey four-wheel drive ute that had driven past the previous day. A tall, well-built man about her age opened the driver's door and stepped out. He was dressed in jeans and a smartly pressed long-sleeved business shirt. His black hair hung in curls around his tanned face, and he wore a beautiful, welcoming smile. He strode towards her, hand outstretched in greeting.

"Hi, I'm Ben Arnold. My family own the farm next door. The house is a bit further up the hill. I should introduce myself and tell you about the sheep." Ben was a very attractive man; she couldn't help noting. His black hair and blue eyes reminded her of her father, who had the same colouring.

"Hi, I'm Emma, and this is Maxie." The dog was standing firmly between them. "And what about the sheep? They're not mine, are they?" Nightmare images of her wrangling sheep flashed through her mind.

"That's what I came to tell you. Clive had to stop farming a few years back when he was diagnosed with dementia. He was a stubborn old bugger and wouldn't move from here, but he was switched on enough to know he couldn't keep up with looking after the animals. He sold me his sheep, and I leased his land."

"The dementia would explain the state of the house then," Emma held up her dirty hands. "I was just about to have a glass of wine. Would you like to come in?"

"No, thanks, another time. I'm just on my way to a dinner meeting in Winsthorpe." With a quick wave, he climbed back into his vehicle and reversed back to the laneway.

"Shame he's already taken," she told Maxie on her way back inside to pour that glass of wine.

Ben climbed into his well-worn farm ute, mentally shaking his head. He knew he'd only been as far as the back door but what he could see was a mess, and that shed! Guilt shot through him as he realised he hadn't been a very good neighbour to Clive. If he'd checked on him more often, then maybe the house and shed wouldn't be in that state. Ben had tried to help in the early days of Clive's illness, but his offers were fiercely rejected.

"If I'm honest, I didn't try too hard after my initial offers," thought Ben, regret settling in his stomach. "Maybe I can do a bit for Emma."

"But why," he wondered, "didn't Carson organise professional cleaners to come through the house before Emma landed? Maybe it cost too much, and Emma couldn't afford it. She certainly has a job on her hands. I hope she sticks it out, though; it'd be nice to have a neighbour again."

CHAPTER 3

DAY 3 SUNDAY

The soothing sound of raindrops hitting the metal roof woke Emma. As she lay in bed, enjoying the peace, she decided to phone Carson to ask about the papers and to take up his offer of help. Given his dealings with Clive, he'd know what should be kept. She thought he might be happy to sort through some papers, and then she'd know what to do with them immediately.

Emma had just grabbed her phone when it rang.

"Hi Carson, I was just about to ring you. If you have some time, I'd like to take up your offer to help."

"I've got a couple of hours this morning, so I can come out now if you like."

She was surprised by his quick acquiescence but was glad of his help.

Emma made herself a coffee, took it into the room she assumed had been Clive's bedroom, and surveyed the scene. Sorting the papers seemed like the first place to start, but she decided to wait for Carson so she wouldn't 'double handle' them.

It wasn't long before Emma heard a car coming down the driveway and went out to meet him, Maxie at her side.

With his door only partly open, Carson paused. "Your dog doesn't look too friendly."

Emma looked down at Maxie, standing alert at her feet.

"She's fine, but I'll put her in my bedroom if you're worried." Emma called the dog and headed back into the house.

"Sorry, girl, but I need this man's help," and she shut the bedroom door on the dog.

"Hi Carson, thanks for this," Emma greeted him as he stepped through the back door.

"No problem." Carson was dressed in ironed jeans with a white business shirt open at the neck. Emma wasn't sure a white shirt was the most sensible wear given what they were about to do, but that was his choice.

Emma took Carson into the kitchen to show him the piles of business papers.

"This looks better and certainly smells better than the last time I was here," Carson laughed. "I'll go through these if you like, and you can go on with something else."

Emma left him to it and headed into Clive's bedroom. She decided to take the same approach as she had in the kitchen and started by collecting all of the papers, again dividing them into two piles; one for recycling, the other for Carson to check.

Forty-five minutes later, Carson joined her in the bedroom and tackled the new pile.

"Did you find anything that needed keeping in that lot?" Emma indicated the kitchen with her head.

"Nothing useful. It's all in the recycle pile now."

"Carson, I wanted to ask if my great uncle left me any money. I don't need it or anything, but I just thought I'd ask."

Carson frowned. "What little there was in his bank account was used for his funeral and legal work in finalising his will. So no, sorry, there wasn't anything."

"No problem, I just thought I'd ask." Emma continued collecting the few papers that were left.

By twelve o'clock, all papers from Clive's bedroom were sorted, checked by Carson where necessary, and stacked beside the kitchen pile.

"I reckon I'd better find the recycling bin and get this lot in it." Emma was quite happy with what they had achieved. Still, she was already over spending her days cleaning and sorting, and it was only the third day.

"What about this room?" Carson opened the door of the room opposite. "It's the dining room if my memory is correct."

Emma shook her head vigorously. "No, Carson, I'm over it. I'm going to vacuum and wash the floor in the lounge room, and then I want to unpack my things. I'm already sick of having to dig things out of boxes. I am leaving that room alone until I have done everything else. It will be weeks before I touch it. I want to enjoy this house."

"That sounds like a very good idea."

Emma thought Carson looked relieved. "Don't worry. I won't drag you into any more work until I'm at the checking stage."

"Good to know. Sorry, have to go. Got a meeting in Bendigo in half an hour." Carson headed out the back door.

"Thanks for your help," Emma called after him, wondering if he realised he had dirt smeared across the bottom of his once-white shirt.

An excited Maxie jumped all over Emma when she opened her bedroom door before running to the back door.

"Let's go, Maxie. Let's find the recycling bin and get this stuff out of here."

Emma and Maxie went out to the driveway and looked around. The bins were not in sight.

Emma had avoided the shed opposite the house, fearing that she would find more rubbish to sort. The shed was about twenty metres long and ten metres deep and was constructed of old corrugated cast iron sheeting. Three of the four sides were fully enclosed, and the fourth side, which faced the house, was only closed off on the first and last quarter of its length. The gap in the middle was wide enough for at least two cars, side by side, to enter the shed. Overall, it was big enough to hold at least four vehicles, or it would be if not for the rubbish it contained. Emma sighed as she looked around the scene before her, her worst fears confirmed.

"Ahhh! This can wait until after the dining room. I don't care if it's still like this next year, as long as I can find the bins now! Uncle Clive, did you ever throw anything out?" she spoke through clenched teeth.

It was hot in the shed, and Emma wanted to get in and out quickly. With her eyes adjusted to the dimness, Emma could make out shapes suggestive of bins to her right. Pushing any obstacles aside with her feet and hands, she crossed the few metres of shed floor to find that the shapes were indeed bins. Emma hauled them out by their handles and dragged them into the warm sunlight on the driveway.

Emma determined which was the recycling bin and pulled it to the back door. It was full when the piles from the kitchen and Clive's bedroom had been loaded.

"I'd better find out which day is bin day, Maxie. With all of this stuff to go, I can't afford to miss a collection."

After eating a quick Vegemite sandwich for lunch, Emma decided to first deal with the lounge room, do one final cleaning of her bedroom, the bathroom, and the kitchen, and then unpack some boxes.

Three hours later, Emma surveyed the back veranda floor, noting with great satisfaction that there were only a few boxes to go. One of them contained her sewing machine, which she decided to set up on the back veranda as the natural light filtering through the louvre windows would be great for sewing. Inspired by the sight of it sitting there ready for use, Emma decided that a trip to town to buy material for curtains for the two front rooms was in order. Every room in the house had some sort of window dressings, albeit rather tatty and dirty in most instances, apart from those two. Emma had again been awakened in the early morning because of the lightness in the room despite the filth on the windows.

"Tomorrow, Maxie, we will have a holiday from work! We'll spend the day in town and treat ourselves to lunch. Shop!"

The dog looked up from her position near the back door and barked. This was immediately followed by a knock at the door.

Emma opened it to see Ben standing there. He was dressed in typical farmers' work clothes, unlike the previous day when he'd been dressed for a meeting.

"I didn't hear your car," she peered past him, looking down the driveway.

"No, I walked. It's not very far. Look, I want to apologise to you. I think I might have been abrupt yesterday when I told you about the sheep." Maxie sat at his feet and rolled her head in for a pat.

Ben extended his hand to oblige. "I've got a soft spot for border collies. When we were younger, my father bred and trained them. His working dogs were highly sought after." Ben crouched down and played with the dog's ears. Maxie was in seventh heaven.

"Where did you get her from?" Ben wanted to know.

"Believe it or not, she was a rescue dog. It was love at first sight for me. She's very smart and has been easy to train. I think she wants to please me because I don't hit or scream at her, as I'm led to believe her previous owner did." Emma's face was grim as she remembered the dog's timid skulking behaviour when she first came home with her.

"It's terrible to think of any animal being mistreated, let alone such an intelligent, gentle dog as this one." Ben stood up. "How are you settling in?"

"I'd be lying if I didn't say I was tempted to tell the moving men to turn around and follow them back to Melbourne."

"That bad?" Ben sympathised.

"Oh, it was. Please take my word for it, but I'm starting to get on top of it. These two boxes are the last I need to unpack for now." Emma waved in their direction. "Carson gave me a few hours this morning to sort business papers, which was helpful."

Ben looked incredulous. "Carson? Our lawyer mate Carson Richardson? How much did he charge for that service?"

Emma blanched. "Oh, I thought he was just being friendly. I can't afford to pay him for his time."

Ben frowned. "Sorry, Emma, but the Carson I know doesn't do anything for free unless there's something in it for him."

"How do you know him? Is he from around here?" Emma wanted to know their connection.

"We were at primary school together. Carson always thought he was many rungs higher up the social ladder than the rest of us, being the son of a lawyer. I didn't see much of him for about ten years because he went away to boarding school and then uni. When he came back to work with his father, he made it very clear that we weren't even in the same stratosphere socially."

"Thanks for the heads up. I won't ask Carson for help again in case I get a bill," Emma declared, and they both laughed.

Then Emma announced, "But now that you're here, you can help me."

Ben looked slightly alarmed.

Noting his reaction, Emma reassured him, "Don't worry, it's just information I need. I want to make curtains for the front rooms. Is there a material shop in Winsthorpe? I also want to buy blinds for those rooms."

Smiling, Ben said, "So you haven't been into Winsthorpe yet? It's a nice place, and it does have quite a range of shops. There's an old-fashioned haberdashery shop. It won't have the range you'd get in Melbourne or Bendigo, but you might find something there. Blinds? It is worth trying the hardware store. They might sell ready-made, but the same applies to the range. Anything else?"

Emma nodded, "Yes, what day does the recycling go out?"

Ben walked back along the lane and up his driveway to the machinery shed, where his tractor awaited attention. He organised the equipment needed to change the oil, and as he worked, his thoughts turned to Emma. "She really loves that dog. It's great that she was kind enough to give a mistreated dog a good home. And bonus points because it's a border collie." He smiled at this, but then thoughts of Carson intruded. He was surprised that Carson had offered to help, and then he realised, "What would I know about Carson. I've hardly seen him in years."

Ben frowned at the thought of Carson helping and himself not offering at all.

CHAPTER 4

DAY 4 MONDAY

Emma woke early, as usual, courtesy of the lightness of her room. The weather promised to be fine, judging by the clear blue sky that Emma encountered as she let Maxie out.

Emma showered and dressed in clean shorts and a shirt... she didn't think her grubby work clothes would be acceptable for her first outing to the town.

After feeding herself and Maxie, it was still too early to head off, so Emma spent time in Clive's bedroom, sorting out his clothes. She hoped that there was a local opportunity shop where she could donate the better ones.

At nine o'clock, she loaded herself and Maxie into the car and drove off down the laneway to rejoin the highway she'd travelled along on her first day. Majestic ghost gums stood tall on the road's verge, their white trunks contrasting beautifully with the dark green of the undergrowth. Warning signs advised drivers to be aware of wildlife crossing, and a 'Help for Wildlife" sign gave a phone number in case a car hit an animal.

Twenty minutes later, the navigation system announced that she was entering the town limits, so she slowed the car. As Ben had said, the town was indeed attractive. Shops lined both sides of the street with wide, old-fashioned awnings protecting shoppers from the elements. A line of ancient peppercorn trees graced the median strip that divided the road in two, their huge branches bending low under the weight of their lacy lime-green foliage.

Emma found a parking space that took advantage of these giants' shade and left Maxie in the car with windows wound down.

"Stay here, Maxie, I won't be too long."

Emma walked the length of the shopping strip on the north side of the road and then crossed over and walked along the other side. She was very impressed that the small township had such a variety of stores. There was an IGA supermarket, a pharmacy, a post office, a clothes shop that appeared to carry shoes, a bakery, a butcher's, a takeaway food shop, and a pub. A hardware and produce store was at the far end of the street on the north side. The haberdashery was at the end of the line of shops on the south side, and the colourful window display was most inviting. When Emma pushed open the door, a bell tinkled, alerting the shop assistant. She was busy with another customer, so Emma happily walked amongst the stands laden with a surprising variety of goods. She found the material section and searched for a pattern that would suit her bedroom and the lounge.

Armed with the bolts of cloth, Emma found threads to match and then headed for the counter to pay for her goods.

"Please, can you tell me if there is an opportunity shop in the town?" Emma addressed the sales assistant when their transactions were complete.

"There certainly is. It's run by the local Uniting Church. Head along the street towards the IGA, turn right at the first road you come to, and you can't miss it. The church has a beautiful spire and stained glass windows, and the Op Shop is in the hall right next to it."

After gathering her purchases, Emma thanked the sales assistant and set off, following the directions. As she turned into the side street, Emma realised she would have found the church without directions. It was a most imposing red brick building, a testament to a time when the town's population was no doubt greater than now and the residents more loyal churchgoers. The windows were edged in white bricks, and so were the corners of the spire's base, which stood at the left side. Emma stopped in front of the portico, admiring the heavy wooden doors at either end, which, she assumed, gave access to the church. Above the portico was a stunning circular stained glass window. Emma decided that she would definitely visit the church when she had more time. Just beyond the church was a sign indicating the Op Shop was down the passageway beside the church. Emma made her way down the path and into the shop. An older woman was behind the counter serving a customer, so Emma browsed the shelves. The woman was dressed in jeans and a light sweater, covered by an apron, and her sleeves were pushed up, ready for work. She had a pleasant face and chatted happily with the person she served.

A few minutes later, the customer left, carrying several bags of purchases, and the woman stepped out from behind the counter.

"Can I help you?"

"My name is Emma. I've moved into Clive Cartwright's house, and I'm clearing out his things. I wondered if you would like any of the clothes?" Emma reached out to shake the other woman's hand.

Margaret smiled as their hands met. "Welcome to Winsthorpe, Emma. I'm Margaret Hudson. Good to meet you, and we can take all of his clothes. The good stuff we can sell and the rest can be torn up for rags. The farmers and tradies are always after bags of rags, so bring the lot."

"Thanks, Margaret. That'd be great." Emma's shoulders relaxed at the news.

Then Margaret asked, "So, how was Clive's place? We haven't seen much of him these past few years. I know he had dementia, so I expect it was a bit of a mess."

Emma's bottom lip trembled as she drew in a deep breath.

"That bad, huh?" Margaret's eyes glistened.

"Yes, I was rather shocked. I thought I would just move in and paint a few walls, and it would all be good." Emma smiled grimly. "But I am getting on top of it."

She turned to go. "It was nice to meet you. I'll try to get back this afternoon with the clothes."

Emma returned to the car via the IGA supermarket. She was delighted to be able to buy many of her favourite brands, and the fruit and vegetables that she stacked into her trolley were all very fresh. As she carried her bags to the car, Emma's nose told her something delicious was nearby. She spotted the bakery and headed over to check the window display. Her mouth watered at the smells that drifted out the door, and suddenly, breakfast seemed a long time ago. Emma didn't hesitate to open the door and head inside.

"Can I help you?" asked the young girl behind the counter. A logo embroidered on her pale green uniform identified the bakery as Harry's.

"Everything smells so wonderful. What would you recommend?"

"My favourite is the beef and bacon pie, but my dad reckons the beef and mushroom is the best."

"Your dad's the baker?"

The girl shook her head. "No, my mum is. Her real name is Harriet, but everyone calls her Harry."

Emma considered the recommended options but reckoned she was hungry enough to try both.

Back at the car with her purchases, Emma was greeted by Maxie. The dog shoved her head into Emma's side as she lowered herself into the driver's seat.

Emma sat in her car, greedily devouring the pies, watched by the envious and drooling dog.

"They were the best, Maxie. Sorry, but not for you. Let's get home now."

At the house, the dog alighted the car quickly, anxious for a chance to relieve herself, while Emma unloaded her purchases.

After putting away the groceries in her fridge and now clean cupboards and stacking the curtain material next to her sewing machine, Emma headed into Clive's bedroom. Now she no longer had to sort the clothes, everything was quickly packed into bags to drop at the Op Shop. She did check the pockets for anything interesting, which was a pointless exercise, it turned out.

After a reviving cup of coffee, Emma carried the bags of clothes to the car. Just enough space was left in the vehicle for herself and Maxie by the time she had finished. On her return to the Op Shop, there was no sign of Margaret. Instead, a young woman stood behind the counter.

"Hi, I'm Emma. I spoke to Margaret this morning about bringing in some bags of clothes."

"Nice to meet you, Emma. I'm Amy, Margaret's daughter. She's just left but told me you might be in this afternoon. Where are the clothes? I can give you a hand."

Amy was about Emma's age and was tall and slender. She was dressed in grey, tailored pants and a colourful fitted shirt. Her black hair was pulled back into a ponytail, allowing her beautiful dark features to be fully appreciated.

The two women headed out to the car and grabbed a couple of bags each, with Emma returning for a second load.

As Emma dropped the final bags in the back room, Amy asked, "Mum said you had moved into Clive's old place. Are you planning to live here permanently, and do you play netball?"

"At this stage, yes, I plan to stay here." Amy's eyes lit up. "And yes, I played netball in high school but haven't played since Year 12."

Emma had barely spoken the words before Amy was clapping her hands together.

"Great, we need another player. Our Goal Shooter has broken her ankle and will be out for the season. You can shoot goals, can't you? Or we could make David the Goal Shooter if you can't...." Amy seemed to be talking to herself now.

"Actually, I did play Goal Shooter, but I will definitely be rusty. Year 12 was a long time ago!"

Amy ignored Emma's reservations and continued speaking. "We normally train here in Winsthorpe at the sports centre on Tuesday nights and play matches on Thursdays, but next week, we're training both nights because the new season begins the week after that. We often go to the pub for a meal after training or a game. Any calories we've lost during play are usually put straight back on," Amy laughed.

"Where are the games played then? Are they just in the local area?" Emma didn't want to be driving all over Victoria.

"The team that's the furthest away is about an hour's drive, so not too bad. Anyway, come along on Tuesday and see what you think."

Emma headed for the door, feeling a bit shocked by the speed with which she'd found herself in a team, playing a game she hadn't played in years. "See you then."

Back in the car, Emma headed towards home but caught sight of the hardware store and decided to call in. The store had two shop fronts, and upon entering, Emma realised that the shop was much deeper than the haberdashery. She could see hay bales stacked neatly on each other through the open back door. The front of the shop, Emma noted, was devoted to products that would definitely come under the banner of hardware; screws, tools such as hammers, spades and rakes and motor-driven ones as well. The middle of the shop seemed devoted to home wares (buckets, glassware and cutlery), and at the back of the shop were outdoor settings, umbrellas and storage units. She was delighted to find a stock of ready-made blinds tucked away in a back corner. Still, as Emma hadn't thought to measure up, she was resigned to returning another day. However, she did collect several paint colour charts and a brochure identifying the size and colour range of the blinds.

Twenty minutes later, Emma, nearing home, felt very satisfied with herself for moving all of Clive's clothes out. As she turned the car into the laneway, Emma brought the car to an abrupt stop as a woman wearing jeans and a tee shirt waved her down.

"Can I help you?" Emma wondered what the woman wanted.

"Hi, I'm Libby, your next-door neighbour. We drove past you the day you moved in. I'm sorry I haven't been down to introduce myself before, but my son has been quite sick with tonsillitis. School started today, and I thought he was well enough to go. Poor kids haven't been able to do anything much during the holidays. All been a bit of a fizzer. So they were champing at the bit to get on that bus this morning, and I was happy for them to go. Two weeks spent at home with one sick and the other grizzling because the other one's sick was a bit much." She looked up as the bus came into sight.

"Anyway, how are you settling in? Can I invite myself for a cuppa in the morning after I put them on the bus? It'll be quite early, around 8 o'clock, if that works for you?"

"That time is fine. My dog doesn't believe in sleep-ins."

For the first time, it seemed, Libby noticed the dog. "Oh, she's beautiful. What do you call her?"

"Her name is Maxie, and she is beautiful in terms of looks and disposition. I'll see you tomorrow morning."

Two hours later, Emma sat on the front step of her house, sipping from a glass of wine and cuddling her dog.

"What a day, Maxie. I've cleaned the clothes out of Clive's room, bought the makings for new curtains, found myself in a netball team, and have a visit arranged for the morning." The dog was only interested in accessing her evening meal, so Emma obliged.

A short while later, Emma stood in the doorway of Clive's bedroom, considering what else she needed to do there. Maxie pressed her snout against Emma's leg. "Not a priority, Maxie, but I do want this room to be a guest bedroom. It'll need to wait until I finish the two front rooms. Come on, Maxie, you've had your dinner. Now it's my turn."

CHAPTER 5

DAY 5 TUESDAY

Emma had been up for a couple of hours when the promised visitor knocked on the backdoor just after eight.

"Come in," Emma had been looking forward to meeting another neighbour.

Libby stepped through the back door and into the kitchen. She was very attractive with long black hair and dark brown eyes. Emma thought she looked about her own age but was taller than Emma. She wore practical jeans and a long-sleeved shirt, the sleeves rolled up to her elbow.

Libby looked around the kitchen. "I'm guessing you've been doing quite a bit of cleaning, judging by the overflowing bins outside the door. Clive was always a bit of a hoarder."

"Cleared and cleaned! I'm working on it. Some rooms are pretty good now, but others…." Emma grimaced at the thought of the work that remained to be done.

"I bought materials for curtains for the two front rooms, and I'm going to paint those rooms too. The first of many rooms to paint, and there's still plenty of sorting and clearing to do." Emma opened the door to the untouched dining room.

"Ouch!" Libby surveyed the scene in front of her. "Was it all like this?"

"Some of it but not all. The two front rooms were quite good, dirty but not cluttered with junk and papers." Emma firmly shut the door on the mess in the dining room and headed back to the kitchen, Libby following her.

"Are you ready for that cuppa?"

"Yes, please, milk and no sugar, thanks." Libby sat at the old Baltic pine table. She smoothed her hand over its surface. "Beautiful grain in this wood. I think I remember it."

Emma explained that all of the large pieces of furniture had been Clive's and that all she'd done was clean and polish their surfaces.

"I definitely remember those dressers from when I was younger," Libby mused. "I often visited Clive with my mother and father before I went to uni. But I got married after finishing my degree, and my husband was a city bloke, so I didn't come home that often. What was your connection to Clive, if you don't mind me asking?"

"I'm his great-niece, but I didn't know he existed until I was contacted by Carson's firm, who told me I was his heir. He was my grandfather's brother, but I do not know why they lost contact. My grandfather never mentioned Clive at all."

"So that's a bit of a mystery then. I wonder if anyone around here knows."

"My grandparents are both dead, and my parents didn't know. They were as surprised as I was by Clive's bequest, so there was no help there." Emma frowned as she realised Libby had said her husband was a city bloke. "I'm a bit confused. You said your husband was a city bloke, but I thought Ben was a farmer."

Now it was Libby's turn to look confused. "Ben is a farmer, but he's my brother. My husband was a city bloke, a nurse just like me. Unfortunately, he died about four years ago."

"I'm sorry to hear that." Emma looked embarrassed. "I don't know how I got things so wrong." Seeking to change the topic, Emma asked about the children.

"Are the children I've seen you with yours or Ben's?"

"They're mine. They're twins; Jess and Tim are ten years old. We moved back here after my husband died. Mum and Dad's house is a big old farmhouse, so there was enough room for us all, and they were happy to have their daughter and grandchildren close by. Tell me about your dog. She seems lovely."

Emma was happy to change the subject and to talk about her favourite animal.

"I got her from the RSPCA. Adopting her was life-changing for us both; she's a very special dog."

"Can I pat her?"

Emma nodded, and Libby crouched down to the dog's level, her right hand extended towards the dog. Maxie sniffed and then pushed her head into the outstretched hand.

"She's got you pegged as a dog lover, for sure."

Libby laughed and stood up, "I need to get going; I start work in forty minutes."

"Where do you work?"

"At the Aged Care Home in Winsthorpe. It's been nice to meet you. Do you play netball, by the way?"

"I've already been asked to join Amy's team, so I'm going to training tonight. I haven't played in years, so I don't know how I'll go."

"That's my team. Thank goodness Amy has already snapped you up. Do you want to come with us to training tonight?"

"No, I think I'll take myself because I'm not confident yet about leaving Maxie here by herself, so I'll take her with me."

"Fair enough. See you tonight!"

After Libby left, Emma decided to take Maxie for a walk and explore where her driveway went. So far, she'd only explored to the end of the shed but was curious to see beyond it now that she had dealt with the most urgent jobs at the house. She knew it went at least some distance around the corner, as Carson's car had been parked there on the day she arrived. Maxie trotted beside Emma, happy to be out for a walk. They set off along the driveway, passing what appeared to be stables on the right-hand side, a short distance past the shed. Emma paused briefly to inspect her property, crossing her fingers that they weren't in the same mess as the shed. It didn't help; the stables would not be accommodating a horse any time soon.

31

"Come on, Maxie, let's keep going. I'll just add this mess to the list of things to be done."

The driveway followed the contour of the hill, so it curved first to the left, straightened and then curved left again. About two hundred metres along from the stables, just where the driveway straightened, Emma saw the next building. As she got closer, she saw that the wooden structure had four doors under an open veranda that ran its length. She opened the first door, holding her breath, hoping she wouldn't find more mess.

"This is a very pleasant surprise, Maxie; it's actually tidy, dusty, but tidy." Every room was the same; a bed on either side of the room with a cupboard at the end next to the door and a window on the wall opposite. When she looked inside, the cupboard only contained 2 pillows and 2 blankets, all smelling somewhat musty as if they hadn't been used in a long time.

"Shearers quarters, do you think Maxie? I'll ask Libby or Ben; I'm sure they'll know."

There were two more rooms at either end of the veranda. Emma discovered one was a bathroom and the other was a very basic kitchen.

"None of this smells the best, but at least there's no rubbish. Come on, Maxie, let's keep walking."

They continued another hundred or so metres to what Emma quickly decided was the shearing shed. She walked around, absorbing the ancient ingrained odours of sheep, manure and lanolin, her imagination taking her into the world of the shearer. She wondered how long it was since the shed had been used, knowing that the sheep running on her property belonged to Ben.

Again, the shed was tidy with very little rubbish.

"Perhaps these buildings were too far from the house for Uncle Clive to leave stuff in them. Let's walk to the drive's end, and then we'll head home."

Emma quickly discovered that the drive finished just beyond the shearing shed. There was a turning circle, big enough to easily accommodate a large truck, presumably so the wool could be taken away and sheep collected for market.

Emma spent the remainder of the day washing the walls and woodwork in the two front rooms. She had already decided to paint everything white. However, looking at the white colour chart gave her a headache.

"Who knew there were so many shades of white?" Emma shoved the chart at Maxie, who helpfully just wagged her tail. "Maybe they will have some ideas at the hardware store."

Emma knew that training began at 5:30 pm, so she packed away her buckets and cleaning cloths just before five.

Ten minutes later, Emma was busy securing Maxie into her doggy seat belt on the front passenger seat of her car. As she turned to walk around to the driver's door, Emma saw Carson's car turn into the driveway. She waited for him to stop beside her vehicle.

"I'm sorry, Carson, I'm about to head into Winsthorpe for netball training. Is there anything I can help you with?"

Carson stepped out of his car. He was dressed immaculately, as always.

"I was just calling past to see how you were getting on and if I could help in any way. Are you training at the sports centre?"

Emma told him what she knew, which wasn't much.

Carson was soon back in his car. "I'll check in with you again. Enjoy the training!" He backed down the driveway and was soon out of sight.

Emma opened the driver's door and slid into her seat. "It's alright, Maxie, he's gone." She ruffled the dog's ears and set off in the direction of Winsthorpe. Emma remembered seeing the sports complex, so she had no trouble locating it. As she pulled into the carpark, she saw that her neighbours, Amy from the Op Shop and a few others, were already throwing a netball around between them.

"You stay here, Maxie. You can watch me make a fool of myself from here." Emma wound down all the windows, shut the door behind her and jogged over to join the others.

Amy waved a welcome and proceeded to introduce Emma. Apart from Ben, Libby, and Libby's children, there were six others. It was the first time Emma had actually met the twins.

"Hi Jess, hi Tim, I've seen you driving past my place with your mum and Ben. It's good to meet you."

The children smiled at her and started to speak just as a tall, good-looking man with tousled blond hair approached, draping his arm around Amy's shoulders when he came to stand beside her.

"This is my boyfriend, Steven. That's his sister, Zoe," she pointed out a young woman nearly as tall as her brother and with the same blond colouring, "and that's David, her husband, and finally, this is Maria and Paolo." A very handsome couple with sparkling brown eyes and curly dark hair approached Emma and shook her hand.

"It's nice of you to come and watch training," Emma told Paolo. He looked a little confused and then broke out laughing.

"Amy hasn't told you, has she? This is a mixed team."

"Oh." Emma's already fragile confidence took a tumble. "How does that work?"

"It's easy. There must be at least one male on the court at any time but no more than three; if there are three, there must be one in each third. Otherwise, it's normal netball rules."

Emma rolled her eyes; this certainly wasn't the netball of her high school memories. Amy called everyone around her and directed the team to practise a dodging drill. Emma was teamed up against the very tall and, as it turned out, nimble Steven. Half an hour later, she sat down on the court and begged for a rest.

The practice broke up soon after, and everyone headed for the pub to have dinner.

"Are you coming?" Libby asked.

"I'll just pop in for the one drink. I've got Maxie in the car, and I think she'll rebel if I make her stay in the car for much longer."

Emma hobbled over to her car, opened her door, and carefully lowered herself into the driver's seat. Maxie licked Emma's hand.

"It's okay, girl. I just hurt all over!" Emma grimaced as she leaned forward to push the start button. "Oh, my calves, my thighs, my back!"

Emma drove slowly from the carpark and followed the other cars along the main street to the hotel.

"I promise I won't be long, girl; I just think I need to get to know my team members a little better," Emma addressed the reproachful dog as she stepped out of the car. When Emma entered the bistro, the team had already pulled several tables together, so there was room for them to sit.

On his way to the bar, Ben asked Emma what she wanted to drink, and he returned with a glass of red.

"See what you think of this. It's a shiraz from a local winery."

Emma took a sip and smiled at Ben. "That's lovely."

Emma was content to listen to the conversation around the table. From the good-natured ribbing of each other, it was evident that these people had known each other for a long time, shared history, and enjoyed each other's company.

While orders were taken for second drinks, David turned to Emma. "So what brought you to our part of the country, Emma?"

"My Great Uncle Clive left me his house, so I moved into it."

Zoe joined their conversation. "Are you a country girl or....?"

"City born and bred, but I'm enjoying getting to know the country," Emma smiled at the group sitting at the table and then stood to leave.

"Thanks for inviting me to join the team. I'll see you at training if I can walk by Thursday." The others laughed. "I'm sorry, but my dog is in the car, so I must head home."

Twenty minutes later, she pulled up at her backdoor and promptly let the dog out of the car.

Maxie immediately rushed towards the back door, her nose to the ground.

"Don't you want to go to the toilet, Maxie?" Maxie ran through the back door as soon as Emma opened it, all the while sniffing the ground. Hackles now raised, she continued to run around the kitchen, and up and down the hall. She eventually came to a stop in front of the dining room door. Emma was becoming increasingly agitated at the dog's behaviour.

Holding her breath, Emma pushed open the dining room door, and Maxie rushed in, her hackles raised impossibly higher. The dog continued to run around the room, but Emma could see that there was nothing and no one unexpected in the room. She spoke soothingly to the dog.

"Come on, there's nothing here for you to worry about," and she stroked Maxie's back until the dog's breathing, and her own, returned to normal.

Emma went straight to the back door which she had failed to lock when they arrived home, so unnerved had she been by the dog's antics. Having secured the door, Emma walked through the entire house to check that the doors and windows were all locked. There didn't seem to be anything to account for the dog's strange behaviour.

"I don't know what that was all about, Maxie, but there's no one here but you and me, so how about you settle down. I'll feed you and then have another glass of wine. I think I need one." Her own heartbeat had slowed to a near-normal rate.

Emma poured herself a large glass of white wine and carried it into the lounge room. She looked out through the dirty window and listened. For the first time since her arrival, she found threat in the silence, not solace.

CHAPTER 6

DAY 6 WEDNESDAY

Emma had found it difficult to sleep, the dog's actions of the night before having unsettled her usually calm self, and her muscles ached. Last night, looking out through the dirty glass made her think that an intruder might also be able to see into the house, so Emma decided that curtain-making was more important than painting.

With her sore muscles objecting, Emma dragged the material onto the veranda floor and spread it out. Her choice of material impressed her; it was a soft, muted grey with threads of gold, silver and red running through it randomly from top to bottom. Emma proceeded to measure and cut curtains for her bedroom and lounge room windows. After last night, she also measured every window for roller blinds.

She was about to start sewing when there was a knock at the back door. Emma was pleased to see Libby and invited her in for a coffee.

Emma related Maxie's behaviour of the previous night when they were settled in the kitchen with their drinks.

"That does seem odd. Does she usually behave like that?" Libby's brow wrinkled.

"No, that was what was so unnerving about it. I walked through the house but couldn't see anything that might account for her actions. I must admit that I felt a little less safe last night."

"You do have locks on all the doors, don't you?"

Emma nodded.

"I will give you my mobile number and Ben's, too, in case you need us, but I don't expect you to have anything to worry about. Nothing happens around here." Libby took a sip of her coffee. "Hmm, delicious! Thanks for the coffee, but I did come to ask how you pulled up after training. I know you found it tough going. And I came to ask if you like horse riding?"

Emma laughed, "I did find it difficult to get out of bed this morning, that's for sure. I'm not sure what hurt the most; my body or my pride. I know I haven't played netball for a long time, but I didn't expect to be quite that rusty. I think my horse riding skills will have suffered the same way."

Libby smiled, "I have a very calm mare who rarely moves faster than a walk unless food is involved, so you could ride her."

"Thank you for the offer. I need to get these curtains made and, I hope, blinds up before I can do that, but perhaps next week?"

"Hand me your phone, Emma, and I'll add our contact details." That task completed, Libby rinsed her coffee mug in the sink and headed to the back door.

"Don't forget, you can call me or Ben if you're worried. And let me know about horse riding. See you tomorrow night at training? Do you want to come with us?"

"No, I think I will bring Maxie with me; she's still getting used to her new surroundings, so I'll make my own way."

Emma carried the now ready-to-sew curtains to the machine and edged the sides and top, attaching clip rings to the top. She left the hems to do at a later date.

When the curtains were ready to hang. Emma dragged the step ladder to her bedroom, climbed it armed with her drill and began the task of installing the curtain rod above the windows. An hour later, she had successfully installed her bedroom curtains. Emma breathed a deep sigh. She knew she'd feel more secure tonight now that her bedroom windows, in particular, were covered.

The lounge room ones were next, which Emma installed faster as she knew exactly what to do.

Emma stood in the passageway between the two rooms and admired her handiwork.

"How much better is that, Maxie?" The dog wasn't even looking at the curtains; she was in the laundry, facing her biscuit bin, more interested in the prospect of dinner.

"Okay, dinner time it is." The dog scampered in front of Emma to her bowl. With the dog fed, Emma turned her attention to the refrigerator. None of its contents inspired her.

"I'm too tired to cook, Maxie. A cheese toasty will do."

Emma took her dinner and a glass of wine into the lounge room, admired her curtains again, turned on the television and sat down for the first time in many hours. "How am I going to train tomorrow night?" Maxie just looked at Emma and snuggled up against her leg.

It was dark when Emma awoke several hours later. Maxie was dancing around the floor, barking at the ceiling. Maxie's volume increased at the sound of small feet running across the corrugated iron roof.

"Just possums, Maxie. Nothing to worry about." Emma had grown up in an old Californian bungalow in the inner city, so she was all too familiar with the sounds of night-time possum activity. The only surprise was that the possum antics had taken a week to disturb them both.

"Come on, mate, bedtime." The dog followed her to the bedroom but sat staring at the ceiling until all sounds of the possums had ceased.

CHAPTER 7

DAY 7 THURSDAY

Emma woke to wet, warm dog breath that was heating her face. She attempted to roll away from Maxie, but the pain in her back stopped her. Instead, she grabbed her phone and checked the time. It was ten o'clock.

"Oh, Maxie, you must be starving." The dog's eyes were large and soulful. Emma moved to the side of the bed and then stood up. "Ouch! And just think, Maxie, I have to go to training tonight. I'm not sure I can walk, let alone run."

Emma shuffled to the veranda, opened the back door to a grateful dog and then put a bowl of dog biscuits on the floor.

She decided that a day spent painting would soothe her, so shortly after her morning coffee and a long hot shower, Emma and Maxie set off for the hardware shop to buy paint.

As she had hoped, the shop assistant was able to advise on paint choices, and Emma also left her with the measurements of the blinds to order. She was soon back home, ready to tackle the lounge room and her bedroom. The first task was to take down the lounge room curtains as she certainly didn't want her new curtains splashed with paint.

Three hours later, Emma completed all the brushwork in the lounge room before rolling the walls. She was about to eat a very late lunch when there was a knock at the back door. Ben was standing there, dressed in jeans and a long-sleeved shirt, ready for work.

"Hi Ben, it's good to see you." And she meant it.

"Libby told me what happened with Maxie after netball training the other night. I wondered if you needed any help making the house more secure if you're still worried."

"Thanks, Ben. Come in. I must admit I was rattled by Maxie's behaviour, but I'm sure there's nothing to worry about. Mind you, I did sleep much better last night, now that I have curtains on my bedroom window."

Ben followed her down the hall to the front rooms.

They walked into the bedroom, where the curtains were still hanging. Ben admired her work and then glanced into the lounge room, noticing the paintwork.

"Impressive," remarked Ben, "I'm a dab hand at painting, so if you have another roller…"

"Thanks, I would appreciate that, but only if you've got time. I was just about to have a late lunch if you'd like to join me."

"No thanks, I eat at normal times!" he laughed. "But give me the roller and paint, and I can do an hour for you now."

Emma quickly made a Vegemite sandwich and returned to the lounge. Ben had already started rolling the wall with the bay windows.

"Thanks for this. I know you must have plenty of farm work to be doing, but my arms and I appreciate what you're doing."

Ben smiled at her over his shoulder as he continued with the painting. The room appeared lighter and brighter with every length of paint.

"I don't think you'll be doing a second coat tonight, given that we have training in two hours, but hopefully, I will get this wall finished with one coat." He turned back to the wall. Emma couldn't help but admire his muscly arms as he rolled paint from the top of the wall to the bottom and back to the top again. She was grateful for his help.

Soon the one wall was complete with its first coat.

"I'd better be going. Do you want a lift to training?" Ben was heading out the door.

"No thanks, but I appreciate the offer and for the painting. See you soon."

Emma picked up the roller and started on the next wall. An hour later, another wall was finished, and it was nearly time to head to training, so she cleaned the brushes and roller, put up the curtains in the lounge again and headed for the door. She called for Maxie to join her in the car, locked the back door, and they were on their way.

Despite earlier misgivings about her ability to participate, given all the heavy physical work she'd been doing, Emma enjoyed the training session but declined the invitation to join the group for dinner at the pub. She set off for home, satisfied that she'd done better than the first session.

Emma pulled up at the back door of her house and let Maxie out of the car. Immediately, the dog began running around with her nose to the ground in the same startling way she had two nights' previously. Emma watched the dog, rapidly debating whether or not to phone Ben or Libby before entering the house.

"Come on, Emma. Don't be so weak," she chided herself. "There's no monster hiding in the wardrobe."

Taking a deep breath, Emma approached the back door, her stomach clenching with fear despite her brave talk. Emma inserted the key in the lock with a trembling hand, quietly pushed the door open and sent Maxie in first. She stood at the door watching the dog. Just like before, Maxie ran up and down the hall, hackles raised, stopping at the dining room door. Which, Emma realised as she made her way down through the house, was standing open.

Emma's hand shook as she entered the room to turn the light on. Despite her fear, Emma forced herself to look in the room. It was empty. She retreated to the back door, locked it, and then walked slowly through the house, turning on all the lights, even though it wasn't yet dark outside, thanks to daylight saving. Back in the dining room, Maxie was still running around, sniffing and whining. Emma slid into the room along the wall. There was no sign of anyone or anything. Not satisfied, she willed herself to enter the last two rooms, her bedroom and the lounge room. There was no unwelcome visitor, and after a cursory glance around, nothing appeared out of place.

Emma let out a breath she didn't realise she was holding and looked at the dog, slowly calming down.

Emma decided to ask Ben and Libby to call in on their way home from the pub. Hands trembling, she managed to message Ben and sat at the kitchen table to wait, her heart still beating fast.

Ben's farm truck pulled up at the back door thirty minutes later. Emma gratefully opened the door and looked out. With the outdoor lights on, she could see the children half asleep in the back seat.

"What happened?" Libby and Ben wanted to know as they climbed out of the car. Emma relayed the dog's behaviour and concluded with information about the open dining room door.

"Are you sure you didn't leave it open yourself?" Libby suggested.

"No, I never open that door because the mess in there is so terrible. I decided to leave it alone until I had done everything else I wanted to do."

Ben and Libby went around the house, checking all the locks were secured.

"Do you want to sleep at ours tonight?" Libby asked.

"No, I will be alright. I probably overreacted."

"If you don't want to come to ours, why don't you put Maxie out for a pit stop now and then you can lock the door behind us when we go?" Ben was already heading to the back door, Maxie following.

With the dog safely back inside, Ben turned to Emma.

"I will call in first thing in the morning, but if you have any concerns during the night, just ring."

Reassured, Emma said goodnight, locked the door behind her neighbours and headed to her bedroom.

Emma lay awake for hours, starting at every creak and groan that the old house surrendered. But eventually, she fell asleep as the first light of the day peeped around the edges of her newly finished curtains.

CHAPTER 8

DAY 8 FRIDAY

Emma woke to the sound of knocking. She stumbled to the back door and was pleased to see Ben standing there.

"I hope you weren't there for long. I was awake for hours after you left, so waking up was a bit hard. I doubt I've slept more than a couple of hours."

"No problem. I have been thinking about what has happened this week. If someone is getting into your house while you're at training, it must be someone with a key. We know that your Uncle Clive had dementia. He could have given keys to anyone. I think you should contact Carson and tell him what has happened, and then I suggest you phone the mobile locksmith who operates out of Bendigo and get them to come and change your door locks."

"I had been thinking along the same lines because there is no sign at all of anyone actually breaking in. I'll take your advice and make both phone calls this morning."

Ben turned to go. "This really is a lovely place to live. I hope you haven't been put off by this."

Emma shook her head. "I want this to be my home." She looked at Ben for a moment. "Back to painting now, I guess."

Emma rang Carson as soon as she was back inside. He was very sorry to hear about her troubles and assured her that, as far as he knew, no one had keys apart from her.

"Do you think it could just be that you're getting used to the place? You know, you're a city girl with a city dog. Maybe it's just all too new for you both."

Emma felt reassured by Carson's possible explanation for a moment until she remembered that Maxie was not a city dog; she had grown up on a farm.

Emma's next phone call was to the locksmith in Bendigo, who was fortunately available after lunch. She knew she would feel better when the locks were changed. Emma decided to leave a spare with Ben and Libby in case she ever needed them to feed Maxie for her, but she didn't think she needed to give a key to anyone else. Having organised the lock change, Emma brewed a mug of coffee and took it to sit on the front veranda to admire the view. Sitting under the corrugated roofline, listening to the birds squabbling in the trees further down the paddock, was very calming.

Emma was tired but thought painting her bedroom would give her more satisfaction than finishing the lounge room. Donning her painting clothes, she dragged the drop sheets across the hall into her room, spread them out and took down the curtains.

Maxie settled down near Emma's bed and prepared to sleep while the work continued. As she had started work quite early, the brushwork was finished by lunchtime. Emma was certainly hungry, and so apparently was Maxie, as she drooled at the sight of the bread and ham coming out of the fridge.

"Here you are, you spoiled dog." Maxie gulped down the small pieces of meat thrown at her.

A knock on the back door announced the arrival of the locksmith. He introduced himself as Ivan, and Emma showed him the door locks she wanted to change.

"Would you like a deadlock fixed to the doors and an ordinary lock?"

When Emma agreed, Ivan returned to his truck, bringing back the extra locks.

"You know you don't use deadlocks when you're inside, don't you?" Emma nodded, and shortly afterwards, the locksmith packed up his gear, handed Emma three sets of keys, and left.

"Back to it, Maxie."

The black and white dog looked at her and followed her into the bedroom. By the end of the day, Emma had applied one coat to the four walls and the ceiling; the woodwork she was leaving at this stage.

After she had cleaned up, Emma stood in the hall between the two rooms and admired her handiwork. She had undoubtedly achieved a great deal, but she also knew much more awaited her.

"Well, Maxie, it certainly looks better than a week ago, that's for sure."

Emma rehung her bedroom curtains, knowing she didn't have enough time to do a second coat, but looked forward to completing her bedroom the next day.

"I'm going to sleep better tonight, Maxie. I am so tired, and now I know no one can get into the house." The dog yawned. "Is my conversation that boring, Maxie? You can't be tired. You slept very well last night if that snoring I could hear was you." With that, the dog took herself to bed. "Great idea, Maxie," and she followed Maxie's lead.

CHAPTER 9

DAY 9 SATURDAY

Emma was up early, wanting to make a start on the painting, so after a quick breakfast for both herself and Maxie, she got to work.

By lunchtime, her bedroom had received a second coat on the walls and ceiling and looked bright and light. Emma was sitting at the kitchen table enjoying a revitalising cup of black coffee and a salad sandwich when she heard a car drive in. She headed to the backdoor in time to see Carson alighting from his car.

She called the dog, "Maxie, quickly, into the laundry." The dog obeyed, albeit with a definite show of reluctance.

"Hi Emma, how's things going? Any more troubles?" Carson looked his usual well-groomed self in a dark suit, white shirt, and blue tie.

"Everything's fine. Thanks for calling in. I've had the locks changed and deadlocks installed, so if there were any spare sets of keys out there, it's no longer a problem."

"That was a good idea, although I can't really imagine there was a problem in the first place. Did you check with your neighbours if they had spare keys? Surely, they'd be the most likely suspects."

Emma ignored the barb. "Can I help you with anything, Carson? Not that I'm not glad to see you, but I need to get back to my painting."

"No, I was just checking to see if you were okay and see if you wanted help."

"Would you like to do some painting?" Emma knew the answer before she asked, before Carson made it clearer.

"I can't paint in these clothes." He actually looked somewhat horrified at the thought. "I actually meant helping with the papers in the dining room."

"No, the dining room is still bottom of the list. But thanks for the offer. I'll let you know when I'm ready to do that room."

After a few more moments of awkward small talk, Carson climbed back into his car, and Emma released Maxie from the laundry.

"Don't look at me like that." The dog's reproach was obvious. "You don't like him for some reason, so it makes sense to keep you two separate. Come on, back to the painting."

The plan was to give a first coat to the other two walls in the lounge and the ceiling if she had time.

Three and a half hours later, that target was met. Emma cleaned up and then settled for a short break with a cold, icy drink and a handful of biscuits and cheese.

"I shouldn't have stopped, Maxie. I've run out of puff. All that painting today…my arms have had it, and so has my neck. Remind me to never paint a ceiling again after I finish this house. Let's go for a walk."

The dog leapt up and danced around Emma.

"I know, I'm sorry, I haven't been very kind to you, have I? I've neglected your walks very badly this past week. So let's go now."

Emma heaved herself out of the chair she'd much rather stay in, but the dog was now raring to go, so she had no choice. The dog instead looked put out when Emma attached a lead to her collar, but Emma didn't know what they might encounter.

They walked down the driveway to the lane and turned right towards the Arnold's farm. There was no traffic, of course, but plenty of sheep were on either side of the lane. The dog was very excited and ran along with the long lead fully extended. Maxie ran forward and backwards, relishing the new sights, sounds and smells. Around four hundred metres up the hill, they came to the driveway of Ben's family farm. It was lined with mature gum trees whose limbs spread into the adjacent paddocks, providing shade for the animals. She could see sheep grazing the grass or lying around the dam. The day had not been hot enough to send them to the trees along the driveway or those growing in the paddocks. Emma was impressed that the sheep were so well provided for and that Ben's parents and perhaps grandparents had had the foresight to keep native trees for the benefit of the sheep. The native animals that undoubtedly shared the paddocks with the sheep would also be very grateful.

A cluster of mature exotic trees seemed to announce the presence of the house several hundred metres up the driveway.

The two of them continued up the lane, the dog still excited by the newness of her surroundings. They passed more sheep. Emma noticed there were buildings to the right of the house. The furthest from the house was surrounded by small yards, so Emma thought this was likely the shearing shed.

The walk continued. Now Emma could see that crops were growing in the paddocks.

"Could be wheat, Maxie, but I really don't have a clue. I must ask Ben or Libby next time I see them. Come on, I think we've walked far enough."

With that, the two of them turned and retraced their steps.

When they arrived home, they were both thirsty and ready for food.

They sat out on the front veranda, enjoying the evening sunset and the fading warmth of the day. Emma felt herself relax as she watched the trees across the valley change colour while the sun slipped behind the horizon.

"I know I made the right decision to come here, Maxie."

CHAPTER 10

Day 10 Sunday

E mma sat up in bed and stretched her aching arms.

"Nothing else for it, Maxie, have to get on with it." The dog looked expectantly at her owner and headed to the kitchen to await breakfast.

After consuming a fried egg on toast and her mandatory morning coffee, Emma headed to the lounge room. As everything was still set up for the painting from the previous day, she could get on with the work immediately. By three o'clock, Emma was rolling the last section of the final wall, having already finished the ceiling.

"What do you think, Maxie? Looks good, doesn't it?" The dog wagged her tail, in approval, Emma decided. She cleaned up the painting gear and debated which room to paint next. She decided on the hall and dragged the drop sheets and paint out of the lounge and into the hall. After a short break, Emma was back at work washing the walls and ceiling before starting to think about dinner.

Her phone rang. Caller ID showed it was Libby.

"Hi, we're having a barbeque tonight as it's such a nice evening. Would you like to come?"

Emma hesitated momentarily, thinking about what she would do with Maxie. She reasoned that Maxie ought to feel secure in her new surroundings by now, and this could be a short test before she tried leaving her for more extended periods, such as going to training or games.

Emma decided to accept. "That sounds lovely. What can I bring? I don't have any meat, but I can make a salad."

"Don't worry about meat; as long as you eat lamb, there'll be no shortage. And don't worry about anything else besides what you want to drink. See you around six?"

"Yes, great, thanks for asking. See you soon." Emma looked forward to spending time with Ben and Libby; she was enjoying getting to know them.

"Now, Maxie, I'm going out for dinner, and I'm afraid you're not invited. Sorry."

After a quick shower, Emma was dressed and ready to head out the door. Maxie followed her.

"No, sorry, you have to stay here. You'll be quite safe, and I won't be very long. You have to be a big girl now." Emma tried to ignore the sad brown eyes as she left. "Back soon, Maxie."

Emma had decided to walk as it was such a lovely evening. Still, she regretted her decision by the time she walked up the driveway of Ben's and Libby's farm, as she underestimated its length and was tired from all the painting.

It was closer to six thirty by the time she reached the house. Voices could be heard from the back, so she followed the sounds. Emma was surprised to find others from the netball team present; she'd thought she was the only guest. She could see the twins sitting at the table, eating. They waved a greeting at her.

Libby spotted Emma and was soon by her side. "I'm so glad you could come."

"Thanks for asking me. I didn't expect there to be so many here."

"Well, after we rang you, we asked the rest of the team. It was short notice, and not everyone could come, but it will be fun. Maria's on duty, so she's not here."

Emma raised an inquiring eyebrow.

"She's a policewoman, a senior constable, to be precise."

Suitably impressed, Emma looked around. She could see Amy and her boyfriend, Steven, and his sister, Zoe, and her husband, David, but Paolo was not seen; he must have been busy too. They stood under a vine-festooned arbour in a beautifully landscaped courtyard. Bluestone pavers covered the ground, and concrete sleepers created a low wall at its boundary. Above the sleepers were garden beds planted with an array of colourful and scented plants, some cascading over the wall. Although not dark enough to create any effect, decorative lights spiralled down the four pergola support posts. To the rear of the area was a barbeque, and a long table surrounded by chairs sat in the middle. Beyond that, Emma thought she spied a swimming pool.

"This is just beautiful," Emma was very impressed by the setting.

"Mum and Dad always wanted an area like this, but they were always too busy running the farm. When they retired and took off to be grey nomads for a year or so, Ben and I decided to build this to have a surprise for them when they get back."

"I don't know what it looked like before, Libby, but it certainly looks lovely now. What a thoughtful surprise for them. How long have they been gone?"

"About eighteen months. If they like a place, they seem to stay for a couple of weeks. They even stayed for a whole month in Palm Cove, in Queensland. They liked it so much."

"So where are they now?"

"In Perth. I think they might stay for quite a while because there's so much to see, and they won't want to cross the Nullarbor in the middle of summer. I don't expect we'll see them until at least April or May next year. Come on, let's join the others."

Libby led her over to where the rest of the guests stood chatting.

"Hi Emma, good to see you again. How did you pull up after Thursday's training?" Amy wanted to know.

"Well, I was a bit sore, to be truthful."

"I think we all were. We don't play or train over the school holidays, so we'd all had a couple of weeks off. We haven't put you off, though, have we?"

"Not at all, Amy. You'll definitely see me on Tuesday for training."

The others smiled at her response, glad they hadn't lost a potential team member.

"So, how's the house going?" Steven asked. "I hear it was a bit of a mess."

"That's an understatement, but I'm getting there. Certainly a slow job," Emma admitted.

The group was interested in knowing exactly what Emma had been doing.

"Well, I've cleaned all the rooms except one, and I do mean cleaned. You should have seen the state of the bathroom and the kitchen." Emma shuddered as she recalled her first impressions. "I've painted the front two rooms and also made curtains for those rooms."

"Wow! All that in what, a week and a bit? You've certainly been busy," Steven was impressed. "By the way, if you need any plumbing done, I'm your tradie. I'm not trying to drum up business for myself but from what I could see from the lane, your roof and guttering should be inspected."

"Thanks for the info, I'll add that to my list of things that need seeing to."

Their conversation was interrupted by the simultaneous ping on several phones, and members of the group quickly grabbed their devices to check the message. Emma looked at Libby with a raised eyebrow.

"Country Fire Authority, you know C.F.A. Most of the people here are volunteers in the local fire brigade," Libby answered.

The phones were all returned to their owners' pockets.

"Nothing for us to worry about at the moment. The crews further west are on to it. Now, tell us, what made you decide to move here," asked David. "People are often in more of a hurry to leave than to arrive."

"Just after a change, and as my great uncle left me the house, it seemed like too good an opportunity. And you're all still here, so it can't be that bad," Emma laughed.

"No, it's not," David said, the others nodding their agreement. "Zoe and I run a building company, and we used to only work in Bendigo because that's where the work was, but lately, we've been doing some work here. The pandemic has certainly seen a mini population explosion in country areas. I think Melburnians finally realised there's more to Victoria than the city."

This started a discussion about the pros and cons of the increase in population in the area. Everyone seemed to agree that, overall, it was a good thing.

"But we don't want it to get too big, do we?" concluded Ben. "We certainly don't want to lose our small-town feel. Anyway, folks, food's on the table."

Emma found herself sitting next to Amy. After helping themselves to food, Amy turned to Emma, "So what do you do for a living? Are you on holiday or something right now?"

"The 'or something'. I'm on leave until next year. I'm a teacher but decided to take a break this year."

"I'm a teacher too. I teach at the local primary school. I was only working in the Op shop to help Mum during the school holidays. I definitely get the attraction of taking some extra time off; it's pretty exhausting, isn't it? So what have you done this year, then? Travelled the world? Studied?"

"None of the above. I just wanted a rest."

"If you're back on duty next year, where will that be? What school were you at last year? Will you go back there? What grade do you teach, or are you in a specialist role?"

Emma was starting to find Amy's barrage of questions hard to keep up with and a little unnerving.

"I haven't made up my mind about next year yet," muttered Emma, hoping that would put an end to the topic.

No such luck.

"But where were you last year?" Amy persisted.

"I taught at a school in inner Melbourne. I taught the older students."

"Oh, did you? I prefer to teach the younger grades." And Amy launched into a speech on the delights of teaching children in their first years at primary school. Emma could imagine that Amy's vivacious and undoubtedly chatty personality would endear herself to young children.

Ben suddenly filled the empty seat on the other side of her, with a tray of biscuits and hummus in his hands.

"Would you like to try my homemade dip. I know we're eating mains, but I just thought you'd like to try it."

Emma helped herself to the offering. She recognised a diversionary tactic even if Amy did not.

"Did you know Emma was a teacher, Ben? We've got heaps to talk about now." Amy was still full of enthusiasm.

"I thought we banned 'shop talk' at our social gatherings, Amy." Ben frowned at Amy.

"Oops, you're right. I just got excited when I found out she was a teacher, too." Amy turned her attention to her cooling lamb chop.

Emma mouthed a thank you to Ben as he stood up from the table. The conversation around the table turned to the upcoming netball season.

"We were beaten in the grand final last season, Emma, so we're looking to improve on that," David told Emma.

"I hope you're not relying on me to be that 'improvement'," Emma laughed.

"Not at all. We're just glad you agreed to play. Anyway folks," David addressed the group, "I've got an early start tomorrow, so we might head off. Been great to see you all. Thanks, Ben and Libby, the food was delicious. See you all on Tuesday night."

Emma took advantage of this to signal that she was also leaving; she was worried about Maxie.

Ben offered to drop Emma off, and she was about to accept when David said he and Zoe could do it as they'd be passing by her driveway anyway on the way back to the highway. Emma felt slightly disappointed; she was enjoying her interactions with Ben and would have liked an opportunity to spend more time with him.

David pulled up at Emma's door and waited while she unlocked it. Both David and Zoe knew about the disturbances at Emma's house, so they waited for her to get inside. Emma struggled to get past Maxie as the dog leapt and twirled in her welcoming excitement. However, Emma immediately sensed nothing was wrong; the dog's behaviour was a normal reaction to being left alone. Emma gave a confident wave to David and Zoe, and they proceeded to back down the driveway.

"Ok, Maxie, you're all right. It wasn't that bad, was it?" The dog seemed to think it was, but she eventually calmed down and went to the back door.

Emma followed and stood there, watching the dog; there were no unsettling antics this time. With Maxie back inside, Emma decided another early night was called for, so they headed for their respective beds.

CHAPTER 11

DAY 11 MONDAY

Emma rewarded her hard work with a trip to Bendigo to purchase rugs for her nearly finished two front rooms. After some online research and breakfast for them both, Maxie was loaded into the car, and they set off.

Emma soon located the shop she sought and, thankfully, a car park in the shade of a gum tree. She knew what size she was looking for, so when the sales assistant approached, Emma told her. Emma was soon poring over the available selection. She found two rugs with colourful modern geometric patterns immediately appealing to her.

They were rolled up and paid for but were too big to fit in her car, so she arranged delivery for the following morning.

Emma headed back towards the car, but her attention was captured by the furniture display in the next shop. She wanted a bookshelf, a sofa for the lounge room, a new wardrobe, and a chest of drawers for her clothes; she was sick of living out of her suitcases and using Clive's old, cramped, slightly unstable wardrobe.

Fifty minutes later, purchases complete and delivery arranged, Emma and Maxie headed back to the house.

After a quick and early lunch, Emma returned to the painting. All she had to do in the two front rooms was paint window surrounds and doors, which was the afternoon's focus. She didn't have time to start painting the hall but was very pleased with how much better both front rooms looked. The arrival of her new purchases the next day was anticipated with much pleasure.

CHAPTER 12

DAY 12 TUESDAY

Emma had barely finished her breakfast when she heard the sound of a truck lumbering up the hill.

It was the rugs being delivered. Not long after that, the furniture arrived. In both cases, the purchases were obligingly taken to their new destination.

Later, Emma stood in the doorway of the lounge room.

"How good does it look now, Maxie? I should have taken more 'before' and 'after' photos. I can't take any more 'before', but I can take the 'after' and I'll send them to Mum. It'll stop her worrying that I'm living in a rat's nest." Emma grabbed her phone, took the photos and sent them off. Her mum came back almost instantly with a thumbs-up emoji and a message to say she would ring later. Emma looked forward to setting her books up on the new shelves.

"Just need the new blinds up, and it'll all be done. I can't wait. No need to ask what you think about the rug, seeing you've been lying on it since it was unrolled!" The dog wagged her approval but didn't leave the comfort of the new floor covering.

Crossing the hall to her bedroom, Emma set about unpacking her suitcases into the set of drawers and transferring her hanging clothes from Clive's old wardrobe to the new one. Emma rolled the new rug out beside her bed and then stood to admire the effect. She had chosen well. The dog trotted out of the lounge room and tested out the bedroom rug; it obviously met with her approval as she lay on it and promptly went to sleep.

"Now I just need to get the old wardrobe out of here. Perhaps Ben can help with that next time he calls in."

Emma spent the afternoon doing the brushwork in the hall. When her phone rang at about 4:30 pm, it was Libby.

"Would you like to come to training with us tonight; we're coming straight home."

"Thanks, yes. Maxie was happy to see me home on Sunday night, but she managed to do it on her own. So, yes, I feel I can leave her. See you around five?"

Emma cleaned up her painting equipment and readied herself for training. When she heard the car coming down the driveway, she turned to Maxie. "I'm going to leave you here, Maxie. You'll be ok." The dog looked crestfallen when she realised that Emma was again leaving her behind.

Emma climbed into the four-wheeled drive, cheerfully greeting her neighbours, and they headed off to training.

"Have you had any further strange behaviour from your dog since you changed the locks," Libby asked.

"No, I haven't. I don't even know if I needed to do it. There's no proof that anyone was actually inside the house. Certainly, nothing seemed to be disturbed or taken."

"And really, you have to ask why? Why would anyone enter your house anyway if nothing was taken? It doesn't make any sense," Ben added his doubts.

"Anyway, the extra security does make me feel safer, so it wasn't a waste of money," Emma concluded.

They arrived at the training court to be greeted cheerfully by the others. Emma was becoming more comfortable around her teammates, especially after Sunday night's barbeque.

Training went well; Emma improved with each session and looked forward to the game on Thursday. She comfortably managed the full hour of activity despite the physical work she'd been doing earlier in the day.

When Libby and Ben dropped Emma at home, she declined their offer to come inside to check everything was okay and headed to the back door. She could hear excited barking coming from behind the door and went in to greet her very indignant dog.

Maxie raced outside to relieve herself but bounded happily back inside, tail wagging profusely. There was no sign of bizarre behaviour from the previous week.

"The change of locks has worked, Maxie," relief evident in Emma's voice.

"Come on, sleep time. I know it's early, but I've had enough for today."

After a quick meal of cheese and bread for Emma and dog biscuits for Maxie, the two headed straight for their beds.

CHAPTER 13

DAY 13 WEDNESDAY

Having gone to bed so early the previous night, Emma and Maxie were awake at first light. Coffee made, Emma headed to the front veranda and sat on the top step, enjoying the dawn chorus coming from the forest as birds either woke to find food or settled to sleep the day through.

"It is really beautiful here, Maxie. I can understand why Clive didn't want to leave."

They sat until the sun was well above the horizon and headed inside for breakfast.

"Let's go for a walk, Maxie. I can get on with the painting when we get back."

On hearing the word 'walk', Maxie leapt up and started excitedly prancing around.

"Come on, let's go."

They walked up the laneway, past the Arnold's farm and over the hill. They were surrounded by sheep in paddocks on either side of the lane. Emma realised that she didn't know where her boundary was and was determined to ask Ben about it. After about half an hour, the dog and owner turned around and retraced their steps.

"So, Maxie, another cup of coffee for me, and then it's back to painting the hall."

Having already done the brushwork the previous day, Emma made good progress with rolling the walls and, after a lunch break, completed a second coat. She was thrilled by how much lighter the front interior of the house looked. Now that it was painted white, she looked forward to moving on to the kitchen. Emma still had to paint the woodwork in the hall, which she knew would take a while, given there were six doorways. Despite that, it all looked so fresh and clean.

CHAPTER 14

DAY 14 THURSDAY

Rising early again, Emma decided to tackle the woodwork in the hall. She sanded where surfaces were rough and filled several chips. It was a quick-drying fill, so by the time she finished washing the wood, it had dried and was ready to paint. The first coat was finished by lunchtime, and she had time to allow the paint to dry and apply a second coat by mid-afternoon. Now that the two front rooms and the hall were finished and she had curtains covering the windows, Emma decided it was time to clean the grime from the glass in the front rooms, starting with those on the outside. It was not an easy job.

"I don't think these windows have ever been cleaned!" Emma grumbled as she changed the water in her bucket for the tenth time in an hour. At first, it seemed all she was doing was smearing mud across the glass, but slowly, the filth disappeared. Eventually, the windows were clean, clean enough to actually see through. Emma marvelled at how much lighter the rooms were from inside, even though she had yet to clean the inside glass.

Later in the day, Emma decided to drive herself to the game because the others were likely heading to the pub for a meal when it was over. She wanted to leave Maxie at the house but wasn't sure how she'd go if she left for that long.

"You stay here, Maxie," Emma patted the dog but pushed her gently away from the back door so she could ease past her unhappy hound. She arrived at the sports complex twenty minutes later and sat in the car briefly to slow her breathing; she was nervous. Her nerves weren't helped when she met her opposition player; he towered over her. Emma's hands were sweating when the whistle blew to start the game. It didn't take her many minutes to realise that height wasn't everything; she was much nimbler than her opposition and faster, too, so she managed to score confidently. The team notched up a win, and Emma was left on the court for most of the game. Her teammates crowded around her at the end of the game.

"Well done, Emma. That was great. The last time we played that team, they beat us by ten goals," Ben enthused.

Libby was excited, too, "It's going to be a great season, Emma. I'm glad Amy nabbed you before anyone else did."

Amy beamed at the praise. "Are you coming to the pub, Emma?"

"Not tonight. Thanks for asking, though."

Emma soon extricated herself from the group amid many cheerful goodbyes and headed home. As she got out of her car, she could hear Maxie barking. She had expected that, but something was different about it, something more strident.

Emma opened the back door, and the dog leapt at her, trembling. Emma went cold. She stroked the dog's head for her comfort as much as the dog's.

"What's the matter, Maxie? Those pesky possums have been on the roof again?" The dog ran off down the hallway, stopped in front of the dining room door and howled. This was not about possums.

Emma could feel her heart beating in her chest.

"What'll I do? Should I call Libby and Ben or open this door?" Emma thought about the other times the dog had carried on at this door. Nobody had been inside then, so why should this be any different? She stopped at the door, put her head against it and listened. No sound came from within. She took a deep breath and slowly opened the door. She reached her hand in to switch on the light and then slammed the door back against the wall, her eyes sweeping the room. No one was there, but her stomach dropped. The window was wide open.

Emma ran across the room, slammed the window shut and secured the latch. Then she rang Ben; she told him what had happened.

"We'll be right there."

Twenty minutes later, the lights of Libby's car lit up Emma's driveway. She went out to meet them, and relief flowed through her. Libby was quickly out of the car, instructing the children to stay put as she and Ben assessed the situation.

"Are you all right?" Libby demanded, ushering Emma inside with her arm wrapped firmly around Emma's shoulder. "Tell us again what happened."

Emma recounted the events from when she pulled up at the back door. Her heart was still beating fast.

"So it's likely Maxie wasn't reacting to possums all those other times, was she?" Ben looked at Emma. "We should call the police."

The police wanted to know if the trespasser was still on the premises and if anyone was hurt. Emma replied negatively to both questions and was informed that a 'Scene of Crime' officer would visit her the next day.

"Come on, Emma, come and sit down. You've had a frightening experience." Ben gave her hand a squeeze. "I'll get the kids out of the car and make us all a hot chocolate."

They sat around the table, Maxie hard against Emma's leg, still panting in her distress. Emma warmed her hands on the hot mug, trying to make sense of what had just happened. The children looked anxious, knowing that someone had broken into her house.

"Will they come to our house next?' Tim grabbed his mother's arm, his eyes wide with alarm.

Libby reassured him and Jess. "I don't think you need to worry. We think the person is looking for something in this house. We don't know what it is, but it's this house they're interested in, not ours."

"Oh, Emma, that's scary. Are you alright?" Jess was very concerned for her family's new friend.

Emma reached out and squeezed Jess's hand. "I'm okay. Thank you for caring."

Jess and Tim nodded.

Emma continued. "This person seems only interested in the dining room if they were actually inside the other times, too. What on earth could be in there that's so desirable?" Emma looked at Libby and Ben.

"You haven't touched that room, have you? No cleaning or sorting?" Ben asked, an idea forming in his mind.

"It was such an incredible mess I just shut the door on it all. I said I'd leave it alone until I'd done everything else." Emma recalled the state of the room on her arrival.

"Then maybe what we have to do is clean it up, sort out the papers and make sure there's nothing in there for your trespasser to want to lay their hands on," Ben suggested.

"You're right," Emma felt better; Ben's plan made sense. "I'll make a start first thing tomorrow."

"I don't start work until 11 in the morning, so I could give you a hand after I drop the kids at the bus stop," Libby offered.

"And I could manage an hour around lunchtime," added Ben.

"Carson has been keen on getting on with that room, so he might give me a hand with that, too. I'll message him in the morning."

"So we have a plan. That's great," Ben's shoulders relaxed at the thought. "Do you want to come back to ours tonight?"

"No, I think I'd prefer to stay here. I don't want to miss the police in case they come extra early. And this person has never broken into the house when I've been home, so I feel quite safe now."

"Good night then, but phone if you're worried." With that, Ben, Libby and the children headed out the door, Jess and Tim dispensing hugs to Emma as they walked past her.

Emma watched them drive back to the laneway before letting Maxie out to relieve herself. Dog back inside, she firmly locked the door. Emma was tempted to use the deadlock but remembered the locksmith's advice.

In bed but wide awake, Emma wondered what could possibly be in that room that was worth breaking into the house, not once, but apparently three times. Had the trespasser found what they were looking for already? Emma started to relax at this thought, but then her eyes flew open. These incidents had only happened when she was away at netball. Who knew that's what she was doing and when?

CHAPTER 15

DAY 15 FRIDAY

Emma was up early, tired after a restless night trying to figure out who knew she was out of the house on Tuesday and Thursday evenings. In her head, Emma attempted to list the people she could think of, but there were too many, so she eventually abandoned this line of thought, knowing she'd get no sleep if she persisted.

Emma made a coffee and, cradling it in her hands, surveyed the dining room's mess.

"I just have to get on with it, Maxie," she sighed. "But I'm finishing this first." And the coffee mug was quickly emptied.

Emma went outside with Maxie close behind her. She dragged the empty recycling bin to the back door and then decided to grab some empty boxes from the shed. Entering it, Emma stared at the mess in front of her. Cleaning this up could be a bigger job than anything she'd already tackled inside the house, she thought. Grabbing the closest boxes, remnants of her moving from Melbourne, she headed back inside.

Emma stood at the dining room door, considering a plan of action. She decided to start with a chair so she'd have somewhere to sit and then tackle the table itself. Dragging out the closest chair from under the table, she commenced sorting. With the chair clear, Emma grabbed the nearest pile of papers. The mammoth task had begun.

Twenty minutes later, Libby called out as she entered the house, "It's me, ready to start work."

Emma poked her head around the dining room door. "In here!"

The two women agreed to sort the papers into piles as Emma had previously done. This reminded Emma to text Carson, and he promptly replied that he'd be over shortly.

Libby started with the mess on the floor next to Emma's chair so that she could clear a path to another seat.

Half an hour later, the women heard Carson's car coming down the driveway.

Emma stood up, calling Maxie to follow, "I'd better put her in my bedroom. She doesn't seem to take to Carson, and the feelings are mutual."

Libby nodded, "I think I'm with Maxie on this."

With the dog safely out of the way, Emma opened the back door to Carson and greeted him warmly.

"Thanks for coming."

"No problem. Does this mean you've completed the rest of the house?"

Emma shook her head.

"So what's prompted the change in plans?" Carson was curious; he knew how adamant Emma had been about leaving the dining room until last. After briefly retelling events over the past few weeks, Carson nodded his understanding. Emma led him to the dining room.

"Hello, Carson." Libby greeted him with none of her usual brightness.

"Hi, Libby. Haven't seen you for ages," Carson put out his hand to shake Libby's, but she pretended not to notice, her eyes fixed firmly on the papers in front of her.

Carson quickly changed his offered handshake into a grab for papers and began sorting. There was little conversation between them, and the papers rapidly disappeared into the recycling bin or were collected into a pile for Carson to vet.

At ten o'clock, Libby stood up. "I have to go; I start work at eleven." With that, she disappeared out the door.

As Emma and Carson worked on, Emma wondered why there was silence between Libby and Carson.

"Do you and Libby not get along?" Emma decided to find out.

"Not really had much to do with each other since primary school." Nothing more was said, so the sorting resumed.

By one o'clock, the table and chairs were clear of the newspapers, papers, advertising brochures, and magazines that had covered them previously.

"Would you like some lunch, Carson?" Emma's stomach reminded her that she hadn't eaten anything since seven.

"No, thank you, I have to head off to a meeting. Just put any papers that you think need checking on the table. I'll call past tomorrow and go through them. We've achieved a lot today. Only the papers in the sideboard are left to do and some piles on the floor."

"Hopefully, Ben and I can get through more this afternoon."

A frown briefly clouded Carson's face at the mention of Ben.

"Well, I'll see you tomorrow." Carson headed out the door, and Emma released Maxie from her confinement.

Ben appeared just as Emma finished her lunch.

"How's it going?" he wanted an update on the sorting.

"Well, you can actually see the table and chairs. I seem to have scored myself a lovely walnut dining setting that appears in good condition. I don't know how old it is, but I'm guessing pretty old 'cos you can't buy furniture like that now. Carson was here for hours. He and Libby hardly said a word to each other. Do you know why that would be?"

Ben frowned, "No, we haven't had much to do with him, like I told you the other day, but I'm sure Carson will get over it. Not much upsets him, or at least that's what my memory would tell me. Anyway, point me toward work, and I'll get started."

Emma took Ben's arm and directed him towards the dining room. He stopped inside the door and stared at the table. The table was rectangular with tapered legs and a drawer at the end nearest to the door. The timber was laid along the length of the table with a border enclosing it all. Arranged around the table were six matching wooden chairs with curved but unadorned backs.

"It's really lovely." Ben ran his hand over the wood. "I didn't realise Clive had anything like this. We only ever sat in the kitchen when we visited. I wonder if it was his parents; it seems unlikely that a man who never married, as far as I know, would have something like this."

"You could be right. Anyway, it is lovely, isn't it? I'm delighted." Emma momentarily considered the table's beauty before her eyes moved from the table to the sideboard. "That's next. If you find anything you're unsure about, stack it on the table; Carson's coming back tomorrow, and he'll check what's there."

An hour later, the floor and the top of the sideboard were clear, leaving only three drawers and two cupboards to be sorted.

"I cannot believe my luck. This matches the table and chairs perfectly. It's beautiful." Emma laughed at her good fortune.

"These are charming pieces. This room will look fabulous when you've waved your decorating wand over it. But I have to go. Sorry, I can't give you more time, but the sheep await!" Ben ruffled Maxie's head as he headed out the door.

Just after Ben left, the police arrived. There were two of them; one young constable and an older woman wearing sergeant's stripes on her arm. Emma explained the situation to them, and they asked to be shown to the dining room.

"And when you got home last night, this window was open, you said." The young man confirmed what Emma had told them. He chatted with his colleague, and they decided to dust the window for fingerprints.

"I'm sorry," the sergeant reported, "but the only prints are on the inside of the window. They are probably yours from when you shut the window last night. But we'll take your fingerprints to make sure that's the case. And you definitely couldn't have left the window open yourself?"

"No, I have left this room alone because it was such a mess."

"It doesn't look messy to me," commented the younger officer.

Frustration tinged Emma's voice, "It doesn't look messy now because my friends have spent most of the day helping me clean it out."

"Well, we'll let you know if we find anything useful. Make sure you keep your doors and windows locked, and phone us if you have any concerns." With that the two officers headed to their car and disappeared down the driveway.

Emma sighed. She knew there was little chance of the police finding anything. She knelt down beside her dog and stroked the lovely soft fur.

"Well, Maxie, at the start of the day, I thought this would take days to sort, but thanks to all the help, I reckon I'll finish this today. So back to it." Emma stood. The dog regarded Emma with her soft brown eyes and settled on the floor, head resting between her paws.

Surprisingly, the cupboards didn't hold much, so were quickly dealt with; the drawers were another matter. It took Emma another hour to deal with the top two drawers.

"Last lot coming up, Maxie, and we'll be done for today." The dog barely lifted her head.

Emma reached into the drawer and pulled out a handful of papers, which were quickly sorted. She returned to the drawer and was surprised to find a thin black booklet. The cover appeared to be made of thick cardboard and was about the size of an A4 sheet. She placed the booklet on the table and opened it.

Emma was looking at an old black-and-white photograph of an attractive young couple; the woman was seated, and the man had his hand protectively on her shoulder. He was dressed in a suit, and she was wearing a long gown and holding a bouquet of flowers. Under the photo was an inscription in beautifully formed handwriting of the date; January 21st 1924. The next photo was of a young baby identified as Clive, and his birthdate was in 1925. Emma wanted to turn the pages quickly, but her fingers were made clumsy by her excitement. She noted that not all photographs had inscriptions, but the final one did. It identified the two young men as Clive and George, her grandfather. Clive was in a suit, and George was in army uniform. It was dated 1944. The pages after this photograph were blank. Emma tried to guess the reason why. Obviously, her grandfather had returned from the war, so that wasn't a reason to stop.

Perhaps the keeper of the album had passed away? Whatever the reason, it was disappointing.

Emma returned to the start. This time, she worked her way through the photos slowly and made sure to read the inscription if there was one. It was obvious that the two boys had been close when they were young as photographs showed them always together, playing games with a nanny goat and little cart, heading off to school together, holding plump little kittens and riding a horse. One photograph had the two boys holding a baby with the inscription 'Clive, George and Louisa, August 1930'. Emma quickly skimmed forward but found no further mention of Louisa. Was she their sister, and why were there no more photos? The album seemed to be creating more mysteries and certainly didn't solve the problem of why she knew nothing about Uncle Clive's existence until he died.

The album had been the last thing in the drawer. Emma returned it to the drawer and surveyed the stack of papers that Carson needed to check. It wasn't very high, so Emma expected it to be dealt with quickly.

Emma surveyed the room, "Well, Maxie, we have a dining room!" The dog looked up at Emma with hopeful eyes. "Okay, I know it's dinner time for both of us."

As Emma closed the room door, she stopped, a cold feeling filling her, when she realised she was no closer to discovering why someone had been so intent on breaking into her dining room.

CHAPTER 16

DAY 16 SATURDAY

Carson messaged Emma first thing in the morning to say he'd be around at half past nine if that suited her. He arrived precisely on time and was, as always, immaculately dressed, his face clean-shaven and hair carefully styled. Leaving Maxie in her bedroom, Emma came out to meet him in her painting clothes.

"Hi Emma, is there much to go through?" Carson wanted to get onto the sorting straight away.

"No, there isn't. Come through." And she led him into the dining room.

"You were right. This won't take long." He made no comment about the beautiful furniture. "Is this the last of the papers?"

"The only other place there are likely to be papers is the shed and maybe the stables, but I reckon tackling that is a long way down the list of things to be done."

Carson nodded his understanding and turned his attention to the small stack of papers on the table.

"Carson, do you know where my great uncle is buried? I think I'd like to pay my respects."

"He's buried in the old Winsthorpe cemetery. It's not used much now, but Clive bought a plot next to his parents years ago, so that's where he is."

"Is it easy to find? I don't remember seeing it?"

"It's out the other side of Winsthorpe, just after you pass the speed de-restriction zone. You turn right up Cemetery Road, and the entrance gate is about five hundred metres up. It should be easy to find his grave 'cos he'd be the only one with a fresh mound of dirt. I can't remember the last time someone was buried there besides Clive."

"Thanks, Carson. I should manage to find him then. Another thing, did you draw up Clive's will?"

"Oh no! That was my father. I think the will was done about ten or twelve years ago when Clive was very much of sound mind."

"Do you think your father would know anything about why Clive left the farm to me? And why I didn't know of his existence?" Emma was anxious to find out and had no answers so far.

"No, I'm sorry, I can't ask him; he died about six years ago." Carson had completed the sorting and was heading towards the back door. "My secretary might have some idea. She worked for my father for many years until he died. I'll let you know if I find anything out. Oh, and that lot," he pointed at the papers he'd just checked, "recycle bin." And he was gone.

Emma decided to wait to hear from Carson before heading to the cemetery. She returned to the dining room and again stood at the door admiring the beautiful furniture. She had planned to move on to painting the kitchen next but now felt she'd like to finish decorating this room. The drop sheets were just in the hall, so they were easily set up. Emma knew she'd have to cover the furniture or move it. She attempted to lift the sideboard away from the wall but was overwhelmed by its weight, so she thought of removing the drawers. The sideboard was still very heavy, but Emma could inch it far enough away from the wall to eventually get in behind it. She then rummaged in her linen supply, found the sheets she liked least, and draped them over the unprotected furniture surfaces.

Emma spent the next couple of hours washing the walls and ceiling while Maxie watched through half-shut eyes. She was finished at lunchtime and gratefully sank onto a chair, with coffee in one hand and sandwich in the other. Maxie eyed the sandwich expectantly.

"No sandwich for you, Maxie. You'll get fat if you eat bread." Emma placed her coffee cup on the sink when she had finished.

"Do you want to go for a walk, Maxie? Those walls have to dry before I can paint." At the word 'walk', the dog sprang up and danced around Emma's feet, nearly tripping her.

"Whoa, Maxie, calm down, or we'll never get out the door!" After another minute of excited jumping, Emma had the lead attached, and they managed to head out.

Their walk followed its usual path, and an hour later, Emma was back painting the dining room walls.

CHAPTER 17

DAY 17 SUNDAY

E mma was still in bed when her phone rang; it was Carson.
"I spoke to my secretary last night. She said she does remember the will being drawn up. She remembers my father expressing his surprise that Clive was leaving the property to you when he'd never mentioned you or any other family, for that matter, in all the years he was my father's client. I'm sorry I can't be more helpful. Anyway, got to go." And with that, Carson hung up.

Emma determined that she would visit Clive's grave, so before starting any work for the day, she bundled Maxie into the car and set off. Carson's instructions proved very easy to follow, and twenty minutes after leaving home, Emma found herself driving up Cemetery Road and through the rusty iron gates that marked the entrance. There was a small carpark where Emma left her car, and clipping an indignant Maxie to her lead, they set off to locate Clive's grave.

The graves appeared to lie in straight lines. Some were marked with legible headstones, and others had headstones leaning at awkward angles with the writing barely discernible. Some graves were carefully tended, and others were barely visible, their headstones obscured by weeds growing through them and around them. Some graves had no markings at all; they were only identifiable as graves because the soil, long covered in grass, was slightly mounded up or, in some cases, sunken. Emma thought it a lonely place, a sad place where the inhabitants seemed to have been discarded; either their loved ones didn't care, or they themselves were dead.

Emma trod carefully, afraid that she might unwittingly stand on a grave. It wasn't until she walked along the third row that she spied the last resting place of Clive Cartwright. His headstone was of black polished marble inscribed in gold lettering. The wording was simple, giving only his name, date of birth, and death. Knowing Clive wanted to be buried with his parents, Emma looked at the graves beside Clive's and realised that the one to his left contained his parents. She struggled to decipher the badly faded writing but eventually identified the names as Henry and Violet Cartwright. When she reached the bottom of the headstone, Emma drew a deep breath. Louisa's name was also inscribed, followed by her age at death: five months. No wonder there was only one photograph of Louisa with the boys. Emma sighed deeply. Sadly, that was one mystery solved.

Back at the house, Emma resumed her painting, hoping to finish the dining room by Tuesday evening.

CHAPTER 18

DAY 19 TUESDAY

After spending almost all of Monday and much of Tuesday painting, Emma nearly achieved her goal; the walls and ceiling were done, but the woodwork was not quite finished. After removing the drop sheets from the furniture, Emma stood at the door of the nearly completed room and cast an eye over her work. She was delighted with the effect but felt the room was missing something. Her eyes fell on the mantelpiece above the fireplace in the corner of the room. This fireplace shared a chimney with the one in the lounge room. She didn't know if the chimneys were in working order; that was something to worry about before next winter and, on this warm spring day, many months away.

"A mirror, that's what it needs, a lovely mirror above the fireplace." Maxie looked up from her resting place at the excitement in Emma's voice. Emma stepped to the lounge room door and decided that a mirror or painting would look great there, too.

"I feel another trip to Bendigo is required, Maxie! We'll go tomorrow. But now it's time to get ready for training."

Emma had just finished cleaning up the painting equipment when her phone rang.

"Hi, Ben."

"Hi Emma, do you want to come to training with us."

"Thank you, I'd like that. I must admit to being a bit anxious about what I might find when I get home tonight."

Ben, Libby and the twins arrived fifteen minutes later. Emma climbed into the back seat and sat beside Jess.

"How's the dining room makeover going?" Ben was keen for an update.

Emma told him of her progress and shared her plans to buy a mirror and a print for the dining and lounge rooms, respectively.

"Can we come and see what you've done to the house?" Jess asked. "Grandma and Grandad have a dining room, too, but nobody uses it; we always eat in the kitchen."

"Of course, you can come and see it. Why don't you call in on your way home from the school bus drop-off tomorrow afternoon?"

Jess looked to her mother for approval. Libby nodded, and Jess clapped her hands. "Cool!"

Training went well; Emma definitely felt she was improving and was satisfied at the end of the session. Jess and Tim entertained themselves by shooting goals on the next court but were glad to join the adults to head home.

Emma felt her insides tightening as they drove down her driveway and was certainly glad Libby and Ben were with her as she opened the back door. Maxie ran out, jumping all over Emma before relieving herself in the grass. When she ran back inside the house, Emma held her breath in anticipation of a reaction that would show someone had been in the house. No such thing occurred. Ben and Libby's tour of the house confirmed all was well. Emma let go of the breath she'd been holding and headed inside as Ben and Libby came out.

"All good. You all right? Do you want us to stay for a while?" Libby's look of concern was appreciated by Emma.

"No, I'm okay. Hopefully, with everything we've done, there'll be no more problems." Emma headed inside, Maxie close beside her.

Libby climbed back into the driver's seat, and the family headed off down the driveway, the children's hands waving at her from the windows.

Emma locked the door behind them and walked into the kitchen. She made a quick salad and sat down to eat it with Maxie at her feet. She had eaten half of it when she had a sudden and unpleasant thought. Was it just a coincidence that there'd been no break-in tonight? Did the intruder know about the added security? Or did the intruder know that the papers were all gone from the dining room? If that was the case, how did they know? Appetite lost, Emma put her plate on the kitchen sink and headed to the bedroom.

CHAPTER 19

Day 20 Wednesday

It was nearly November, so it wasn't surprising that the next day, it was already very warm by nine o'clock when Emma was preparing to go to Bendigo. She decided against taking Maxie in case she couldn't find any shade to park her car. When Emma grabbed her keys and wallet to head out, Maxie trotted along expectantly.

"No, Maxie, it's too hot to take you today." The dog's ears drooped, and she lay down on the mat just inside the back door, looking forlorn.

"I won't be very long, I hope." With that, Emma shut and locked the door and headed to her car.

Emma had decided to return to the same shops she'd bought from on her last visit. She wandered around in the first shop and finally found a beautiful rectangular gold-edged mirror that she knew would look great in the dining room. She didn't find a print she liked, so she headed into the next-door shop. It didn't take her long to find an attractively framed print of a pair of magpies sitting on a barbed wire fence. It reminded her of the birds she could hear around her house.

Back home, having given Maxie a big hug, Emma hung her new purchases in place, albeit with some difficulty, and was delighted that they looked as good in place as they had in her imagination. Now all she had to do to finish the dining room was a little bit of painting around the window.

Emma hoped her new blinds would arrive soon as the old one over the dining room window barely covered the glass and certainly did nothing to add any charm.

A knock at the back door interrupted Emma's painting clean-up. When she opened the door, Jess and Tim stood there, school bags over their shoulders and smiles on their red faces.

"Come in, you look hot," Emma was glad to see them. "Just leave your bags here and go into the kitchen. I'll be with you in a moment."

When Emma arrived in the kitchen, she asked the children, "What about a cold drink and some cookies?" Emma had bought cordial and biscuits when she was shopping in Bendigo.

"Yes, please," they said in unison. While the twins consumed their snacks, Emma studied their appearance. Jess was slightly taller than Tim, but they both had the dark hair and eyes of their mother and uncle. They seemed to be very friendly, confident children if her interactions with them were anything to go by.

When the children had finished their refreshments, Emma invited the twins to walk around the house with her. They were intrigued by the shape of the fireplace in her bedroom,

"Are they all like this? Why is it a triangle? Does it work? Can we light a fire?" Jess was excited at the thought.

Emma laughed, "I don't know if they work, and don't you think it's too hot to find out? I think we'll have to wait until winter."

"But that's ages away," Tim objected.

Emma explained that the fireplaces sat in the corner of the rooms so they could share a chimney; there were five fireplaces, including the one for the kitchen stove, but only three chimneys.

"Can you show us the old furniture in your dining room? Uncle Ben said it was really special," Tim asked.

"Come on then," And Emma showed them the room. Both children seemed to appreciate the beauty of the wood because they stood in the room near the table, touching the surface carefully.

"Have you used it yet?" Jess questioned Emma.

"Well, no, I only just finished this room today. Which reminds me, don't touch the window sill. It's still wet."

"Do you have special plates to use in here?" asked Jess.

"No, I don't...." but then Emma thought of Clive's beautiful setting, decorated with peacocks and rosebuds. "Let's have a look in the kitchen. There might be something."

The twins raced into the kitchen and opened the doors of the two dressers. Jess went to the cupboard that held Clive's special crockery. She crouched down in front of the door, opened it and pulled out a plate decorated with peacocks and rosebuds.

"Look at this one, it's lovely, Emma."

Tim abandoned the search in his cupboards; obviously, Emma's own modern crockery didn't hold his interest.

Tim and Jess carefully pulled out more plates.

"Are these old, like the table and chairs in your dining room?" asked Tim.

"I expect so. They belonged to my great uncle who lived here before me."

"I don't remember meeting him. Mum said he wasn't very well and that we shouldn't bother him," Jess said. She suddenly lifted her chin and looked at Emma thoughtfully. "Are we bothering you?"

"Not at all. It's fun for me to show you my things and what I've done to the house." A look of relief passed over the twins' faces.

"Can we take these plates into the dining room?" asked Tim.

Emma nodded.

"It'd be good to find out what there is. I haven't done that, so let's go." Although not quite true, Emma didn't want to spoil their fun. They set off carrying the crockery slowly, a few pieces at a time, to place on the dining room table.

"Let's stack all the same type of pieces on top of one another, and it will be easier to count," suggested Jess.

When the inventory was complete, Jess and Tim were delighted to find six of most items, although one dinner plate and one cup were missing. There were cups and saucers, bread and butter plates, bowls and two different sizes of dinner plates.

"Why is that? Are the small ones for children?" Tim wondered aloud.

"I think the small ones are for an entrée?" Emma hoped she was right.

"What's an entrée?" asked Jess.

"It's the first course, a small portion of something before the main course."

"I get it. Grandma always serves soup before a roast if she's having visitors. I thought it was just called soup, not entrée."

"An entrée doesn't have to be soup, but it could be. It could also be something like a few prawns or some calamari or savoury mousse."

"We could have a dinner party; there's enough big plates for Mum, Uncle Ben and the three of us. That'd be fun, wouldn't it?" Tim and Jess looked at Emma, their eyes sparkling with anticipation.

Emma thought about it. "We could do that, couldn't we? What about Friday night? You could come here after school and help me. What do you think? Will we ask Mum and Uncle Ben when I take you home?"

"Yes, please. What are we going to cook? We have to have three courses. That's what Grandma does when she has visitors for dinner."

Things were going faster than Emma had anticipated, but then she thought, "Why not?"

Emma went into the lounge room to find her recipe books on the new shelves. When she returned, Jess and Tim had their heads together, talking quietly.

"We want to do invitations for Mum and Uncle Ben; we know how to do them 'cos we had to write invites to our family to come to the school's Open Day back in May. Do you have any nice cardboard?"

"I don't have cardboard, but I do have some pretty notepaper." (One of the standard gifts to teachers at Christmas time.) "I'll have a look for it, and yes, I think that's a really nice idea."

The children pounced on the recipe books while Emma went to find the notepaper. She found some packed into her bookshelf and took it back to the children.

"Find anything you'd like us to cook?"

"Us?"

"Well, we are doing this together, aren't we?"

The smiles on their faces said it all.

"Now, you'd better get those invitations done, or it'll be too late, and I'll have to take you home."

"Do you have any coloured pens or pencils?" Tim asked.

Emma laughed, "I'm a teacher. I've got heaps. I've even got gel pens!"

"Awesome, can we use those?" Jess's face lit up at the thought of using the highly colourful pens.

As soon as Emma set the various writing implements down on the kitchen table, the twins got to work. They did indeed know how to word an invitation, and after decorating them, Tim asked for envelopes.

Emma handed them over, "It's time I took you home, so grab your stuff and let's get going. I'll sort the menu if that's okay, and I'll tell you what I've come up with at the game tomorrow night."

Back at home, Emma fed the dog and herself before sitting down to plan the menu for the dinner party. She wanted to keep it simple so that the children would be able to help her. Knowing the weather was forecast to be very warm on Friday, Emma decided on an entrée of prawn cocktails, a main course of fish, chips and salad, and a Basque cheesecake for dessert. Libby had told her that there was a fish monger in Bendigo that sold fresh seafood, so Emma's plan was to take her ice-filled Esky to Bendigo for Thursday's game and shop before she played.

Decisions made, Emma and Maxie headed to the lounge room to enjoy a movie, Emma from the comfort of her new sofa and the disgruntled dog from the new rug on the floor. Maxie's relegation to the rug didn't stop her from placing an optimistic paw on the soft material of the sofa.

"Not happening, Maxie, not happening."

CHAPTER 20

DAY 21 THURSDAY

Emma decided to start the day with a walk and took a very happy Maxie up the laneway past the Arnold's farm. The excited dog dashed from one side of the laneway to the other, uncovering new smells at every step.

When they arrived home, Emma set about washing the walls in Clive's room. She had planned to do the kitchen next, but now that the dinner party was happening, she'd deferred that. Stepping around wet walls while she cooked was not a good idea.

When the cleaning was finished, it was time to leave for her shopping trip and training. Emma stowed the icepacks she kept in the fridge into the Esky and hugged a disappointed Maxie.

"Sorry, girl, you'd be in the car for too long this time, and it's very warm. Safer for you to stay here."

Emma had directions from Libby as to the location of the fishmonger, so it didn't take her too long to find it. She bought fresh Australian prawns and five beautiful pieces of snapper, all of which she loaded into her Esky. She also made a quick trip to the supermarket to buy everything else she needed for Friday night's dinner before heading to the game.

Emma greeted her team members and was introduced to the opposition. She was undaunted by the size of the man who was to be her opponent; after all, she'd done very well the previous week. She quickly found out that he was tall but, unlike last week's opponent, was also nimble. Emma promptly found herself struggling. At half-time, Amy offered to let her sit out the rest of the game, an offer that was gratefully accepted. It also gave her time to chat with the twins and tell them about her plans for their dinner party.

"I love fish and chips!" Jess was delighted with Emma's menu.

"And so do I," Tim joined in.

The twins and Emma cheered their team on from the sidelines, and when the final quarter ended, their team won by just one goal. Amy had done really well against the opponent who had subdued Emma's efforts.

The team members congratulated each other on the win before separating to go to the local pub for a meal while Emma headed for her car, anxious to get the food in the Esky transferred to the fridge at home.

"See you tomorrow night," Emma called to Ben and Libby as she headed to her car. She stopped beside the twins, who were standing at their mother's car.

"I'll see you two after school," and the twins nodded, excitement showing in their sparkling eyes.

As she drove up the laneway, Emma could see that the sensor lights outside her back door had been activated.

"Those pesky possums, again! Poor Maxie will be beside herself," she thought, bringing the car to a stop. "At least I hope it's possums." She suddenly felt cold despite the warmth of the evening.

She paused before unlocking her car door. Emma looked around cautiously but could see nothing to cause alarm other than the outdoor lights being on.

She climbed out of the car, grabbed the Esky from the boot and headed for the back door. When she opened the door, a panting Maxie flew out, jumping up at Emma, tail wagging furiously.

"Come on, go to the toilet. You must need to go." The dog obliged, but instead of running back inside, she pushed her nose to the ground and ran backwards and forwards from the car to the shed and finally into the shed.

"Come on, Maxie, it's just possums," Emma was reassuring herself as much as the dog. "I want to get inside. I'm hungry, and you must be too." The dog ignored her and continued to run around, tail high in the air and nose still to the ground. Emma shrugged and took herself and the Esky inside, closing and locking the door firmly behind her.

"I'm sure your stomach will bring you inside soon, Maxie." Dropping the Esky in the kitchen, Emma went straight to the dining room, but no windows were open, and nothing was out of place. Emma let out a sigh of relief, but still, she checked the whole house, confirming that all windows and doors were secure.

Emma filled the fridge with her earlier purchases and set about preparing her own meal. The smell of chicken stir fry proved too much for Maxie, and she finally barked at the door to be let in. With the back door locked and the dog fed, her rumbling stomach reminded her she hadn't eaten for many hours, and Emma attacked her meal with enthusiasm. But all the while, Emma wondered what had triggered Maxie's behaviour, and she didn't think it was possums.

CHAPTER 21

DAY 22 FRIDAY

Emma woke filled with happy anticipation of the day and evening ahead. She had decided the previous night to give the house a quick clean with specific attention focused on the dining room. She also planned to set one person's place on the dining table with all the crockery, cutlery and glassware required for the special dinner so that the children would be able to follow her example when they arrived later in the day.

Before she could do anything else, though, she needed to make the cheesecake so that it would last the longest time possible to cool in the fridge.

It was the first time she had actually used the oven, so Emma was filled with trepidation as she placed the dessert into it, but after the prescribed hour, the cake appeared to be cooked.

By lunchtime, Emma had achieved all that she had planned to do in preparation for the evening ahead, so she decided to start painting in Clive's room. She continued until she heard the happy sounds of two excited children arriving.

"Hi Tim and Jess, there's biscuits and juice for your afternoon tea. I'll clean up my painting stuff while you snack."

The children headed straight for Maxie, who had been lying in the hallway outside Clive's room while Emma was painting. She was very pleased to see the children and happily submitted to many pats and cuddles. Eventually, Jess and Tim decided they needed refreshments, so they washed their hands and started on the biscuits and pineapple juice, which was refreshingly cold and straight from the fridge.

Emma shut the door of Clive's room just as the children finished their afternoon tea.

"So, what I need you to do first is set the table." She showed them her example and left them to follow it.

"Come and see what you think," Jess called out about half an hour later.

Emma stood in the doorway of the dining room and surveyed the children's work.

"Wow! Great job, everything is so neat. Do you think we need flowers to decorate the table?"

The children nodded their enthusiasm. "Where will we get flowers? You don't have any growing, do you?" Tim asked.

"No, but I bought a lovely bunch yesterday, so you can choose some from it to go on the table."

Tim and Jess chose three flowers each from the vase on the mantelpiece and took them to the kitchen to cut the stems to fit the small vase that Emma produced for them.

"What about candles?" Jess suggested.

Emma sent her to look in the cupboards in the kitchen in the hope of locating some.

After a few minutes and a victorious yell, Emma knew that the search had been successful.

With the candles placed at either end of the table, the children and Emma admired their handiwork.

"That looks really good, very professional. You two have done a great job." The children beamed their satisfaction.

"What now?" Jess was ready for the next challenge.

"I need you to prepare the salad. We're going to serve the prawn cocktail on a bed of lettuce and with a dressing on it. Then, we need to wash all the ingredients for the salad to go with the fish and chips. Jess, you can do the lettuce and Tim, you're going to make the dressing for the prawns."

Emma showed the children what they needed to do, and they both set about completing their tasks. Emma peeled the prawns and removed the alimentary canal.

"Oh, that's disgusting." Tim was repulsed by the parts of the prawn that Emma was removing.

"Well, you don't eat that bit. That's why I'm taking it out." Emma could tell that Tim was not convinced.

"Don't be such a baby, Tim. I'll eat yours if you don't want them." Jess was not in the least bothered by the mess that was accumulating in front of Emma.

By half past five, everything had been prepared, so Emma sent Tim and Jess to her bedroom to get changed into their party clothes, which Libby had dropped off on her way to work. They were both smiling when they reappeared wearing dark blue denim jeans and short-sleeved tee shirts with colourful designs across their fronts.

"Don't you look smart," Emma complimented the children, and their smiles grew even wider. "Now I just have to get changed, and we'll be all set. Can you look after Maxie for me? She'd like to be fed. Can you do that? Her food's in the laundry."

The dog skipped around the children as they headed through the kitchen. Emma went to her bedroom, slipped off her painting clothes and donned a body-hugging, knee-length green dress that complimented her chestnut hair.

Right on six o'clock, a knock was heard at the back door. Tim raced to open it, and Jess welcomed Libby and Ben inside. They'd both joined in the formalities of the evening and were smartly dressed; Ben in a suit and open-neck shirt and Libby in a navy blue slip dress.

"Please follow us to the dining room," announced Tim, and he and Jess led the way.

Libby stared at the beautifully set and decorated table. "Did you do this? Aren't you clever? I'm so impressed." Her praise was rewarded with huge smiles from the children.

"There's so much cutlery and crockery. I won't know what to use." Ben looked confused, but the wink he gave Emma showed that he was playing up the situation for the benefit of the children.

"Oh, we'll show you, it's easy." Both children looked thrilled that they would be able to help their uncle.

"Tim, Jess, I need to get our guests a drink, and you need to bring the tray of canapés here. When you have done that, you can get yourself a glass of soft drink from the fridge." Now all business, the children headed to the kitchen to follow out their instructions.

They were all soon sitting around the table eating canapés and enjoying their drinks.

Much of the conversation centred on the improvements that Emma had accomplished in the house.

"I haven't been in here since that morning I spent sorting Clive's papers." Libby's eyes swept the room, "It's amazing what you have achieved."

Delighted with the compliment, Emma's face blushed pink. "I'm really happy with it. I know there's still a long way to go, but compared to when I first arrived, it's a palace."

When most of the canapés had been consumed, Emma ushered the children into the kitchen and gave them instructions on what to do to serve the prawn cocktails. Jess and Tim took turns carrying the finished entrées into the dining room; their efforts were greeted with much acclaim.

"So now, what do I eat this with?" Ben asked innocently, his hands sweeping across the array of implements in front of him.

"It's easy; just work from the outside," Jess parroted Emma's earlier instructions.

Everyone agreed that the prawns were delicious, even Tim.

"Now we have to clear the table. Tim, Jess, let's go." And the twins immediately leapt to attention.

In the kitchen, Jess scraped the dirty bowls into the bin, and Tim carried the salad into the dining room while Emma cooked the fish and chips. As soon as the main course was ready, the children brought the plates, again one at a time, into the dining room. There was little conversation while the meal was consumed; everyone's enjoyment evident.

"Well done, Jess and Tim, that was delicious." Libby was full of praise.

"Come on, team. Time to clear the table." Emma stood to gather up some of the plates while the children picked up others.

This time, Tim scraped the plates, Jess carried the cream to the table for dessert, and Emma cut portions of cheesecake for everyone. Then, the children took the plates into the dining room.

When the meal was over, Ben stood up. "I'd like to make a speech…Thank you for a beautiful meal, Emma, Tim and Jess. We have felt really very spoilt. And a special thank you to Emma for letting us be the first guests in her new dining room."

Enthusiastic clapping greeted Ben's words, which brought Maxie out of her resting place under the table.

"Is that where you were, you cheeky animal?" Emma reached out her hand to pat her beloved dog. "Would you like a cup of tea or coffee to finish off the meal?" Emma offered Ben and Libby.

"No, thank you, I'd better get these two off to bed. Come on, you've had a long and exciting day. Time to get you home." Libby's words brought groans from the children.

"You've got tennis in the morning." The children visibly brightened at that reminder.

They all walked towards the back door.

"Thanks for your help, you two. You were both tremendous. We'll have to do this again." Emma was all smiles but was taken by surprise when, first, Jess and then Tim flung their arms around her waist and hugged tightly.

"Thanks so much, Emma." Two tired but very happy children headed out the door.

"Are you coming, Ben?" Libby asked.

He shook his head, "No, I think I'll have that cuppa after all. I'll walk home. It's a lovely night, so that won't be a problem."

Emma returned to the kitchen with Ben.

"Tea or coffee?" Emma asked as she collected the cups that the children had carried into the dining room earlier in the day.

"A cup of herbal tea would be great, any flavour."

Emma placed peppermint tea bags into the cups before adding the boiling water.

Ben accepted his tea. "Will we sit on the front veranda to drink this? It's such a pleasant night."

Emma nodded and followed Ben out to the front steps of the house. It was certainly a beautiful night; there was warmth still in the air, and the sounds of nighttime animals carried on the gentle breeze. Emma looked up at the clear night sky and sighed as she sat down on the top step. "I could never tire of looking at the stars here. It's so dark, without street lights, and you can see so many more than you can in the city."

Ben sat beside her. "I never get tired of the view," but he wasn't looking at the sky.

They sat in silence for a while, enjoying the ambience and the company. Ben then commented, "You've done an amazing job with the house. I expect you'll be glad when you've done everything."

Emma nodded. "I feel I'm in the home stretch with the house, but the mess in the shed is daunting. I think there's more rubbish in there than there was in the whole house. When I'm ready to tackle it, I think I'll rent a skip bin so I can just throw stuff in there as I sort."

"Well, when you want to start, just give me a yell. We sorted the dining room very quickly when there were a few of us, so hopefully, we can achieve the same with the shed. You haven't had any more problems with intruders since we cleaned up the dining room, have you?"

"No, thank goodness. My biggest problem now seems to be possums. Maxie was beside herself when I got home from the game last night, running around backwards and forwards to the shed. She stayed outside for ages after I went in. She didn't even come for her dinner."

Ben frowned at this news. "That seems a bit odd. Does she usually behave like that if she hears possums?"

"Well, no, but I wasn't home, and maybe she got spooked. Why? Do you think I have something else to worry about?" Emma's voice was pitching higher.

"Probably not, but maybe we will come home when you do on Tuesday night. I'm not trying to worry you, but the dog's behaviour seems unusual, so let's call it an insurance policy." Finishing his tea, Ben stood up. "I'd better get going; I have to be up early."

They headed inside, Ben locking the front door after them, and then walked through the house to the kitchen.

"Thank you for such a lovely evening. It was great to see how happy the kids were. Libby and I both appreciate you involving them in the meal." Ben wrapped his arms around Emma and gave her a quick hug and a light kiss on her cheek. "See you soon." With that, Ben headed out the back door.

Emma stood still, touching her cheek where Ben had planted the kiss.

"I didn't see that coming, Maxie. Come on, it's time for you to have a toilet stop before I do these dishes.

Ben walked down the driveway, reflecting on how much he had enjoyed the evening. Emma really was a kind and caring person, he thought.

"I bet her students love her, judging by her interactions with Tim and Jess; she made them feel so important and appreciated. It's so good for them to have another reliable adult in their lives." Ben's thoughts turned to Emma's story about Maxie and the possums in the shed. He hoped that it really was possums that had upset Maxie. He preferred not to think about the alternative.

CHAPTER 22

DAY 23 SATURDAY

Saturday morning was beautiful, with a very clear blue sky, a hint of chill in the air, and no breeze, as Emma discovered when she let Maxie outside just after 7:00am. It didn't feel like the day was going to be too hot, which pleased Emma. It would become more challenging to finish the painting when the summer heat set in.

"Come on, Maxie; breakfast, a walk, and then painting."

Their meals were finished when Libby knocked on Emma's back door and opened it to be greeted by enthusiastic licks from Maxie. Emma came out of the kitchen holding a tea towel.

"Come on, Emma, let's go. It's a great day for horse riding."

Emma baulked at the idea. "Um, I don't think I have time," she mumbled.

"Not taking no for an answer today. So come on."

Emma thought for a moment. She really did want to go; it was just nerves holding her back.

"Come on, let's do it." Libby smiled widely, grabbed Emma's hand and pulled her towards the back door.

"Leave Maxie here, she'll be fine," Libby advised.

Realising she was to be left behind and without her promised walk, the dog's ears drooped in disappointment.

"Sorry, Maxie." Emma dropped down beside the dog and ruffled her soft, black ears before heading out the back door. The two women chatted as they strode up the laneway to Ben's and Libby's farm.

They headed to the stables at the side of the house, where two horses stood side by side, already saddled.

"You were confident I'd come, weren't you?" Emma laughed.

The visibly younger horse shook her head and neighed at the women.

Libby touched the neck of the younger horse. "She's mine. Her name is Bella. The other one is my daughter's. She's a very calm older lady."

Emma looked at the horse and felt herself start to relax a little. The horse stood quietly, making eye contact with her. She was a beautiful solid chestnut colour, broken only by a white star above her eyes. Her coat shone, no doubt the result of much tender care from Libby and the children.

"Can I touch her?" Libby nodded her assent, and Emma reached out a hand to the horse.

"What's her name?" Emma asked softly, stroking the face of the horse.

"What do you think she's called?" Libby giggled.

Emma looked at the white star. Surely not?

"Is it Star?"

"Got it in one! But we can't take credit for such a clever name. It was her previous owner. Now, let's get you up, and we'll be on our way."

Taking a deep breath and trying to remember what she'd learned from her childhood riding experiences, Emma grabbed the pommel and swung herself into the saddle. She hoped her nervousness would not be conveyed to the horse underneath her.

"You okay?" Libby asked as she expertly mounted her horse.

"I think so; I hope Star doesn't hold my lack of experience against me."

Libby led the way out of the stables and onto the laneway, turning downhill towards Emma's house.

"We're not going to the highway, are we?" Emma's voice held a note of panic.

"Of course not. You probably haven't noticed it, but there's a little track where your farm and ours share a boundary. It's on our land, but it runs down to the river, and there's a bridle path beside it. We'll ride there today."

Emma's shoulders relaxed a little more.

The horses seemed to know where they were going as Star turned down the track alongside Bella without Emma doing anything. As they approached the river, Emma became aware of the sounds of water running over rocks. Horses and riders stopped when they reached the bridle path at the bottom of the track. The trees grew tall here, beautiful towering gums climbing straight up to the sky, branches outstretched to the sun. Smaller tree ferns and bracken grew in their shade. The smell of damp soil was all around them, and the call of birds was constant and loud.

"What a beautiful place," Emma sighed in appreciation.

"One of my favourite places in the world," agreed Libby. "Come on, we'll ride along the path for a while. We can go as far as you feel comfortable with. Are you going okay?"

"Yes, fine. Happy to keep going."

They turned to the left, and the horses meandered slowly along. Emma felt herself relax into the rhythm of her horse's movement. She closed her eyes and listened to the sounds of the bush around her, the calling of the birds, the burbling of the water as it flowed over the rocks and animals scurrying through the undergrowth. A sense of calm descended on her, and Emma realised she felt more at peace than she had in a long time.

"Emma... Emma?" Libby's voice called her back from her revelry.

"Thanks for bringing me here. It's just so peaceful."

"You wouldn't say that if we were here just after a rain storm. This shallow river turns nasty then," Libby warned her. "Come on, let's stop for a break. I brought morning tea along," and she tapped the bag that was on her back. The women slid from their horses, tied them to a branch, and found a smooth, flat rock in the shade of the same tree, large enough for them both to sit on.

Libby produced a flask of coffee, two mugs and a packet of Tim Tams, which she set down between them.

When Libby had poured their drinks, Emma sipped gratefully from her mug. She dipped her chocolate-covered biscuit into the hot coffee before nibbling on the softened end. "Hmmm, this is heaven. Thanks for bringing the supplies."

"No problem. So tell me, are you happy with your move to Winsthorpe? Did you know the house was going to be such a mess?" Libby was curious.

"Yes, I am very happy I moved here. I have a house that I'm enjoying renovating…. well, okay, enjoying might be too strong a word, but it is a challenge, a good challenge, I've made friends with a big group of people, and I'm doing things I haven't done in years…. like playing netball and riding horses," Emma laughed.

"So why did you come here?" Libby could see Emma was about to interrupt her. "I know you inherited the house. You could have just sold it, but you didn't. You seem to have just rushed up here without any thought to the condition of the house. I'm not being critical, but it does seem rather impetuous."

Emma considered how to answer her friend. She knew she could just lie, but Emma felt she and Libby were developing a strong bond, and she didn't want to compromise that by not being honest. It would be difficult to tell the truth; she hadn't told anyone, not even her mother, the full story.

She made a decision; she wouldn't lie, but she wouldn't tell the whole story either. One day, she might tell it all, but she wasn't ready to do that yet.

Emma began, "About eight years ago, I married a man I had been with since uni. I thought he was the love of my life."

"You're married," Libby's face showed all the surprise she was feeling.

"Technically, yes, emotionally, no, and our divorce should be finalised very soon," Emma continued. "He is in finance, and, as you know, I'm a teacher. He did very well at his job, so we decided to buy a house in Hawthorn, which was a very expensive house. It was a stretch, but as we didn't plan to have children, it seemed a reasonable idea. The house needed lots of work, a bit like Clive's, but without the rubbish, so we were going to renovate and make a killing when we sold it. The problem is that you need plenty of money to renovate, even if you're doing as much work as you can yourselves. Needing money meant my husband was working long hours, which translated to him not having much time to work on the house. I think he also didn't realise how much time my work took up until he had to notice. So the one, maybe two-year turnaround became a lot longer. We never had time for each other because if we weren't working on paid jobs, we were working on the house. Over time, we both came to resent it, but he refused to sell until we had finished the house. I think he chose profit over us. Eventually, we were sleeping in separate bedrooms. Neither of us wanted to move out because we couldn't afford to, and then COVID hit. It made it easier for him to work on the house because he was no longer travelling to his office, but it made it more difficult for me because teaching remotely took up even more time than being in a classroom. He became more resentful, and we finally reached a point of no return."

"That's sad for you both," Libby nodded, her eyes full of sympathy.

"He was right about the house making us money, though. You know how prices of houses skyrocketed after the lockdowns ended? Well, we'd finished the house by then so we sold in a hot market and walked away with a very healthy profit. It's why I could afford to take this time off work."

"Thanks for telling me. Do you want this kept between ourselves?" Libby asked.

Emma appreciated her new friend's thoughtfulness. "I don't mind if you tell Ben, but no one else, please. He wouldn't tell anyone, would he?"

Libby shook her head. "So, did you come here after the house was sold?"

"It was an absolute gift. The timing couldn't have been better. And I didn't care about its condition. The roof doesn't leak, the property is sound, and everything that needs doing is cosmetic, so no, I didn't care about its state. I admit it was worse than I expected, but it'll be great when everything is finished."

Libby collected the mugs and what was left of the Tim Tams. "Are you ready to head back now?"

Emma straightened up and stretched to relieve the pain that was developing in her lower back. "Yes, let's go."

The women mounted their horses, Emma with greater confidence this time, and set off at a slightly faster rate than earlier. Emma felt a sense of loss as the beauty of the river was left behind but knew she would definitely accept any further invitations from Libby to ride with her.

Back at the stables, they removed the saddles from the horses and slung them over a low wall before taking the horses to be hosed down in the adjacent small paddock. They rubbed the horses down then and left them to dry in the warming morning sun.

"Thank you for making me go; I really enjoyed that." Emma turned in the direction of her house. "I'd better get back to it. I want to paint Clive's room today."

Libby waved Emma off and walked up the path that connected the stables to the house.

Emma was welcomed home by Maxie, rubbing her head into Emma's hands.

"Sorry you couldn't come with us, Maxie. I'll take you for a walk after I've had a rest. I think I need to sit on something that isn't moving 'cos I'm already feeling it." Emma rubbed her hands over her stiffening spine.

Dog and owner sat together on the front veranda steps while Emma consumed a very welcome cup of her favourite coffee.

"Come on, Maxie, let's go for that walk. When I get back, I want to paint." The dog jumped up and barked excitedly at the mention of the word 'walk'. They headed along the same path that Emma and Libby had ridden earlier in the day. Enjoying the exercise, Emma hoped that it would ease the pain in her lower back.

Back at the house, Emma decided on an early lunch to be followed by an afternoon spent painting in Clive's room. The previous day, she had managed to paint the ceiling and two of the walls, so she planned to continue from there, hopefully managing a second coat of the walls and ceiling if she had time before nightfall.

It was growing dark just as Emma rolled the final section of wall. She was thrilled with how fresh the room now looked and smelled.

"What do you think, Maxie?" The dog lifted her head in approval, Emma was sure. "Come on, time for your dinner, you poor thing. You must be starving," which made Emma realise how very hungry she was herself.

Emma fed the dog, poured herself a glass of wine and pulled out the leftover prawns from the previous night.

Maxie finished her food and followed Emma out to the front step. This was definitely becoming Emma's favourite place to sit. She balanced the prawns on her knees and sipped at the wine.

"I think I need to buy a table and some chairs so it's more comfortable to eat and drink out here. What do you think, Maxie? Perhaps I should look in the shed first. There's so much stuff in there. Maybe I'll find a lovely wooden chair or something like that."

Maxie seemed to wag her tail in agreement.

Emma stood up, stretching her tired muscles. "Come on, Maxie, inside. I think we'll watch TV for half an hour and head to bed. It's certainly been an exercise-filled day."

CHAPTER 23

Day 24 Sunday

Emma eased herself out of bed. Those muscles unfamiliar with horse riding definitely objected to the previous day's exercise.

"Oh, Maxie, I think I need to do some stretches or something. This is painful." The dog looked up from her mat on the floor and decided that Emma's movements meant breakfast was on its way.

"Okay, okay, I'm coming." Emma shuffled to the laundry and fed the dog before opening the back door so that Maxie could head out when she was ready. Emma moved slowly back to her bedroom, stopping only to switch on the coffee machine in the kitchen. She dressed in her painting clothes and plodded back to the kitchen for a strong cup of coffee and two paracetamols.

Maxie came bounding back into the kitchen.

"I wish I had that much energy today, Maxie. I want to paint the woodwork in Clive's room and get started on the back veranda."

After a second cup of coffee and two slices of Vegemite toast, Emma felt she could make a start. She completed a first coat on all of the woodwork in Clive's room as planned and then decided that she would wash the walls of the back veranda and then stop. She really was finding the physical work challenging today and figured that a rest for the latter part of the day would do her good.

Emma had just cleaned up from painting when she heard a car coming down the driveway. She stepped out of the back door in time to see Carson emerging from his car. He was dressed more casually than Emma had previously seen him; he wore jeans and an open-necked shirt. Sensing Carson's arrival, Maxie rushed from her mat in the kitchen and planted herself firmly against Emma's legs.

"Hello, Emma, I haven't been in touch for a few days, and I thought you might need help with some papers. The last time I was here, I noticed how bad the shed was. Could you do with a hand cleaning it up?" He took a few steps towards Emma, and Maxie stood, wary of his presence. Carson stopped. "Is she alright? She's not going to bite, is she?"

"Of course not. She must have just been surprised there was someone here, that's all." Emma reached down to calm the dog's hackles. While patting the dog, she thought about Carson's offer. Emma hadn't planned to touch the shed until she'd finished in the house, but as Carson had made the offer, perhaps she could rethink it.

"It's such a big job, Carson. But if you've got time to spare, your help would be much appreciated. I was going to wash the walls in the veranda this afternoon, but that can wait."

"You don't have to help me. After all, you won't know what papers to keep; you'd only be asking me to go through them for you anyway. I can just sort papers while you focus on the veranda; that makes more sense."

"Well, I guess it does. Thank you. The recycling bin is reasonably empty, so you should just be able to put stuff straight in there." With that, Emma headed back inside, her hand firmly guiding Maxie to accompany her.

"I don't know why you don't like him," Emma scolded Maxie as they entered the house. "Obviously, he's not a dog person, but he hasn't done anything bad to you. Come on, you can watch me work on the veranda."

After an hour of washing followed by a late lunch, Emma thought she should offer Carson some refreshments. Carrying a cup of tea and a plate of biscuits, Emma firmly shut Maxie inside the house, not wanting a repeat of the earlier behaviour.

"How are you going, Carson? I brought you a cup of tea. Hope I remembered how you like it."

Carson didn't look up from the papers in his hand but mumbled a thank you. Emma looked at the messy pile of papers on the floor beside him.

"Are these ready for recycling?" Emma wondered why Carson hadn't put the unwanted papers directly into the bin, but as he was giving up his time to help her, she wasn't going to be critical.

"Yes," he nodded.

Emma bent down, swept the papers into her arms and dumped them into the recycling bin.

"You've been through heaps already, Carson. Thank you." Emma surveyed the boxes of papers stacked haphazardly behind Carson. "Don't feel you have to keep going. There's still so much here."

"I can keep going until four o'clock. Maybe I can help you again next weekend." He sipped his tea. "My secretary had an idea about finding out why Clive left this farm to you and what happened between him and your grandfather."

He immediately had Emma's attention.

"I don't want to get your hopes up, but my secretary, whose name is Bettina, thought you might be able to look up old newspapers to see if there's anything that sheds light." Emma was disappointed that there wasn't an immediate solution but appreciated that Bettina had given it thought.

"Oh." Emma was immediately deflated. "I don't think their story would have made it to the Melbourne papers."

"No, the local papers. Bettina said there was a Winsthorpe Weekly newspaper until 1990, and she thought the library might have kept copies or at least digitized them. You could try the Winsthorpe library first, although it might be too small to store back copies, or the Bendigo library."

"Thanks, Carson, I'll give that a go." Emma thought this the longest conversation they'd ever had.

Emma returned to the house to be met by an indignant Maxie.

"I'm sorry. I thought it would be better for you and Carson if you stayed inside." The dog's expression showed her opinion differed.

Back inside, Emma continued washing. Although the veranda was almost as wide as the whole house, the upper half of the back wall had mostly windows, so it was not as bad as some of the other rooms.

"Come on, ten more minutes, and this will be done," Emma willed herself to keep going. "You can do it. You just have to shift the ladder one more time." She climbed down the ladder holding the bucket, but as she stepped from the last rung, a yelp from Maxie filled the air. The bucket slipped from Emma's hand, and its contents spilt across the floor. "Oh, Maxie, I'm so sorry." She flung the washcloth down in frustration. "That's it! I've had it! I'll clean up this mess, and then I'll stop."

Emma grabbed some towels from the bathroom and threw them onto the water on the floor.

"I'm going to see what Carson has done. You stay here, Maxie." Emma headed out the back door and was surprised to see no sign of Carson's car. She reached into her pocket for her phone and understood why he'd left; it was after four o'clock. She crossed the driveway to check his progress and found another pile of papers beside the recycling bin.

"I wonder if Carson even knows how to recycle," Emma muttered through gritted teeth as she picked up the second large pile of papers for the day. Her phone pinged; there was a message from Libby, "Kids are on their way on bikes. Please let me know when they have arrived. Send them back in fifteen."

Emma hadn't made it to her back door when the children swung into her driveway, riding their bikes as fast as they could.

"Hi Emma, we've got something for you," they called, their excitement palpable.

As they reached the house, both children flung their bikes sideways and rushed over to her, holding a large card. On the front of the card was a drawing of a dog that could only be Maxie. Inside was a message. "Thanks for having us for dinner and for letting us help you. We hope we can do it again." It was signed with heavily decorated signatures.

"Do you like it?" they clamoured. "We both did the drawing."

"I did the writing 'cos I'm a better writer. I got my pen licence in grade 3, but Jess didn't get hers until Grade 4." Tim's tone was just a little smug.

"I really like all of it, thank you. And yes, we will do it again. It was so much fun, wasn't it? Now, have you got time for a drink and some biscuits before you need to head back?"

The twins dashed in through the back door, stopping only to pat Maxie. The dog was thrilled with the attention, having been relegated to the inside of the house for most of the day. Very much at home now in Emma's kitchen, the twins needed little encouragement to help themselves to the promised biscuits and cordial. Ten minutes later, they hugged Emma and Maxie before racing back to the bikes for the return ride home. Emma coaxed Maxie to accompany her in saying goodbye to the children.

"Come on, Maxie, you can come out now," Emma felt a little guilty for keeping the dog locked up for so long, but if that was the price of Carson helping her, she'd gladly do it again. Emma texted Libby to let her know the children were on their way home and then went to the veranda to finish mopping up the water.

CHAPTER 24

DAY 25 MONDAY

E mma was wakened by Maxie's hot breath as she leapt up on the bed.
"What are you doing, dog? Let me sleep," Emma pushed at the dog, but
Maxie was immovable.

"Oh, come on, get off." Emma rolled over in the bed and came face to face
with her bedside clock.

She sat up instantly; it was nearly midday.

"Oh, poor Maxie, you must be desperate."

Emma rolled out of bed, mindful of her aches and pains, and headed, as
quickly as she could, to the back door. The dog rushed gratefully outside and
returned, expecting her breakfast.

"Here it is, you poor thing. Oh, I need coffee, Maxie." And she switched on
the machine.

With a large coffee in hand, Emma headed out to the front veranda and sat
down on the top step to enjoy the reviving drink. She looked out across the
valley and listened to the calming sounds that surrounded her. Emma checked
her phone and saw there was a message from the hardware store informing
her that the blinds had arrived. Energised by the thought of being able to have
greater privacy and a darker bedroom for sleeping, she determined to head to
town as soon as she was ready.

As the focus of her attention was now the enclosed back veranda, Emma also wanted to buy material to make curtains for the windows in there. Emma thought that the veranda had once been open on all sides, but at some time in the past, the sides had been filled in with weatherboards and windows, which was quite a common practice to make a small house one room bigger. The back wall was constructed of boards to waist height, and above that, louvre windows extended to the ceiling. She would need a considerable length of material to cover the windows as they ran from one end of the veranda to the other. Measurements taken, Emma headed to her car. She had planned to take Maxie with her, but the temperature had really climbed in the past hour.

"You stay here, Maxie. It's too hot for you to sit in the car, even if I can find a park in the shade." The crestfallen dog sat on her mat and looked mournfully at Emma.

Full of excited anticipation, the drive to the store went quickly, and Emma was soon at the hardware store to collect the blinds. A young assistant helped her load the car. "You've got plenty of work ahead of you with this lot," she said.

Emma just nodded her thanks and walked in the direction of the haberdashery store. Now that she knew her way around the store from her previous visit, it didn't take long to locate the materials and choose what she wanted. Realising she should have bought the curtain fixtures when she was in the hardware store, Emma retraced her steps.

"Back again?" remarked the young assistant with a smile.

"Yes, I forgot I needed curtain rings and poles for the curtains I'm making."

The assistant directed her to the right location, and Emma soon purchased her requirements. Again, the assistant helped load the car.

"Thanks," Emma called as she opened the driver's door.

Greeted with excited licks and jumps from Maxie when she arrived home, it took several trips to carry her purchases from the car to the two front rooms.

"I'm only going to hang the blinds in the rooms that I've finished, Maxie. Hopefully, it's not going to take long."

While the installation of the blinds was quite simple, there were ten of them to install, four of them in each of the front rooms alone. It took most of the afternoon and many trips up and down ladders for Emma to complete the task.

"Well, Maxie, thank goodness that's done. Come on, rest time. I need a very large mug of tea." The dog jumped up from where she had been resting all afternoon while Emma worked; she was ready for exercise and began leaping around Emma in anticipation of a walk.

"Okay, okay, but I'm having that cuppa first."

The restless dog padded up and down the passageway while Emma drank her tea, ensuring the walk was not forgotten. At last, Emma was ready to go. The dog capered around her, hardly standing still long enough for Emma to attach a lead. Then, when they set off, Maxie tried to drag her up the hill towards Libby's and Ben's house.

"That's not where we're going. We're going down to the bridle path." Emma kept a tight hold on the lead; she didn't want the dog to slip from her grasp.

When they reached the river, Emma again marvelled at the beauty of the location. She could hear kookaburras in the distance, laughing as they staked their territory. Too tired to walk any great distance, Emma decided to free Maxie from her lead. She was confident that the dog would return to her, although she hadn't let her off-lead since taking up residence in Clive's house.

Five minutes later, Emma's confidence in Maxie was beginning to wane. She hadn't seen the dog since unclipping the lead. Maxie had headed up the bridle path in the direction that she and Libby had ridden two days earlier. Emma decided to follow and called out Maxie's name as she walked. With no response to her calls, Emma walked faster and faster until she was jogging. Her breaths were coming quicker and shorter, made worse by her rising sense of panic.

"Maxie, Maxie, come on, where are you?" Tears of frustration began to fill Emma's eyes as she scoured the path and bush around her. She didn't see the tree root that caught her foot, sending her sprawling into the dust and gravel.

"Oh, that hurt," she gasped, winded. Emma fought for breath, and as her breathing eased, she became aware of the pain shooting through her left ankle. She sat up and gingerly dragged her leg out in front of her to check the source of the pain.

"That doesn't look too bad, but will I be able to stand up? One way to find out." Emma shuffled on her bottom to the base of the culprit tree and, using the trunk for assistance, managed to stand. At this point, only her right foot was weight-bearing, but slowly, she tested the left foot. She was reassured to find that, although the ankle was painful and swelling badly, she could stand on it, just. Now, Emma faced a conundrum. How was she going to get home, and how was she going to find Maxie?

Emma reached into her jeans pocket and was relieved to discover her phone was intact. As she checked her contact list for Ben's number, her phone rang; it was him.

"Are you alright? I rang to say that Maxie arrived here a couple of minutes ago. I thought you must have been right behind her, but when you weren't, I was worried."

"I'm on the bridle path. We went for a walk. I took Maxie off the lead, and she ran away and wouldn't come back. I was running after her, but I tripped, and I hurt my ankle." Emma was crying now from either the pain or relief at knowing Maxie was safe; she wasn't sure. "Could you possibly help me get home?"

"I'll lock Maxie in a stable and then come for you. I'll bring my first-aid kit. Now tell me exactly where you are."

Emma had no idea how far she had run to find Maxie, but she knew she had come further up the bridle track than she and Libby had on Saturday morning. She looked around her for something that would be identifiable to Ben, but all she could see was bush.

"I'm sorry, but other than being on the bridle path, I don't know where I am. I turned left when I reached the river. Which I know isn't much help."

"Okay. That's something, at least. See you soon."

Emma slid down the tree trunk to wait for Ben.

It was about half an hour later when Emma first saw flashes of a blue shirt through the trees. She lumbered to her feet and called out to Ben. He waved to acknowledge that he'd heard her and soon arrived with the first aid kit under his arm.

Ben bent down to check her ankle. "I don't think you're going to train tomorrow night with that. But maybe you'll be right for the game on Thursday;

it doesn't look that bad. I'll strap it for you, though; it'll make it easier to get you home."

Ben knelt down and lifted her foot onto his thigh to strap the ankle with a stretch bandage that he pulled from his kit. Emma relaxed as he secured the bandage, grateful that her dog was safe and that her injury wasn't worse.

Resisting the urge to cry again, Emma tested the foot on the ground and managed to shuffle forward in small, slow steps.

"Lean on me, or it'll be dark before we even reach the ute," Ben laughed.

Emma gratefully accepted his outstretched arm, and they moved faster. Even so, it seemed an age before his vehicle came into view.

"Thank goodness we're nearly there." A relieved Emma wanted nothing more than to collect Maxie and get home to rest her ankle. "I hope that silly dog of mine is suitably apologetic for her behaviour."

"Did you hear or see anything that could have frightened her?" Ben asked.

"I'm not sure, but I will give her the benefit of the doubt and say she just made a big mistake!"

They drove to Ben's stables, and he returned to the car with a somewhat chastened black and white dog. When Maxie jumped into the ute, she landed in Emma's lap and proceeded to lick any exposed skin she could reach.

"Enough! I'm going to drown in your slobber," Emma growled, but she was hugging Maxie tightly.

Ben swung the ute into Emma's driveway and pulled up at the back door.

"If you give me the keys, I'll open up for you." He let Maxie out of the car and hurried to unlock the door of the house.

Ben helped Emma into the lounge room, where she could recline on the sofa.

"Thanks for rescuing Maxie and me, I really appreciate your help."

"No problem. I'm just glad it wasn't worse for you and that Maxie was smart enough to run to the stables. Is there anything else I can do for you?"

When Emma shook her head, Ben started to leave. "Obviously, you won't come to training tomorrow night. I'll call in, though, to see how you're doing." And with a ruffle of Maxie's head, Ben was gone.

Emma rearranged the cushions on the couch to make herself as comfortable as possible and was quickly joined by Maxie, who snuggled up hard against Emma's side.

"Just as well I love you, you silly dog."

Ben backed down the driveway, glad that Emma's injury seemed reasonably minor. He felt that his role in getting her and Maxie home safely had brought them all a little closer together, which, on consideration, he decided, was just what he wanted.

CHAPTER 25

DAY 26 TUESDAY

Whether it was from the discomfort in her ankle or the close quarters of a remorseful dog who insisted on snuggling against her human's body, Emma didn't sleep well. She struggled out of bed, resigned to doing little in the way of painting for the day.

The dog fed, and with a cup of coffee in hand, Emma hobbled out to the front steps and sat down to enjoy the quiet of the early morning. It was already warm sitting in the sun, so after drinking her coffee, Emma returned inside.

"What am I going to do? I can't just sit here all day." Emma had never been a person to lounge around, and the thought of doing nothing didn't appeal when there was still so much to be done.

"I know, Maxie, I can make the curtains for the veranda." Maxie didn't even raise her head from the mat where she was lying.

Collecting the material from where she'd dropped it on the lounge room floor the previous day, Emma made her way to the enclosed veranda and laid it out on the floor. As awkward as it was crawling around the floor while protecting her injured ankle, Emma managed to measure and cut the material to the right lengths before seeking refuge in a chair.

"Ooh, well, that was a bit more challenging than I'd hoped. A rest and some morning tea is required, Maxie."

With her ankle up on the chair opposite, Emma enjoyed a cup of tea and a few chocolate biscuits.

"Don't look at me like that, Maxie. A girl just needs chocolate sometimes, you know."

After resting her ankle for about half an hour, Emma felt ready to sew the curtains. She seated herself at the sewing machine, propped her ankle on a small box and began work.

It was just after four o'clock when Emma sewed the final hem. She folded the finished curtains into neat piles and carried them, somewhat clumsily, into the dining room. She was just filling the kettle for a cup of tea when she heard a vehicle in the driveway. The twins, Ben and Libby, were at the door.

"Ben says you can't come with us. He said you hurt your ankle. Can we look at it?" The twins looked at the bandaged ankle and, finding there wasn't much to see, redirected their attention to the dog.

"So, not very exciting, after all," Emma laughed at the children's response.

"We came to see how you were getting on and to ask if there was anything you'd like us to buy for you when we're in Winsthorpe. I'm sorry I didn't get here yesterday, but I ended up doing an extended shift because we were short-staffed," Libby was apologetic.

"No problem. I've been fine, apart from sharing my bed last night with this silly dog."

The children laughed when they heard this. "Mum, can we have the farm dogs sleep on our beds?"

"Definitely not. They smell a lot like sheep, and then you'd smell like sheep, too. And I don't think you'd like that."

The looks of disappointment on the children's faces gave Emma an idea. "I tell you what... one day, when the house is finished, you can spend the night here in the spare room, and Maxie can sleep with you. That's if it's alright with your mum. What do you think?"

"Mum, can we, can we stay?"

"Yes, but not until Emma has finished the house. Agreed? I know you'd love to stay, but we can't stop Emma from getting on with her renovations," Libby explained.

Ben signalled it was time to go. "Come on, everyone, back in the car, we've got to get to training."

With a last hug for Maxie, the children headed out the door, followed by Libby and Ben.

"I'll call in tomorrow. See how you're going. Phone me if you have any unexpected visitors tonight. There shouldn't be any issues given everything that's been done, but don't hesitate to phone if you're worried." With that, Ben left, closing the door behind him.

Ben's words stayed with Emma, and so, after they had gone, she shuffled around the house, making sure that all windows and external doors were locked. After feeding Maxie and eating an early dinner herself, she couldn't settle to watch television; she didn't want any noise to cover the potential sounds of intruders, so she decided to investigate if the local library held any copies of the now-defunct weekly paper. She googled Winsthorpe Library to discover that it only opened two days a week, and the service was provided by the central Bendigo library.

"I think I'll have to go to Bendigo, but it's probably worth a visit to Winsthorpe, just in case. Now, when are they open?"

Having ascertained that the local library operated on Tuesdays and Thursdays, Emma thought she would begin by phoning on Thursday.

When Emma received a text from Ben saying they had just arrived home, asking if she was okay, Emma relaxed and settled down to watch television.

CHAPTER 26

DAY 27 WEDNESDAY

Emma slept much better as her ankle was giving her less pain, and Maxie, apparently feeling she'd apologised enough, spent the night curled up on her rug on the bedroom floor.

Coffee brewed, Emma carried her cup out to the front steps, followed closely by Maxie, who promptly lay down on the sun-warmed veranda floorboards.

"What am I going to do today? The ankle's improved but I still don't fancy climbing up and down ladders to paint." The dog sat up at the sound of Emma's voice. "And no, I'm not taking you for a walk."

The dog lay back down, disappointed eyes looking up at her mistress.

While she enjoyed her coffee, Emma pondered the jobs she could do while seated. The papers in the shed quickly came to mind.

"I can sit on a chair and sort out a few of those boxes. Even if I have to get Carson to check some papers later, it would still move the process along."

Feeling invigorated now she had a plan, Emma quickly ate two slices of toast and Vegemite and made her way across to the shed.

The mess in the shed was still overwhelming despite the start that Carson had made. It didn't take Emma long to set herself up on an old chair with the recycling bin beside her and her ankle supported on an upturned container.

She dragged the nearest box over and began. An hour later, that box was finished, and she had not saved any papers from it.

"Which one now, Maxie?" The dog made no response other than to wag her bushy tail.

"This one'll do." The box was the middle one of a stack of three, the one she'd just sorted having been the top one. Emma stood up and made to grab the box.

"Wow! This is heavier than I expected."

She decided to leave the box where it was until she had sorted the top papers and then move it when it was lighter. The first few centimetres were just papers similar to those in the first box and held no importance. The next thing she lifted out was a bound book. When she opened it, Emma realised it was a journal, not a journal of personal experiences but of the goings-on of the farm.

As Emma turned the pages, she realised that Clive, she presumed, had recorded the temperature at 5:00am and 5:00pm every day, the rainfall, too little on many pages, it seemed, wind direction, and then there were observations of life on the farm. Entries told of cutting hay, baling and storing it, sheep shearing and animals being sent to market. There was an entry about a ewe giving birth to quintuplets and the care Clive took of them, keeping them in the stables at night and supplementing the milk they got from their mother with bottles. He also noted the wool clip and arrangements with shearers, crop production and many other details associated with the farm. Across the front of the book was handwritten 1954.

Emma was fascinated by the detail and the commitment to the weather recordings, in particular.

"He won't have just done one for 1954, Maxie. There must be others."

Spurred on by the thought, Emma dived into the next box and, under a pile of unimportant papers, found journals for 1955, 1956 and 1957. Skimming through these confirmed no personal details appeared on the pages. By the time she broke for lunch, Emma had found ten journals, but all for the 1950s.

"Are there more to find, I wonder?"

After a quick lunch and a glass of cold water, Emma resumed her task. Despite working her way through another six boxes, she found no more journals. The recycling bin was bulging with discarded papers. Emma decided to stop sorting until after the weekend, when the bin would be emptied, as tempted as she was to continue.

When she stood up, Emma stretched to ease her back, and Maxie leapt up, hoping this was a sign that a walk was imminent.

"Sorry, Maxie, the answer's still no. Maybe tomorrow. But come on, it's dinner time for you, so it's not all bad, is it?" The dog wagged her tail and trotted after Emma into the house.

CHAPTER 27

DAY 28 THURSDAY

When Emma woke up and first put her injured foot to the ground, she realised that it felt considerably better. Encouraged by the improvement, Emma decided to paint the veranda if her ankle tolerated the activity. So, after breakfast for both Maxie and herself, Emma organised the drop sheets and other painting gear. She decided to start on the back wall as she wouldn't need to climb a ladder to paint it. If she managed that, then she'd try the ladder for the higher walls. Emma was very pleased when, two hours later, she had successfully painted the whole back wall, and her ankle wasn't feeling any worse. It had been slow going as the timber had been very thirsty for fresh paint and the wall almost as wide as the house, but it was done.

After a break for lunch, Emma turned her attention to the other walls in the veranda and managed the end walls in the afternoon. By four o'clock, Emma decided she'd done enough, so after cleaning up and making a cup of tea, she rang the Winsthorpe library to ask about the back copies of the defunct local paper.

She spoke to a young woman who said she'd need to check and would get back to Emma when she had.

Five minutes later, her phone pinged; the message was from Ben asking if she wanted to come to watch the game and then join the team for dinner at the pub in Capstown where they were playing.

Emma declined, thinking she'd prefer to rest her ankle to hopefully heal it faster. Ben messaged back, "Ok. Phone if you have any worries tonight."

Emma sat out on her veranda to enjoy a glass of wine and her dinner. There was still a little light at 7:30, thanks to daylight saving, which had begun the weekend she'd arrived at the farm. It was warm with little wind, and Emma felt herself relaxing as she listened to the sounds of animals just ending or just starting their day.

Half an hour later, her revelry was interrupted by the headlights of a car, which she could see making its way up the laneway. Thinking it too early for her neighbours to return as Capstown was an hour away, and very mindful of the intrusions she had experienced, Emma felt her heart and breathing rate increase and her stomach muscles tighten. She called Maxie to follow her inside and locked the front door. Not turning any lights on, Emma carefully made her way to the back door. She opened it a crack and watched the vehicle turn into her driveway. Emma took a step out, Maxie at her heels. The sensor light, detecting their movements, sent bright light streaming across the yard. The vehicle slowed, the driver seeming to hesitate, then rapidly reversed backwards, wheels churning the gravel as it shot back to the lane.

Heart now pounding, Emma hurried back inside the house, Maxie close by her side. She locked the door and phoned Ben.

CHAPTER 28

DAY 29 FRIDAY

She hadn't slept well, the events of the previous night swirling around in her head. Had the car belonged to her intruders? Was it just someone who'd taken a wrong turn? If it had been an innocent misdirection, why did the car reverse in such a hurry? If only she'd been able to identify the car.... Ben and Emma had discussed the possibilities at length when he arrived nearly thirty minutes after she'd called. The family had already been on their way back when she'd phoned. Libby had dropped Ben at Emma's door and then taken the twins home to bed.

"If it was the intruder, they must have taken fright when they realised you were home," Ben had said, his concern obvious. "That's a good thing, really, because it means they don't want to hurt you. But there must still be something in the shed or house that they want."

Emma had nodded her agreement. "The only thing of any interest that I've found so far are journals from the 1950s. And they only hold statistics and information about the farm and the weather; I didn't find anything personal in the ones I've looked at."

"Was that Clive's doing? I'd really like to see them, but I can't imagine a log of statistics being the target, can you?"

Emma had shaken her head. "I think I'll head back to the shed again tomorrow and leave the painting for now. Carson said he might be able to help on Saturday, too."

Ben had frowned at that piece of news.

"I'll try to get over on the weekend too. If you're okay, I'll head home. Why don't you put Maxie out while I'm here, and then you can lock up when I leave?"

When Ben had gone, Emma closed the blinds and curtains and checked the doors again before heading to bed.

Now that it was morning, Emma felt very disappointed that the intruders were possibly still looking for something on the property. Emma knew she had no choice but to keep cleaning out the boxes despite her ankle feeling much better.

After breakfast, Emma took her cup of coffee into the shed, set herself up as she'd done previously, and began on another box. She determined that as there was no room in the recycling bin, she would put discarded papers into one of the now empty boxes. She'd label these boxes in large red letters to show they were for recycling to hopefully deter any intruders should they come back.

After three unproductive hours, Emma was becoming increasingly bored by her task; she'd found no more journals and nothing interesting amongst the papers, certainly nothing she'd need to ask Carson to scrutinize.

"At least," she thought, "I have the satisfaction of knowing the pile of boxes left to check is shrinking."

After lunch, Emma forced herself to continue sorting, but again, nothing of interest was found in the papers.

"One last box today, Maxie." Emma sighed heavily and eyed the top box of another stack. When it was dragged to the floor, she was delighted to see what appeared to be a raffia and cane chair, a relic from the 1950s. It had been hidden behind the stack of boxes and was covered in bags of clothes or maybe rags.

"Oh, this could be perfect for the front veranda, Maxie. I wonder if there are any more."

Now more than happy to abandon her sorting, Emma decided that she needed to create a pathway through the remaining boxes to reach the area behind them. This proved difficult as some of the boxes in her path were heavy, and her ankle was still something of a handicap. By stacking the boxes even higher than they'd been and dragging a few items to the side, Emma managed to create a narrow way through. She reached the chair, threw the bags to the floor, and lifted it above her head to carry it out, moving awkwardly past the piles.

The chair was eventually carried to the driveway and inspected in the daylight.

"It's lovely, Maxie. I can't see anything wrong with it other than it being dirty. I wonder if it has a mate?"

Emma headed back inside the shed to begin a search. If there were more, she was determined to find them. Heading back down the path she'd made through the boxes, Emma arrived at the back of the shed and looked around. Moments later, she spotted another raffia and cane chair, partially covered by a tarp and close to where the first chair had been. Dragging the tarp away, Emma was delighted to find this chair was a match for the first. This, too, she carried to the driveway.

"Oh, Maxie, this one's in even better condition, apart from the bit that wasn't covered up. I wonder if there's more?"

Despite further searching, no more chairs were found. Emma was about to carry her bounty to the front veranda when she thought it wise to check under the seats for redback spiders. Dark places were their preferred habitat, and she didn't fancy being bitten by one.

Emma grimaced, "I should have thought about that before I carried them out, Maxie!"

Upending the first chair revealed nothing sinister, but the second one provided a comfortable abode for a beautiful but venomous shiny black spider, with the tell-tale bright orange-red flash across its abdomen.

"Sorry, spider, you have to go." Emma grabbed a long, thin stick and prodded the spider until it jumped off the chair and disappeared into the shed where it had come from. She then carried the chairs, one at a time, to the front veranda, where they looked right at home.

"What do you think, Maxie? Look good, don't you think? Now I just need a small table between the chairs that can hold drinks so they don't have to go on the floorboards. Maybe I'll get lucky, and there'll be one of those in the shed, too." Emma laughed, delighted at her finds.

Spurred on by that thought, Emma headed back to the shed, her faithful dog beside her. She was just about to make her way down the makeshift path to the back of the shed again when her phone rang; it was the librarian that she'd spoken to the day before.

"Hi Emma, I think I've found out what you want to know. Some of the papers are stored on microfiche in Bendigo. We also have some hard copies of the old local paper stored here, so it's probably best if you come in when we're next open and have a look for yourself."

"Thank you, I really appreciate your help. I'll come in on Tuesday. Thanks again."

Excited by this news, Emma hoped that Tuesday might see the start of solving the mystery of Clive's will.

CHAPTER 29

Day 30 Saturday

As she stepped out onto the front veranda holding her morning coffee, Emma felt the heat immediately.

"I don't think we'll be out here for too long, Maxie." The dog was soon panting her agreement. As they turned to head back inside, Emma saw Carson's car coming up the hill. Leaving Maxie inside, she headed out the back door to meet him.

Emma waved a welcome to Carson as he stopped in front of her.

"I thought I'd help you sort more boxes today if that suits," Carson offered as he climbed out of his car. Ben's warning from weeks ago that Carson didn't do anything for free suddenly sprang into her mind.

"Thanks, Carson, I appreciate your offer, but……." Emma struggled to find the appropriate words to ask the question but then decided to come right out with it, "Are you expecting me to pay for your time?"

Carson stared at Emma, his face turning red. "No, of course, I'm not. Whatever made you think that?" He was clearly offended by her suggestion.

Emma didn't want to implicate Ben in this accusation, so she just blustered, "I'm sorry, I have just been a bit overwhelmed by you helping so much, and I thought maybe you were doing it for payment."

"I can assure you, I haven't any thoughts of billing you for my time. I just wanted to help you with this terrible mess, but if you'd rather I didn't, I'll be on my way." And he made to get back in the car.

Seeing Carson's distress made her feel foolish for taking Ben's laughingly offered comment seriously.

"I'm so sorry, Carson, I didn't mean to upset you. You've been a fabulous help. I guess I'm just not used to people helping unless there's something in it for them. I'm from the 'big smoke', you know." She tried to make light of her accusation, but Carson had obvioulsy taken offence.

"Well, it's certainly not the way it's done around here," he huffed, "but I accept your apology, and I'm willing to just get on with this sorting if you are."

"Thanks, Carson. Again, I am so sorry to have upset you, and I appreciate the help you've given me."

Emma followed Carson to the shed, where she pointed out the boxes that were already sorted and labelled.

"I'll get started then." Carson made to grab one of the unsorted boxes.

Feeling contrite, Emma offered Carson another excuse to leave the sorting for the day.

"Are you quite sure you want to be out here? It's already very hot in the shed."

Carson retorted, "This isn't that hot. Wait until January when it's over forty for days on end."

Emma shrugged and headed back into the house. Carson grabbed a handful of papers and got to work.

An hour and a half later, Carson was still out in the shed, so Emma decided to try to appease him by taking him morning tea.

"I think I remembered how you have your coffee. Milk and two sugars?"

"Thanks, Emma, and I'll have one of those shortbread biscuits too."

"Found anything interesting yet?"

"Absolutely not. Just more of the same... old pamphlets, magazines, receipts, but I'll keep going. I'd hate to throw out his secret cache of loot," Carson laughed.

"It's pretty hot out here. Are you okay? What can I do to help?"

"Yes, I'm okay, but you can help by having a poke around the rest of the shed for any more boxes of papers."

Emma liked the sound of this; she hoped her searching might reveal more useful stuff like the two chairs she'd recovered the previous day.

They worked on, breaking only for a lunch of salad sandwiches and for Emma to take Maxie for a brief walk. By around five o'clock, they decided to call it quits. Carson had sorted through all of the remaining boxes of papers, and Emma had unearthed an attractive coffee table in need of some restoration and a great deal of junk.

"I think I need to hire a skip to get rid of this stuff. Do you know of anyone around here who does that sort of thing?" Emma assumed Carson would have contacts of all sorts.

"Yes, I do. I'll write his number down for you." He promptly pulled out a business card and a pen from his top pocket and handed the card to Emma with a name and phone number now on the back of it.

"Thanks, Carson. And again, I'm sorry for what I said this morning."

"All good. I'm glad this job is finished. Once you've got rid of the junk, you'll have somewhere to park your car under shelter and, believe me, you'll be glad of that once the real heat hits."

Carson climbed into his car and reversed down the driveway. He slowed when he saw Ben walking through the gate. They gave a brief nod to each other, and then both continued on.

"Hi Emma, has Carson been helping you again?"

"He's just spent most of the day here. I just have to get a skip in and fill my recycling bin about ten times, and I'll have a garage!"

"He's been here all day! Wow! What's your secret in getting him to help you so much? Perhaps he fancies you," Ben joked.

Emma blanched, and she certainly didn't laugh. "Don't be ridiculous. He's not interested in me, and I'm certainly not interested in him other than as a friend."

Ben looked at Emma, "I'm glad to hear that," he smiled. "He's not my favourite person, but enough about Carson! I came to ask if you'd like to come up to ours for a swim and dinner tonight. With the weather heating up, the twins convinced me to get the pool into working order, which I've had time to do today, and we're planning the first swim of the season tonight."

Emma looked uncertain. "How cold is the water going to be? I don't want to freeze!"

"Don't worry, it's solar heated, and the weather has been plenty warm enough anyway."

"Okay. I believe you, then. I'll dig out my bathers. They'll be in a drawer somewhere, I'm sure. Can I bring something?"

"If you have the makings of salad, that'd be great. See you in about an hour." Ben headed back down the driveway.

With the visitors gone, Maxie looked up from where she'd been lying in the shade expectantly.

"Come on, Maxie. We've time for a walk and dinner for you before I leave. I think my ankle will take it."

The dog leapt up and bounced around Emma, ready to head out for the promised walk, the heat not discouraging her at all.

An hour later, Emma was ready to head off for the promised swim and dinner, leaving a disappointed dog skulking on her bed.

It was certainly a very warm evening, and Emma decided she was more than ready for that swim by the time she walked to Ben's and Libby's. The twins ran at Emma as she came around the side of the house, hugging her quickly.

"Come on, we've been waiting for you so we can all get into the pool at the same time; it's tradition!"

"I'm ready! Let me just drop the salad inside, and I'll be right back."

Three adults and two children stood around the outside of the beautifully clean pool. The water sparkled in the late sunlight, making it hard to see how deep the water was. The large pool was set at the side of the barbeque and courtyard area that Emma had so admired on the night with the netball team.

"Ready, set, go!" Five bodies jumped in as one. Yells and gasps resonated around the courtyard as the cold of the water took their breath away. Ben had neglected to tell Emma that the solar heating unit hadn't actually been turned on, and the recent bout of warm weather had not raised the temperature of the water by much. Still, it didn't take long for their bodies to acclimatize, and all five of them were soon engaged in a game of Marco Polo with Tim as 'it'.

"Marco," Tim called out. A chorus of 'Polo' met him, and Tim, eyes tightly closed, pushed through the water in the direction of a caller.

They played for ages, enjoying the childish fun, stopping only when the twins complained they were hungry.

It was still warm, so getting changed wasn't necessary. Ben cooked the meat on the barbeque, and the twins helped their mother bring out the salads, bread, and plates.

Conversation flowed easily around the table while dinner was consumed, the children joining in confidently.

Emma asked about something that she'd been considering all day. "It has been hot today, and it's only early November. Everyone tells me it will get hotter, so I'm thinking of installing an evaporative cooler. Do you know anyone who installs them?"

"I'm not sure, but David, Zoe, or Steven certainly will have contacts in the trade, given their line of work," Libby volunteered. "You can ask them at training on Tuesday evening."

Emma wanted to find out more about the sheep that surrounded her house, and Ben was happy to oblige. Ben told her about his family's farming history and about the care that needed to be provided to the sheep. Emma wanted to know what Ben did with the lambs that had been appearing in the paddocks.

"How rare is it for a ewe to have quintuplets? Clive wrote in one of his journals about helping a ewe to raise her five lambs?"

"Twins are quite common, but you don't get many triplets and certainly not where all three thrive. I've never heard of a ewe having five lambs."

"That's a lot of babies, isn't it Uncle Ben?" Tim said, trying to sound every bit like the farmer that he wanted to be.

"It certainly is, Tim. It's hard to imagine them all surviving," Ben agreed with his nephew.

"Well, according to Clive's journal, the lambs survived with what, I suspect, was a lot of intervention from him. You have working dogs, don't you? Do they do most of the work rounding up the sheep when it's needed?"

"Yes, a well-trained working dog is worth its weight in gold. I give them a hand from my motorcycle, but they do the work."

"I know the sheep at my house were already shorn when I arrived here, but did you use your own facilities or mine?"

"I used my own facilities. It's easier that way."

The children had listened attentively.

"I want to be a farmer when I grow up," announced Jess. "I'll grow horses, though, not sheep."

"And so do I!" Tim concurred with his sister. "But I'm going grow sheep just like Uncle Ben."

The conversations continued, and by the time the meal was finished, it was dark.

"I'd better be getting home. Maxie has been somewhat neglected today, with Carson around for so long. It's fair to say that Carson isn't Maxie's favourite."

"That dog's got excellent taste," Ben nodded. "Come on, I'll walk you home."

"How very quaint, Mr Arnold, but thank you, I accept the offer." Emma thanked Libby and the children for their hospitality, gathered her things, and set off with Ben.

"I don't think I've told you that the librarian from the Winsthorpe Library rang on Friday to say that they do have old copies of the Winsthorpe Weekly and that I can look at them on Tuesday when the library's next open. The selection they have may not answer my questions about Clive, but it's a start."

"That sounds promising," agreed Ben.

"And I need to take issue with you; you caused me a great deal of embarrassment today," Emma said indignantly.

"What are you talking about? I was only at your place for about five minutes. What can I have possibly done in that short a time?" Ben was all innocence.

"When I first moved here, you said that Carson never did anything without charging for it. So when he turned up this morning to volunteer his time in cleaning the shed, I asked him if his time was costing me." Emma frowned at the memory and felt her cheeks warming. "He was affronted by the suggestion and certainly let me know it."

Ben burst out laughing. "I wish I could have seen the look on his face."

"It was all your fault. I had to backtrack very quickly. I nearly lost his help because of it," she snapped.

Ben was still chuckling five minutes later as they headed down the hill towards Emma's driveway.

"What a beautiful night it is; look at all the stars. The night skies are so much more impressive here than in the city, with so little light pollution." Emma stopped when she realised that Ben was no longer beside her.

"Ben?" she turned around. Ben was about 5 metres further back up the hill, staring intently in the direction of her shearing shed.

"What's the matter? Why have you stopped?"

"I thought I saw a light near your shed."

Emma walked back up the hill and stood beside Ben, both staring intently in the direction of the sheds. They kept watch for another ten minutes but saw nothing.

"Sorry, must have been my imagination. I guess I'm just seeing things that don't exist because I'm worried about everything that's happened at yours in the past month."

Emma turned and gave Ben a hug.

"Thank you for worrying. I appreciate it." She let him go, and they continued without further conversation to Emma's house.

Maxie leapt around them when the backdoor was opened and dashed outside. Ben and Emma checked that all was well inside the house while they waited for Maxie to return.

Planting a friendly kiss on Emma's cheek, Ben said, "I'll get home now she's back inside. Sleep well. See you in the morning."

Ben was glad he had accompanied Emma home; every minute he spent in her company made him happy. "And Carson is just a friend. That's good to know." And he smiled to himself as he strolled up the laneway.

Emma locked the door behind Ben, showered the chlorine off her skin and headed to bed when her hair was dry.

Emma fell asleep straight away and dreamt of Maxie rounding up sheep in the paddocks in front of the house, herself helping from the back of a motorcycle. And then she was awake, the sound of a bike receding in the distance.

CHAPTER 30

DAY 31 SUNDAY

Emma had barely had time to drink her morning coffee when she heard the sound of voices at her back door.

Libby and the twins were standing there when she opened the door.

"Hi Emma, we've come to do some work for you." Tim bounced up and down in front of her, his excitement obvious.

"What are you going to do?" Emma asked, her mind ticking over quickly, trying to come up with jobs for the children.

"We're going to clean up your orchard!" Jess informed her.

Then Emma noticed the tools the family was holding.

"That's some serious stuff you've got there!" Emma admired the whipper snipper, chain saw and brush cutter she could see in their hands. "You're not going to use the chainsaw, though, are you?" Dreadful images of lost fingers or worse popped into her head.

"Don't be silly, that's for me to use, not the children," Libby smiled at the relief evident on Emma's face. "But we do have some serious cleaning up to do! Your orchard is a fire hazard, and the poor fruit trees haven't seen a prune since who knows when. It's not the best time of year to prune, but I reckon the trees will appreciate being tidied up no matter what season they are in. Ben's bringing the slasher on the back of the tractor. He should be here soon."

The sound of a tractor coming down the laneway was easily identifiable. It reminded Emma to ask about the motorcycle she thought she'd heard during the night.

"Did you hear a motorcycle at all last night?" Emma hoped she had imagined it.

"No, I didn't. Why? Did you?" Libby looked concerned.

"I'm not sure. I was dreaming about rounding up sheep on a motorcycle, and then I heard it, so I'm not sure whether I really heard one or not."

Libby nodded sympathetically. "We'll check in with Ben in a minute."

The tractor stopped halfway between the laneway and the house where the gate into the front paddock was located. Ben alighted and jogged the gap to the house.

Libby asked Ben immediately if he'd heard a motorcycle during the night.

"No, did you?" It was Emma, he was asking. She repeated the information she'd already given Libby.

"Have you checked if anything is out of place this morning?" Ben looked worried.

"I haven't had a chance. If I'm honest, part of me didn't want to look because that would make it real," Emma admitted.

"Well, come on, we'll look now. Libby, do you want to start slashing the paddock? We'll be back shortly."

Ben and Emma walked across the drive to first look in the shed opposite the house, and although it was still a mess, it didn't seem to Emma that it looked any different to the day before. The stables were another matter; she'd only looked in there briefly weeks earlier. They were a mess then, and they still were.

"I haven't any idea if things have been touched in here!" Emma was frustrated that she couldn't be more certain.

They walked on to the shearers' quarters. Opening the door of the first room, Emma drew in a deep breath. "This has definitely been disturbed."

"Are you sure? It all looks very neat." Ben doubted anyone had searched in here; it was so tidy.

"I'm sure all right. When I was here a few weeks ago, everything was very neat, but the mattresses were on the beds, not leaning on the wall, and the wardrobe doors were definitely shut," she said grimly.

They checked the other rooms and found similar evidence of things having been moved in every one; the mattresses had all been shifted and blankets tossed around.

Depressed by what she'd seen, Emma accompanied Ben to the shearing shed. However, it was difficult to determine if anything had been touched there.

"Oh, Ben, I can't believe this. The intruder has changed their pattern. To my knowledge, they have never been on the property while I've been here; it's always been when we've been at netball training or games. Last night, they were here, and so was I. I'm really so sick of it. What on earth are they looking for? There's nothing interesting left in the shed." Emma started to cry. Ben reached for her and hugged her tightly against his chest. Her crying slowed, and she took a step back.

"What am I going to do?"

Ben continued to hold Emma and spoke over her head, "I know they came when you were home, but they made no attempt to enter your house. They also didn't stop at the shed, which tells me we just have to keep sorting the papers and rubbish in the last few buildings, and that should stop them altogether. That theory has worked with the house and with the shed, so just keep going with the clean-up."

Emma felt cheered by Ben's logic and determined that she would do just that; keep cleaning and sorting.

As they made their way back to the house, Ben commented, "I noticed the doors of the shearers' quarters had locks but weren't locked. Do you have keys for them? That might provide a simple security solution if you do."

"I have several keys in the bunch that Carson gave me that I haven't found homes for yet, so I could start with them."

"Why don't you go back with the extra keys to see if they work while we get on with tidying up your orchard?"

They parted ways at her back door. Emma found the keys and whistled for Maxie to follow her.

"Oh, Maxie, is it ever going to stop? I'm so fed up with looking for whatever I'm looking for and being worried. I came here for peace, and whoever this creep is, he's disrupting my life." The dog just trotted along at Emma's heels, happy to be out for a walk.

Emma tried the extra keys in the locks on the doors of the shearers' accommodation and was relieved to find they worked. She locked the windows in each room before doing the same to the doors.

Back at the house, she left the keys on the kitchen table and headed to join the others in the orchard.

By lunchtime, the orchard was looking a different creature than it had at 8:00 am. The grass was slashed and raked into piles, the weeds around the trees had been trimmed back with the whipper snipper, and the chain saw was used vigorously to trim dead wood and larger branches from the fruit trees. Libby had cut the larger timber into pieces suitable to fuel fires in winter, and the rest were piled up in the bottom corner of the fenced orchard.

"Thank you all so much." Emma was thrilled with the morning's work and was very impressed by the contribution of the twins. "You two have been fantastic. I don't know how you managed to carry so much of the pruning to the bottom of the orchard and rake all that grass into piles."

The twins beamed with pride at Emma's words.

"I bet you get a better view now," Tim called as he ran up onto the front veranda. He stopped when he saw the state of the narrow windows on either side of the front door.

"These are disgusting. Why haven't you washed them?"

"I was waiting for you to volunteer, Tim," Emma joked.

"We'll do it!" yelled Jess. "Come on, Tim, it'll be fun."

Tim rolled his eyes but agreed.

"You don't have to do it," Emma was sorry she'd made the suggestion now, but Jess wanted to get on with it.

"We'll need a bucket, cloths, the hose and a ladder, I reckon," Jess called out.

"Okay, I'll collect what you need, but I reckon this deserves a trip into Winsthorpe for one of those soft-serve things."

Tim suddenly became more motivated.

"Can we have one dipped in chocolate with a little bar of chocolate sticking out of it?"

"Yes, you can as long as your mother agrees." Emma and the twins all looked to Libby for her consent.

When she nodded, the children ran off to locate the hose while Emma set off to find the other items.

"Ben and I will head home now," Libby called after Emma.

"Thank you, thank you," Emma yelled out from the veranda. She knew how very lucky she was to have the Arnold family as neighbours.

The children returned at the same time as Emma, and Tim soon hosed down the windows. All three of them grabbed soapy cloths and scrubbed at the dirt, Emma standing on the ladder to tackle the highest parts. Jess then grabbed the hose to wash off the soap. Tim and Emma were busy packing up the buckets and cloths and didn't see what was coming.

"Hey! What are you doing?" Emma squealed as Jess turned the water onto her and Tim. Tim launched himself at Jess, and they wrestled over the hose, water going everywhere but onto the soapy windows. Maxie jumped up and down, barking with excitement at the game that was unfolding. Emma left the melee and headed for the tap. With the water turned off, the game lost its fun and order was restored.

"Come on, you two. Let's just quickly hose off these windows and go get that ice cream."

Children, dog and Emma were soon on their way to enjoy a cold treat. The car was full of the smell of wet humans and dog, but nobody minded a bit.

CHAPTER 31

Day 32 Monday

Emma had not slept well; she kept expecting to hear the noise of a motorcycle again. No such thing happened, but her restless night made Emma even more determined to deal with the remaining papers and rubbish as fast as possible. As soon as it seemed a polite time to phone, Emma made contact with Carson's skip bin provider, who was able, he told her, to drop two large skips to her on Wednesday morning.

"You can't bring one today?" Emma knew she sounded rather desperate, but she really wanted to get on with it.

"No, I'm sorry, my bins are all in use already. Wednesday really is the best I can do."

Emma resigned herself to the wait and decided to return to painting the back veranda, which she had abandoned several days previously after hurting her ankle, in favour of sorting the shed and making the curtains for the veranda.

Having already applied one coat of paint to three of the four walls, it didn't take long for Emma to paint the fourth, but the ceiling was another matter as it was such a large area. Nevertheless, she was finished by lunchtime and was able to apply a second coat to the walls and ceiling by dinnertime. She looked forward to painting the woodwork around the windows and being able to hang the new curtains in the next few days.

CHAPTER 32

DAY 33 TUESDAY

Emma awoke early, excited at the prospect of hopefully getting some clues to the estrangement between her grandfather and great-uncle. She took her morning coffee to the front veranda, Maxie at her heels. The sky was clear of clouds, and the temperature was already unpleasant.

"You'll have to stay home, Maxie. It's too hot for you to be in the car for any length of time."

When Emma grabbed her keys, Maxie rushed to the back door, not intending to be left behind.

"Sorry," Emma patted the dog's head as she shut the door on a very disappointed dog.

Emma arrived at the library just as the doors were opened by a woman dressed in garish, clashing colours, and her hair was in disarray.

"Are you the librarian?" Emma tried to keep the astonishment from her voice. "I'm Emma. I think it was you who rang on Friday about the newspapers?" Emma queried, all the while trying to look unperturbed by the woman's appearance.

The librarian laughed at the expression on Emma's face, "It's storytelling morning for the pre-schoolers. I always dress to impress; they're a tough audience. Come on, I'll show you where the papers are stored."

As they entered the room at the back of the library, Emma smelt the slightly damp mustiness of old newspapers. Large brown folders stood in neat vertical lines on the shelves lining the room.

"Each folder is devoted to one year; the date is written on the front," the librarian informed Emma. "I've got to get ready for the little ones, so I will leave you to it. If you need any help, you can catch me after they leave."

Emma decided that she needed to start with 1943 if the library held that folder; she wasn't really sure what years the collection would cover. She knew from one of the photographs she'd found that the boys still appeared close in the summer of that year.

The first folder that she pulled out had 1952 across the front. Hoping that every year was represented, Emma counted back and dragged out the ninth folder. She was relieved to see 1943 on the front cover.

"Fantastic! That wasn't too difficult!" Emma delved into the first paper, all the while conscious of the excited chatter of the young children and their squeals of delight as the librarian entertained them, role-playing characters from a favourite and familiar children's book in the next room.

Ninety minutes later, her early optimism was gone. She had skimmed through every paper in the folder and found nothing about Clive or George. Devastating stories about local boys lost in battle dominated the pages. Sadness overwhelmed Emma. One, two and even, in one case, three sons were killed or missing in action.

A tear rolled down her cheek. "I can't begin to understand the impact on families and the community. Losing one child is horrendous, but two or three ...?" She shook her head.

Emma decided to take a break, feeling weighed down by the tragedies. She left the library and headed for the bakery, taking her purchases to consume in the shade of a giant peppercorn tree.

Fortified by the break, Emma headed back to the library. She dragged out the 1944 folder and started again. Unfortunately, the papers' sad contents were very similar to those of 1943. When she reached the final paper for 1944, she didn't hold much hope, but on page 3, she found a photograph of Clive and George, George in soldier's uniform. The caption informed the readers that

George Cartwright had joined the army the week that he'd turned 18, on the 12th of December, and that the writer was sure that the community wished him a safe return. No animosity between the brothers was apparent in the photograph, so Emma pushed on to the 1945 folder.

In the late January edition, she saw a photo of a familiar face, her grandmother, or at least she thought it was. The caption informed her that Miss Enright of Melbourne had arrived to take up a teaching position at the Winsthorpe school.

"Is that how my grandfather met my grandmother?" Emma wondered.

Emma continued her search, eventually unearthing a photograph of Miss Enright and Clive in the late July edition, announcing their engagement.

"That's strange. There must have been two Miss Enright if she had married Clive. Maybe two sisters married the two brothers." Then she stopped.

"I thought he left the property to me because he never married. Maybe I misunderstood…. Maybe he married Miss Enright, but they had no children." She sighed. "I am no closer to finding the reason for them falling out. I guess I just have to push on."

Emma continued on with the papers from 1945 until she reached the edition for the first week in September, which was filled with articles about peace in the Pacific. Subsequent editions were filled with joy and sorrow in equal measure as families found out the fate of their beloved sons, fathers, husbands and even daughters in some cases. She reached the end of the editions for 1945 with no further understanding of the apparent reason for the falling out between the brothers.

The librarian came into the room just as Emma was returning the 1945 folder to the shelf.

"Any luck with what you were looking for?"

"No, but I'll come back on Thursday if that's okay."

Emma headed back to her car and drove home, pondering what she'd found.

"Were there two, Miss Enright? Did Clive marry? Is any of this connected to their falling out?"

Opening the door to her house, Emma was almost bowled over by Maxie, who rushed outside and then danced around her beloved human for at least ten minutes. She was so excited to see her.

Emma had spent much of the day on her feet. Her ankle was telling her to give netball training a miss, so Emma messaged Libby, grabbed a glass of wine, and went out to the front veranda to enjoy the view. She kept a watchful eye on the laneway, but no motorcycle or vehicle was sighted, much to Emma's relief. It wasn't until she saw Libby's vehicle head up the driveway that she fully relaxed and headed inside.

CHAPTER 33

DAY 34 WEDNESDAY

Emma was just finishing her morning coffee when she heard a knock on the back door and stood up from the table to greet Libby.

"Hi. I wanted an update on what you found out yesterday. I'm not on duty for another hour, so spill!"

With the coffee machine switched on, Emma told Libby about her discoveries.

"So, I'm not really any further ahead. I know Clive was engaged to a Miss Enright, but I don't know if that person is my grandmother Miss Enright, her sister, or it's just a coincidence that the surnames are the same."

"So the mystery continues… Have you thought of checking with the Victorian Births, Deaths and Marriages Registry? When I was researching my family tree, I found their site to be very helpful. You know Clive's name and his possible bride's. You have some idea of when they could have married, and you have the same information on your grandparents. All you need is your computer!"

"I hadn't thought of that at all. Thanks, Libby. I'll give that a try."

When Libby had finished her coffee and headed off to work, Emma sat down at her computer and typed 'Births, Deaths and Marriages Registry Victoria' into the search bar. She was soon engrossed in finding out what information the site could provide.

"So, Maxie, I should certainly be able to find out if Clive ever married Miss Enright or anyone else for that matter."

Emma started with 1945, the year the couple's engagement photograph appeared in the local paper. She typed in Clive's name and ticked the box for the marriage registry. Nothing came up. She checked every year until 1950 and then started entering time spans of five years, right up to the year 2000. Still nothing. Emma took the same approach with her grandfather. And after only two tries, there it was. George Cartwright married Georgina Enright on the 20th of December 1947, just after he turned 21 if she had done the maths correctly. Georgina was 24 at the time of their marriage, which took place in Melbourne.

"Is this the answer for why we didn't know about Clive? Did George marry the woman who was Clive's intended?" Maxie looked up from her place on the floor at Emma's feet. "Or were there two Miss Enright who were sisters or two Miss Enright who had no connection to each other at all? And I've only searched Victorian records. What if Clive married in New South Wales or Queensland or Tasmania?" Emma shook her head in frustration. The dog put her head on Emma's knee.

"Thank you, Maxie. I guess I just have to go back to the newspapers tomorrow to see if I can turn up anything new."

As she closed down her computer, Emma heard the sound of a truck coming up the lane.

"That'll be the skips, I hope, Maxie." She headed out the back door and was pleased to see it was indeed the truck bringing the two skips.

The driver wound down his window. "Where do you want them?"

Emma directed him, "Can you place one just over there," pointing to the area in front of the shed, "and the other one in front of the stables, just down there?"

"No problem," and the driver moved his truck into position to offload the skips. He had just turned his vehicle to head back down the driveway when Emma saw Carson's car coming towards her.

As Carson pulled up beside Emma, Maxie scrambled to her feet, instantly alert.

"I have a few hours to spare today, so I thought I could give you a hand?"

Emma was somewhat taken aback. How did Carson know the skips were coming? Had the driver told him? Did she want to be in his debt again? Before she had time to think the matter through, Carson spoke again.

"I had a client cancel our arrangement for today, so I have the time. Now, why don't I start on the stables, and you keep going here at the shed?" Without giving Emma time to object, Carson drove to the stables and disappeared inside.

Shaking her head at the speed with which events had just unfolded, Emma called to her dog, whose eyes had followed Carson's every move.

"Okay, Maxie, I guess that's settled." And she headed into the shed, pulling the dog after her.

The boxes of papers, waiting to be recycled, sat in one pile, making it easier to access what remained. Surveying the scene in front of her, Emma decided to work on one section of the shed at a time. She dragged two old car tyres to the skip, wrangled a badly stained and smelly single bed mattress into it and then shoved boxes of broken glasses and crockery on top of that. Propped against the back wall was an old window frame, which she managed to drag into the skip along with other pieces of useless, broken furniture. When that was done, she could see there was an old washing machine and a metal bed frame stacked on the back wall further along from where the window frame had been.

Looking at her now full skip, Emma decided to keep the metal pieces until she could find a way to recycle them.

"And if I can't, I'll just get another skip," she reasoned.

Calling Maxie to follow, Emma went into the house to get a drink of water; emptying the shed had been hot work. As she sat at the kitchen table enjoying the cold water, her thoughts turned to Carson.

"Is he just being friendly, or is he angling to take me out?" she asked the dog as she drank her water. "Do I tell him I'm not interested and risk offending him? I'd feel like an absolute idiot if he really is only being helpful." The dog just looked up from her resting place under the table. Emma vacillated between being grateful for Carson's help and wanting to make it clear that she had no interest in a relationship with him. Refreshed by her break and drink, Emma collected a drink for Carson. Leaving the dog inside the house, she marched resolutely out the door and headed to the stables. Emma had made up her mind; she'd be a coward and say nothing to Carson.

"Hi Carson, how's it going? I see there's plenty of space still in your skip. Mine's full, but I've finished, so what would you like me to do?" she asked as she handed him the water.

Carson waved her off. "It's better if I just do this myself; I know where I'm up to. You have a break or do something else. You haven't finished the painting yet, have you?"

"Are you sure?" Maybe this answered Emma's concerns; Carson certainly wasn't looking for an opportunity to spend more time with her. Thank goodness she hadn't said anything.

"There's certainly plenty of painting left to do, so thanks."

Walking through the unpainted rooms, Emma tried to gather the enthusiasm to start on one of them or, at least, to paint the veranda woodwork. In her first couple of weeks she'd been highly motivated to tackle the front rooms but now found it difficult to muster that same feeling of urgency. Perhaps she should do something else.

"But what, Maxie?"

Her thoughts turned to the windows beside the front door that were now clean on the outside, thanks to the twin's efforts.

"I'll clean the inside of those windows and then move on to any others that haven't been done, and that'll be another box ticked." Right now, that was a much more appealing job to Emma than painting.

It was mid-afternoon by the time she finished. Emma stood in her bedroom, looking through the now spotless glass at the view across the paddock. The sheep were grazing under the shade of the ancient gums or seeking water at the dam. Beyond them lay the national park and its dense grey-green foliage. Despite the worry that the intruder had created, Emma knew, as she absorbed this tranquil scene, that she'd made the right decision in coming to this place.

"I could just stand here all day, Maxie, but work awaits." She bent to the dog, who promptly rolled on her back for a tummy rub.

"Now you'd like me to do this all day, wouldn't you? But I've got things to do." Emma laughed as she collected the cleaning tools she'd been using. She headed to the laundry, thinking about what to eat for a very late lunch, when thoughts of Carson suddenly popped into her head. Her face flushed with guilt as she realised she hadn't offered him anything since the glass of water hours earlier. She didn't even know if he was still at the stables.

"Oops, Maxie. I'd better make amends, hadn't I? You stay here. I know he's not your favourite person."

Carson's car was still in front of the stable block, so she knew he was still there. She stepped inside the passage that connected the three rooms and stopped to listen. She could hear movement coming from the tack room.

Carson was sitting in the middle of the room, surrounded by piles of paper.

"Is this all for recycling?" Emma eyed the mess with horror.

"Yes, it is."

Emma mentally growled, "So why aren't they in the bin then? Can you not bring yourself to 'file' them?" But she stooped down, swept up as many papers as she could hold, dropped them into an empty box, and repeated the action to fill another four boxes.

"I'll have to label these like I did the ones in the shed," Emma grumbled.

Carson barely looked up; he was so engrossed in his sorting.

Emma hurried back to the house and returned with her marker pen in hand. She labelled the boxes and stacked them on one side of the tack room.

"Have you finished in the two stables?"

When Carson nodded, she asked, "Did you find anything interesting?"

"Only some journals. I stacked them in a box in the first stable. Otherwise, just more papers."

"I don't suppose those are stacked in boxes?"

"No, I was too busy sorting."

Emma gritted her teeth, swivelled quickly and headed into the stable next door. A very messy collection of papers spread across the floor. Flushed with anger, Emma bit back the words that instantly flashed into her mouth, reminding herself that Carson was doing her a favour. She simmered as she stacked the papers into empty boxes, labelling them as she went. When that was done, Emma stood to take a breath. That's when she realised that the stable was actually very tidy; only the checked papers were waiting for disposal. Her breathing slowed, and her shoulders relaxed as she prepared to enter the other stable.

The mess that greeted her was similar; the only difference was that there was one box already filled with the journals that Carson had spoken about. As much as Emma wanted to read those, she left them alone to pack papers into the now labelled, empty boxes. Again, Emma noted with satisfaction how little was left to do. She returned to the tack room and set about picking up old musty-smelling hessian bags that, she presumed, had once held horse food and dragged them to the skip. There were some rusty metal feed bins that she thought were in too poor a shape to bother with recycling, so she dragged them out, too. As Emma re-entered the tack room, Carson stood up, an island in the middle of more discarded papers.

"Well, that's all done."

Emma eyed the pile of papers on the floor and wanted to disagree with him.

"So I'll leave you to it. That's excellent, isn't it? I think that's everything sorted now." Carson looked happier than she'd ever seen him, probably, she thought, because he wouldn't have to volunteer his time again. "Just need a few trips with the recycling bin now," he commented.

"Thank you so much, Carson. You've been a great help," Emma tried to keep any hint of sarcasm from her voice. Carson grinned at her and headed for his car. As he drove away, he turned back and gave her a wide, toothy smile.

Emma jogged along to the house to let Maxie out and then headed back to finish up in the tack room.

An hour later, the stables were very presentable; all that was left of the previous mess was the boxes of papers ready for recycling. Emma was immensely satisfied with the day's work, even if she'd had to pick up every sheet of paper that Carson had checked.

"Surely, that must be the end of the intrusions; there's nothing left for anyone to be interested in. The shearers' quarters and shearing shed hold nothing that you wouldn't expect, so I don't need to touch them. Come on, Maxie, time for a walk."

Emma headed back to the house to collect Maxie's lead, feeling more light-hearted than she had been since the intrusions began.

They walked up past the Arnold's farm, the dog enjoying the exercise after being locked in the house, away from Carson.

As they neared her property on their return, Emma saw Ben's farm truck coming up the hill and turn into her driveway. He descended and walked around the truck to meet her. Maxie pranced around Ben, settling only when he'd given her ears a rub.

"How did the skip filling go today? I saw you had your faithful helper in tow, and I don't mean Maxie."

"Don't get me started. He does sort the papers but then just throws them on the floor, expecting someone else, that is me, to pick them up. He left piles of papers all over the floor in all three rooms of the stable block today and made no attempt to get them into boxes or the recycling bin," Emma huffed.

"Sounds like good old Carson, although the fact that he is actually helping, and for free, is something of a miracle. Are you sure he's not sweet on you?" Ben grinned at Emma's expression.

"Definitely not!" Indignation made her voice loud. "He made it very clear he didn't want to spend time alone with me. When he first arrived this morning, I nearly said something to him about me not wanting to go out with him if that's why he was helping me so much. Very, very fortunate that I didn't because he made it quite clear that wasn't the case."

Ben laughed loudly at this, "I hope you're not offended by his lack of interest in you."

Emma pulled a face that left him in no doubt of her feelings.

Then she wrinkled her nose. "Where have you been? You smell like dirty, wet wool?"

"I took some lambs to the Bendigo Sales yard. Lambs are selling at a good price right now."

"Oh," Emma didn't want to ask what fate held for those lambs, so she changed the subject. "Where are we playing tomorrow night? I think I will be right to play, or at least I hope I will be?"

"That's why I called in. We are playing at home so we'll definitely get together for a meal at the pub after the game. If it suits, we can pick you up at five."

"That would be great, I'd like that. Thanks."

By now, they had reached the shed. Ben looked in and let out a long whistle.

"Wow! That's amazing. When you think about what it looked like when you first got here…. And the stables?" He followed Emma and Maxie to the stable block and looked around.

"Congratulations, Emma, you really have done an incredible job." Emma beamed her satisfaction at Ben's compliment.

"Surely you will have no more unwelcome visitors. There's nothing anywhere that could hide any secrets or treasures now."

"That's what I'm hoping. I haven't enjoyed coming home to find I've been broken into, that's for sure."

"Now you've cleared the stables, you'll have to get yourself a horse. Libby said you enjoyed the ride with her. She said you were pretty good."

"I don't think my bottom would agree with her. I definitely exercised muscles that hadn't been used in a long time."

"Well, if you ride more often, those muscles would get used to the workout. What about a ride with me on Saturday morning?"

"You ride?"

"Oh yes. Mum ferried the two of us to pony club every Sunday morning for years."

"That'd be good. I'd enjoy that."

They were back at Ben's truck by now.

"Pick you up at five for the game," Ben called as he climbed into the truck cabin and backed down the drive.

"Come on, Maxie, time for a rest, then dinner for us both." The dog trotted along beside Emma, happy to have her special person to herself again.

Ben was thoughtful as he drove towards his farm. "She's done amazing things to that house and cleaned up so much rubbish. But what is Carson up to? Why is he being so helpful? What's in it for him? I certainly hope he isn't angling for a date with Emma?" That, he realised, was the last thing he wanted to happen.

CHAPTER 34

DAY 35 THURSDAY

After a quick breakfast, Emma gathered her things, ready to head to the library. Maxie hung close to Emma's side, not wanting to be left behind.

"I'm so sorry, Maxie, but it's too hot for you to come with me, and I don't know how long I'm going to be." The dog's sad eyes followed Emma to the door, but still, she left without her canine friend.

Twenty minutes later, Emma arrived at the library just before opening time and just like before, the librarian arrived looking extremely colourful. Emma suspected she always dressed like this, despite her previous protestations that it was for the benefit of the young children.

"You're here for the newspapers again?" the librarian queried. "Well, help yourself. You know where they are."

Emma headed to the little room at the back of the library and looked for the folder for 1946. As she now had a fair idea of the set-up, it didn't take long to put her hands on the correct one.

As she skimmed through the newspapers, Emma could see that, as the months progressed, there was less talk of the fallout from the war and more about the goings on in the community. It was in the July issue that Emma found what she had been looking for; a photograph of Miss Enright and another young woman. The attached article informed her that Winsthorpe welcomed Miss Bromley, who was replacing Miss Enright at the local school, and that Miss Enright was returning to Melbourne. There was nothing about her engagement, broken or otherwise, to Clive. This seemed to support the information from the Births Deaths and Marriages Registry that Clive had never married. What wasn't clear was if this Miss Enright was the same one as her grandmother. Perhaps if she showed the photograph to her father, he'd be able to confirm if she was his mother or not. Emma carefully angled her camera over the newspaper and captured the image. Although it wasn't very clear, she still sent it to her father.

Moments later, he replied, "Where'd you get this photo? My mother looks so young."

Emma looked at the image again; her father's response seemed to decide it. George, her grandfather, had married the girl Clive loved enough to ask her to marry him. How that happened: They were not likely ever to find out, but what was possible was that it was the reason the brothers fell out. How very sad for the family and for Clive especially, thought Emma. Clive had lost his fiancé, his brother and his future.

Emma messaged back that she would phone her father later to explain all.

After replacing the folder, Emma collected her phone and keys and prepared to leave. The librarian had just finished her storytelling session and was back at the main desk. She called out as Emma headed for the exit.

"Did you find what you were looking for?"

"Yes, thanks for your help. Those papers were really very interesting."

As Emma drove home, she pondered the choices made by both her grandfather and Clive. They both must have really loved Georgina Enright to have been prepared to sacrifice so much. While George may not have expected Clive to cut him from his life, he must have known that taking up with Clive's former fiancé would hurt his brother tremendously.

"How would I feel if one of my friends started dating my ex? Actually, I wouldn't care, but then I don't love him, so it's not the same at all. Poor Clive, poor Georgina, poor George."

Back at the house, with thoughts of her family weighing heavily on her mind, Emma again prevaricated over what to paint; she really had lost her enthusiasm for it.

"It's gotta be done, Maxie. I might choose the smallest room and paint the laundry." Emma knew it was the least important room to have finished, but its small size definitely held its appeal.

She collected her bucket and washcloths and set about cleaning the walls and ceiling. It didn't take long, so she decided to wash the bathroom while the laundry dried.

After a quick lunch, Emma commenced the painting and, much to her delight, found that she had completed one coat of the walls in both rooms by the time she needed to get ready for netball.

Just after five, Emma heard Libby's vehicle coming down the driveway.

"You stay here, Maxie. I'll be a while, so don't stress." She gave the dog a hug and hurried out to meet her neighbours, locking the door behind her.

As she settled herself between the children in the back seat, Emma told them what she'd found at the library earlier in the day.

"Poor Clive," lamented Libby, "he lost his love and his brother."

Emma agreed, "He must have been so hurt by their actions to have cut himself off from George. In the photographs I've found of them together, the boys seemed very close before this happened. I know it's possible that Clive and Georgina had separated before she became involved with George, but given Clive's reaction, that seems improbable."

"Perhaps leaving you the farm was Clive's way of saying he eventually forgave George and Georgina." Ben looked over his shoulder at Emma and gave her a sympathetic smile.

The twins scrambled out of the car as quickly as they could when Libby pulled up at the sports ground; they were keen to see if any of their friends were on the playground next to the stadium. Emma, Libby and Ben greeted their team members, and the group spoke briefly about tactics to beat the opposition.

The game went well, and Emma was delighted that her ankle gave no problems. She could not say the same about her opposition player, who seemed to tower over her and frequently stole the ball. Even so, Emma managed to score a number of goals, and although their team lost, it was a close and exciting game.

When the game was over, both teams descended on the pub for a meal. They managed to pull enough tables together to accommodate everyone. Emma found herself sitting next to David, and she took the opportunity to ask him about evaporative air cooling.

"Of course, we can do that for you, but I think you should ask Steven to check your roof first. I wouldn't want to organise the installation and then find out that the roof has problems. It doesn't look like it's received too much TLC in recent times," David advised.

Steven was sitting opposite Emma, but he was involved in an intense conversation with an opposition player, so she waited until there was a gap in the conversation.

"Steven, I want to get a cooler installed at my house. It's already so hot, and everyone says it's only going to get hotter. I've spoken to David, and he suggested I get you to check the roof out first."

"He's right, Emma. Definitely worth doing. I can come past first thing tomorrow if you like before it gets too hot. I definitely don't want to be crawling around on a metal roof at four o'clock in the afternoon. It's like roaming around the hotplate on a stove once the sun hits."

"Thanks, Steven. That would be really great. It's already so hot. I just can't imagine how hot the house will be in January if I don't do something about cooling it."

It was a fun evening; her team seemed to know the opposition team very well, and there were many shared and entertaining anecdotes exchanged. Emma was worried about Maxie and hoped they wouldn't stay too long, so she was relieved when Libby stood to leave.

"Come on, school tomorrow. Time to get you home." There were no grumbles from the twins; they were ready for bed.

As they drove home, Emma asked Ben how they knew the other team members so well.

"We all went to secondary school together and were in many of the same teams during our teenage years. We were the sporty cohort back in the day, so we hung out together," Ben explained. "We like it when we play against them and always go out for dinner afterwards."

"They seem like a great group of people. I had a really good time with them, both on and off the court," Emma smiled.

When they arrived back at Emma's, Ben suggested he accompany her inside to check everything was okay.

"Do you want me to wait?" Libby asked.

He waved them off, "No, I'll walk home."

Maxie was excited to see Emma and Ben and jumped around the two of them for several minutes.

"Come on, Maxie. It's dinner time for you," Emma called the dog to follow her to the laundry.

Ben walked around the house, checking to make sure everything was secure. "Looks like all the cleaning up has finally stopped the intrusions."

"I'm just so thankful for all the help I've been given. I'd still be wading through it if I'd done it on my own. Carson has done so much. He's been wonderful, even if he doesn't know how to put papers into the recycle bin," Emma could smile at the memory now.

"If you're still up for that ride on Saturday," Ben said, "I thought we could head off around noon and take a picnic with us."

"Where would we ride? I don't want to go anywhere near the road."

"Of course not. We'll go along the bridle path again."

"Would you like a glass of wine or a cup of tea? Coffee?" Emma wanted Ben to stay for longer; she'd had a little conversation with him at the pub.

"I'd like that. A glass of wine would be lovely if you've got one open."

Taking a bottle of wine from the fridge, Emma poured two glasses. They carried their drinks to the lounge room and settled themselves on the new sofa. Prompted by the conversations at the pub and wanting to know more about Libby's and Ben's childhood, Emma asked him to tell her about his early life. "What sort of mischief did you get up to?"

"One day, we let all of the farm dogs out of their kennels. We thought they'd like to have a play. Dad was furious because the dogs all ran off, and he had to find them. Which he did, eventually."

"I don't suppose he would have liked to lose his dogs; aren't they very valuable?"

"Yes, they are. We had to pick up sheep poo in the home paddock for weeks after that." Ben laughed at the memory and then looked more serious. "Libby and I used to love climbing around in the hayshed. We'd leap off the highest bale onto the ones below; it was rather prickly, but we never minded. One day, I came close to suffocating doing that, so we stopped. Libby saved me."

"What happened?" Emma looked aghast.

"I jumped from a bale and landed in a gap in the stack. I just disappeared down the hole. Fortunately, my arms were above my head, so Libby was able to reach my hands and drag me out. It was very frightening for us both, and we never went back." Ben looked distressed by the memory.

Emma took his hand and squeezed it. "Did you tell your parents? Did they wonder why you never played there again?"

"Well, here's the thing. We weren't allowed to play there because what happened to me was always a risk." Ben looked a little shame-faced.

"What else did you do? Apart from disobeying your parents."

"Horse riding was a big feature, as I've said, and we often tagged along behind Mum and Dad when they worked around the farm on weekends. That's how you learn to farm most of the time; it's like being an apprentice." Ben finished his glass of wine and stood up to go.

"I'll see you on Saturday." At the back door, Ben put his hands on Emma's shoulders and kissed her lightly on the cheek before heading off down the driveway.

As he walked, Ben smiled to himself. He really enjoyed Emma's company and hoped to be more than just friends. Maybe in time, that could happen.

Emma locked the door behind Ben and headed in the direction of her bedroom. Just as she made to get into bed, Emma remembered that she'd promised to ring her father. Checking the time, she decided it was still early enough to make the call.

He answered on the second ring.

"So tell me all about the photo," her father urged. He listened carefully as Emma relayed everything she'd found out.

"Poor Clive. It seems a cruel thing to do to yourself, to cut yourself off from your family," he said when she reached the end of her story. "Perhaps it's why he left you the farm. So how's it going?"

"To be honest, Dad, I didn't want Mum to know how bad it was when I arrived, so I've kind of fobbed her off when she's asked for details. You would not have believed the state of it. Rubbish was absolutely everywhere, with dirty plates and even dirtier appliances, and mould was growing in the fridge." Emma heard her father groan at the image she'd created in his mind. "But it's nearly done now. I have to finish painting the bathroom and laundry and then do the kitchen work, and then everything inside will be finished. Perhaps you and Mum can visit in a couple of weeks when hopefully that'll be finished, and when I hope the evaporative cooler is installed. Some days have been really hot already. I don't know how Clive put up with it."

"No doubt he just accepted the weather, no matter what it was like because it's what he had grown up with," her father mused. "Anyway, it would be lovely to see you and Maxie. Be in touch soon."

The pressure was on Emma now; she had to finish that painting.

CHAPTER 35

DAY 36 FRIDAY

After breakfast, Emma returned to the bathroom to tackle the ceiling when there was a knock on her back door, and Libby appeared.

"I thought I should check out the sheds and stables. I haven't seen the 'after' shots yet, but Ben tells me it's pretty impressive."

The two women and Maxie walked across the drive to look in the shed. Libby stared at the scene in front of her.

"Amazing! I hope you took lots of photos to show what it was like before."

"Oh, I did. Come on and see the stables."

Libby was shocked by the transformation. "I can't believe it's the same place. You can get a horse for yourself now!"

"That's what Ben suggested, too. But I think I need a few more test runs to be sure it's what I want before I commit to buying my own."

"Is there a paddock attached to the back of the stables for a horse?" Libby led the way around to the side of the stable block and surveyed the fences. "A bit of repair work is required, and a few sheep need to be moved, but it's certainly doable if you decide to buy a horse."

Libby continued to extol the virtues of owning a horse as she, Emma and Maxie walked back to the house.

"I'll think about it." And then, changing the topic, "Would you like a cold drink?"

"No thanks, I'm actually on my way to work. I just wanted to see for myself what you'd done. I'll see you later."

Back inside the house, Emma tackled the ceilings in the bathroom and laundry and then completed a second coat of their walls. She still had to paint the woodwork and give a second coat to the ceilings, so she decided to tackle that after a late lunch.

"By this time tomorrow, Maxie, I should be able to tick two more rooms off the list."

CHAPTER 36

Day 37 Saturday

Emma spent the morning painting the windows in the bathroom and laundry for the second time and then prepared for her ride with Ben. She was really looking forward to improving her riding skills and, if she was honest, the prospect of spending time alone with Ben.

As arranged, Emma arrived at their stables at midday. Ben had the horses saddled and a picnic lunch in his backpack, which he slung over his shoulders as they mounted their horses.

They rode side by side down to the bridlepath and then turned in the same direction as Emma had travelled with Libby.

"Are we going along here? I've already ridden this with Libby and walked it with Maxie. I thought we would go somewhere new." Emma felt embarrassed as soon she said the words; she knew she sounded like a petulant child.

"You won't have been as far up the path as I'm planning to take you. You'll see. Besides, you didn't want to go on the roads, so this is the best choice."

Emma just nodded and walked on, her horse planting its feet firmly on the rough path.

They rode on for well over an hour, and just when Emma was beginning to think she'd tested her skills more than enough for the day, the path opened into a grassy meadow. They were high above the river now, and although she could hear the water running, the trees and grasses hid it from view.

"This is lovely!" Emma enthused as she slid from her horse. Ben joined her, and they tied their charges to a branch in the shade.

Ben spread out a picnic rug at the base of a nearby eucalyptus tree and then unpacked the picnic.

"Wow! What a spread. Thank you, Ben." Emma could see several cheeses, pate, grapes, olives, hummus, and a fresh loaf of bread, which was plaited so it could be pulled apart easily.

"Glass of wine? Water? Juice?" Ben held each up in turn.

"Water and wine, please, but not in the same glass."

"Never, madam." And Ben poured her a glass of both.

Grinning, Emma drank the water quickly and then sat back to savour the wine and the various foods on offer. They chatted about the progress of the netball team and Emma's restoration of her house while they ate. Ben refilled their glasses, and they both sat back against the smooth grey trunk of the gum tree.

After a few minutes of companionable silence, Ben said, "So Libby tells me that you're in the process of getting divorced."

Ben frowned at Emma's grimace. "Sorry, I thought Libby said it was okay for her to tell me."

"I did. I'm sorry. I didn't mean to make you feel uncomfortable." Emma regretted her grim look; she didn't want to embarrass Ben.

"Do you mind if I ask how long you were together?"

"Around twelve years. We met at Uni. We were probably too young. What I thought I wanted at twenty turned out to not be what I wanted at thirty-two."

Ben nodded his head. "I know what you mean. I met a girl at Ag College who I assumed wanted to be a farmer and that we'd finish our course, come back here and farm. Probably get married along the way. But I was wrong, very wrong; it took us both a while to work that out."

"I'm sorry," Emma said gently.

"I was at the time, but I know that we would have made each other miserable if we'd stayed together."

They sat on in silence, and Emma could feel her eyelids grow heavy. The warmth of the sun combined with the alcohol was having a soporific effect on her. Lulled by the sounds of insects and the wind rustling the leaves, she leant into Ben's shoulder for support and drifted into sleep.

When Emma woke, it had grown cooler. Embarrassed, she realised her head still lay against Ben's shoulder. She eased herself into a standing position, muscles complaining.

"Come on, Ben, we'd better get back," Emma said and gave Ben a gentle nudge.

Ben shook his head and blinked, "What time is it?"

Emma pulled out her phone to check. "No wonder it's cooler; it's nearly four o'clock. We must have slept for at least an hour."

Ben scrambled to his feet and looked over towards the horses, shuffling their feet in the dirt.

"Poor things must think we've forgotten all about them."

They gathered the remains of the picnic, untied the horses and mounted.

It was an uneventful ride back, but Emma was glad to arrive at Ben's stables an hour later. She slid off the horse, giving a grunt as her feet touched the ground.

"Bit sore then?" Ben laughed.

"Not sure whether it's from riding or sleeping for an hour sitting on tree roots!"

"Probably both. You go, Emma, I'll look after the horses."

"Are you sure? That'd be great. Poor Maxie will be wondering if I'm ever coming home. Thank you for a wonderful afternoon. I really enjoyed myself." Emma kissed Ben on the cheek quickly before turning and heading down the drive.

CHAPTER 37

DAY 38 SUNDAY

Emma grunted as she grabbed her phone to turn off the alarm; it was eight o'clock, and Maxie was on her feet immediately.

"Come on girl; toilet time and food for both of us."

After a slow start, thanks to her aching muscles, Emma returned to painting. She completed the remaining woodwork in the laundry and bathroom and then headed to the kitchen. As she stood in the doorway, Emma stared at the two heavy dressers.

"I have to move them to paint, but how?"

The dog just wagged her bushy tail.

"Perhaps if I unpack their contents…." With that idea in mind, Emma made her way to the shed to look for flattened cardboard boxes. She carried a number back inside, reconstructed them, taped the seams firmly and set about emptying the contents of the first dresser. Emma filled the boxes with as much as she could carry and then placed the boxes on the dining room table. When the first dresser was empty, Emma manoeuvred herself to the end of it, took a strong hold and tried to lift. Nothing happened. Then, she tried to use her shoulder against the wall as a lever to push it forward but had the same result.

"I think I'm going to need help here, Maxie. When I've emptied both dressers, I'll phone Ben and see if he can come over. I hate to admit it, but a bit of male muscle may be called for."

It was lunchtime when Emma messaged Ben, but he didn't get back to her until later in the day.

"Sorry, but I had problems with a boundary fence on the other side of the hill; reception isn't so good over there."

"That's fine, nothing urgent," and she explained the issue.

"I can come over around five if that's okay."

When Ben arrived, they headed into the kitchen, and together, they managed to inch the heavy dressers far enough away from the wall to allow Emma access.

"They really are heavy. I think the tops can probably be separated from their bottoms, which you'd do if you were moving house. This is your last room to paint, isn't it?"

"Yes, it is. Thanks for that, Ben. You can see why I couldn't move them myself. Would you like a drink? Coffee, wine, beer?"

Ben looked at his watch. "A glass of wine would be great, thank you."

Drinks in hand, they headed out to the front veranda, Maxie close by Emma. It was a beautiful evening, a cloudless sky and still quite warm. In silence, they stood together, looking over the blue-green of the forest over the valley.

"It's a beautiful view; I love the colour of the gums in the evening light," Ben sighed, looking into the distance before turning to sit.

"Do you like my chairs?" Emma asked as they settled into her salvaged seats.

"They're great. Where did they come from?"

"The shed. They were behind all of the rubbish."

"What a find," Ben smiled his appreciation. "Did you check for redbacks?"

"There was a huge female under your chair, actually."

Ben jumped up. Emma laughed at his discomfort.

"Of course, I checked, and I also washed them down." Ben settled back onto his chair and lifted his glass towards Emma's.

"Congratulations, Emma, you've done an amazing job. The house and sheds are unrecognisable from how they were when you arrived."

"I feel very lucky to have had so much help. I think I'd still be sorting papers at Christmas if I hadn't. I need to finish the kitchen work, and that will take a while. Then, I need to think about what to do with the outside and when I'm going to do it. The weatherboards really need painting, but I might just give myself a rest. Mum and Dad are keen to visit, too. I didn't want them to come until I finished inside because I didn't want them to see what a terrible mess it was; I knew they'd have worried about me. And I definitely need that cooler installed. I think Steven is coming around tomorrow morning."

"If you didn't want them worrying about you living in a mess, I bet you didn't tell them anything about the intrusions."

A shame-faced Emma admitted, "No, you're right, I didn't."

"Nothing odd has happened since the incident with the motorcycle, has it?" Ben counted on his fingers. "And that's about eight days ago. Do you have any theories about what they were after?"

"I've thought about it a lot, and the only conclusion I can come to is that they were looking for some sort of document. I think that accounts for their focus on the dining room. It was their most urgent target because I moved into the house, and they couldn't risk me finding whatever it was while I was cleaning up. Then, they shifted their attention to the sheds and stables just as we finished clearing the papers inside the house. Again, there was box after box of papers. Finally, when that was finished, they checked out the shearers' quarters and possibly the shearing shed. As you pointed out, the fact that they only did anything when I was out or, at least, thought I was out shows they meant me no harm," Emma sighed. "I really hope it's over now."

"What you're saying makes sense, but neither you nor Carson ever found anything that would account for the intrusions?"

"No, nothing. I can't imagine what information could hold a threat. Maybe I'm wrong about the papers, but they were looking for a box of Uncle Clive's treasure, like half-empty cans of food and dirty frypans!" Emma laughed. "Would you like to have dinner here? Won't be anything fancy, just cold meat and salad. We could eat out here if you like; it's certainly warm enough."

"Thanks, Emma, I'd like that. I'll give you a hand." Ben followed Emma inside to the kitchen, which was now dominated by the dressers standing away from the walls. The dog danced around them as they worked together to prepare the meal.

When everything was ready, Emma said to Ben, "Could you feed her, or she'll give us no peace when we're eating? I'll refill our glasses and carry the food out."

They chatted easily as they ate, conjecturing what could have been the attraction for the intruders. Early suggestions were quite sensible, but ideas soon became ridiculous.

"Perhaps they wanted his journals," Ben suggested.

"Maybe they were into vintage clothing! Everything in Clive's wardrobe met that criteria." Emma giggled at the thought.

"Perhaps it was his false teeth they were after."

"Or maybe his art collection." They both knew that the only thing on Clive's wall had been an out-of-date calendar.

Later, Emma walked Ben to the back door. "Thanks for your help this evening, Ben. I expect I'll be calling on you again when the painting's done."

"No problem, I'm glad I could help." Ben leaned forward and kissed Emma's cheek. "I'm really glad you came to live here, Emma." He turned and headed down the driveway.

"Me too, Ben," she whispered so that only the dog could hear and watched Ben walk to the end of her driveway. He seemed to sense it because he turned on reaching the lane and waved to her.

"Come on, Maxie, time for bed."

She really is lovely, Ben thought as he walked home, enjoying a feeling of contentment he hadn't experienced in a long time.

CHAPTER 38

DAY 39 MONDAY

As arranged, Steven arrived at seven to check the roof and guttering. He called out through the back door, and Emma responded with an offer of tea or coffee before he started his inspection.

"No thanks. I need to get on with this before the sun heats it up too much."

Emma could hear Steven clumping around on the roof as she ate her breakfast, and then, just as she was gathering her buckets and cloths to wash the kitchen walls, he appeared at the door.

"I'll have that cuppa now if that's alright. It was getting warm up there." Steven took his hat off and looked around the veranda before following Emma into the kitchen.

"This looks great, Emma. Ben told me the state it was in when you arrived. I gather that the condition was something of a surprise, and I don't mean a pleasant one."

"It was certainly a much worse mess than I had expected, but I'm nearly there." Emma put a cup of tea down in front of Steven. "So, what did you find?" Whatever it was, Emma hoped the cost wouldn't be too great.

"The roof needs to be painted, but it's in surprisingly good condition. The gutters are another matter; there's rust and holes in quite a bit of it, so I would suggest replacing them."

"Oh, so this means I'll have to delay getting the cooler." Her disappointment was evident.

"No, I don't think so," Steven reassured Emma. "I suggest you ask David to organise the painting of the roof and the installation of the cooler, and when that's done, I'll replace the guttering."

Emma brightened, liking Steven's idea. "So you're saying that the two things are independent of each other?"

"Exactly. All you need to do is choose the colour. Can I suggest you go with a lighter colour; that will reflect heat better than a dark colour. Do you know if there's any insulation in the roof space?'

Emma shook her head.

"Why don't I have a look before I go?"

"Thank you, Steven. That's really kind of you. What do I owe you for today?"

"Nothing, all part of the service for friends." Steven smiled at Emma and headed out to his vehicle to grab a ladder to allow access to the manhole in the laundry.

Steven set up the ladder, disappeared through the manhole and then reappeared minutes later.

"Good news, there's insulation batts in the ceiling, so that's one thing less for you to worry about."

"So, no buried treasure?" Emma grinned.

"Not unless you count two dead rats as treasure. Now, I think I have a Colourbond colour chart in the truck. I'll just get it for you."

"Why don't I walk out with you? It'll save you having to come back inside."

At the truck, Steven reached into a cardboard box on his backseat and dug around it briefly before bringing out the one he wanted.

"Either of these would be my suggestion." He pointed to a very pale off-white sample and a light grey one.

"That's easy, I like this one." She pointed to the pale grey.

"It's called Southbeach. Tell David this is the colour to paint the roof, and I'll order the same for your guttering. I'd better get going; a blocked toilet in

Winsthorpe is calling." Steven grinned at Emma, climbed into his vehicle and headed off.

In no hurry to start washing the walls, Emma ambled inside and surveyed her next paint job. The kitchen walls were grimy from years of frying eggs and bacon, lamb chops and steak, potatoes and tomatoes, and all without the modern convenience of an exhaust fan. Emma shuddered at the memory of the lamb chops cooked by her grandparents when she was a child; they swam in a pool of fat.

Emma filled her bucket, doubling the amount of sugar soap. Starting behind the first dresser, she found that section of the wall to be slightly better than the rest; presumably, the dresser had sheltered the wall to a certain extent.

Several hours and many changes of water later, Emma stood back and looked at the one wall she'd cleaned; it already looked much better than the rest of the kitchen. Tired from the strenuous task, she knew she'd only get one more wall washed before evening.

"That's alright, though, Maxie; the walls can dry overnight."

After eating and allowing herself a rest, Emma tackled the wall behind the second dresser; it was as hard to clean as the first one, and it was six o'clock by the time she'd finished.

"That's enough for today, Maxie. My arms are aching from all that scrubbing. Let's go for a walk before dinner. You've been so patient today."

Emma and Maxie headed off down the bridle path, enjoying the warm evening and the sounds of the birds. Emma could make out the laughing call of a kookaburra and the chortling of magpies. This time, Emma kept Maxie on her lead, not trusting her to stay close otherwise. On their return home, Emma flexed her arms, happy that they no longer ached. After dinner, the dog and owner settled in front of the television to watch Emma's favourite television show.

CHAPTER 39

Day 40 Tuesday

Wanting the dressers back where they started as soon as possible, Emma focussed on the walls she'd made ready the previous day. Both were done with a first coat by lunchtime, and Emma was thrilled by the light in the room.

After a quick lunch, Emma was ready to tackle the second coat. She hoped Ben would have time after training to help her return the dressers to their original position.

She was just cleaning up and admiring the two finished walls when Libby messaged to say they'd pick Emma up at five o'clock for training.

"Just time for a quick walk, Maxie." The dog dashed to the back door, excited at the prospect.

After a brisk walk, Emma quickly changed, ready for the family to collect her.

The twins greeted Emma with enthusiasm.

"When are we going to do dinner again?" they wanted to know.

Emma thought quickly. "How would you like to help out when my Mum and Dad come to stay?

The twins looked dubious.

"What do you mean?"

"Well, if it's alright with your mum, I thought we could have another dinner party but with two extra people."

A look of relief passed over the children's faces.

"I thought you were leaving Mum and Uncle Ben out," Tim hadn't liked that thought.

"Of course not. The first dinner party was your idea, so we can't leave the family out of it."

"Then count us in," Jess enthused.

"So when are they coming?" Libby asked.

"I haven't actually asked them for a specific date yet. I wanted the kitchen to be finished, but I'm sure I will have that done in the next few days. I planned to phone Mum tonight to get it organised. They are both champing at the bit to come."

"Why would they be champing at the bit? They're not horses!" Jess scoffed.

"It means they are really keen to come. It's just an old saying," Libby told her.

"But Emma's not old, is she?"

Emma thought she'd better ask Ben about moving the dressers before the conversation became even sillier.

"Ben, I've finished painting those two walls where the dresses were. Can you help me move them back?"

"No problem. I'll come in on our way home."

"Great," Emma smiled, "that's what I hoped would you say."

A couple of hours later, they were back at Emma's, and the twins were keen to see the newly painted parts of the kitchen.

Seeing the small shake of Libby's head, Emma made another suggestion. "Why don't you come in after school on Friday when the whole thing should be done."

"Great idea." Libby put the car into gear and headed off before the children could object.

"Let's shift these dressers." Ben led the way into the house, greeted by a very enthusiastic canine rushing around his feet, followed by Emma before the dog dashed outside.

Ben smiled as he walked into the kitchen. "It's stunning what a difference it makes. I can't wait to see the whole room painted."

Emma agreed, "I'm amazed by how much lighter it looks with only the two walls done. Tomorrow, I'll start on the rest."

Ben and Emma worked together to move the two dressers back into place; it was no easier than moving them off the walls, and they were both relieved when it was done.

"If there's nothing else I can help you with, I'll get home. Libby has cooked dinner for me."

"No, that's all. Thank you," she said, kissing Ben's cheek briefly as he went out the back door. He took three steps along the driveway, stopped and turned.

"Emma, I might be reading the signs all wrong; I'm very out of practice with dating, but I think our friendship could grow into something more if we both want it to. If I'm wrong, please put me straight. I don't want to compromise our friendship if you don't feel the same."

Emma hesitated, staring at Ben. Then, she seemed to make up her mind. "I think so, too, but I want to tell you something before this goes further. Will you have dinner here with me on Saturday night so we can talk?"

Ben filled the space between them, put his arms around Emma and landed a gentle kiss on her forehead.

"I look forward to that," he said and was gone.

"Well, that was a surprise, Maxie."

The dog looked at Emma as if to say, "Only to you."

CHAPTER 40

DAY 41 WEDNESDAY

By the end of the day, Emma had scrubbed the two remaining walls in the kitchen. They were even dirtier than the first two, but being on the short sides of the rectangular-shaped room meant it took less time. She even had time to apply a first coat on the wall that held the window and wood-fired stove.

Feeling sure she would finish the painting in the next few days, Emma was confident enough to telephone her mother to invite her parents to stay.

"That'd be wonderful, Emma. We've been dying to see the place. Would it suit you if we came the weekend after next? I've got a bowls tournament this weekend, which I don't want to miss."

"That works well for me, Mum. I'm looking forward to seeing you and Dad." They chatted for a few more minutes before ending the call.

Emma looked around the kitchen again and then at the dog.

"Tomorrow, I finish the walls and start on the ceiling and woodwork." Steely determination gave an edge to her voice.

CHAPTER 41

DAY 42 THURSDAY

A delighted but tired Emma almost met her goal by the time she needed to leave for the game. The team was playing in Smithton, about half an hour away. Emma was driving herself as she knew the others were going to the pub for a meal. She intended getting home quickly so she could enjoy a restorative soak in the bath.

Ben, Libby, and the twins were already at the court when she arrived.

"Is the kitchen finished?" Jess was excited to know if it'd be finished before their visit the next day.

"Not quite, but I'm getting there." Seeing the disappointment on the children's faces, she added, "But you can still call in after school to see it."

The twins brightened. "That's great. That's okay, isn't it, Mum, if we take a look at the kitchen tomorrow?"

Libby agreed and then asked Emma if she'd made arrangements for her parents to visit.

When Emma answered in the affirmative, Libby said, "It'll be good to meet them. I'm sure they'll be blown away by what you've done at the house."

Emma hesitated. "Well, actually, I didn't send them any 'before' photos; I didn't want them to know how bad it was, so they might not be as impressed as you think."

"They don't need to have seen what it was like when you arrived to appreciate how good it all looks now. Come on, the umpire's about to blow her whistle."

The game went well, with Emma scoring the winning goal. The jubilant team pressed Emma to come to the pub with them.

"Come on, Emma. We have to celebrate when we have a win. They don't happen that often," Amy was very persuasive, and Emma decided to join them for one drink before heading home; it would give her a chance to talk to David about the roof and evaporative cooler. She managed to grab a chair beside him and pass on the information that Steven had provided.

Back at home, Emma enjoyed her bath every bit as much as she had anticipated, her sore muscles definitely benefitting from the magnesium she'd added to the water. After feeding herself and Maxie, they headed to bed, even though it was still quite early; she wanted to be well-rested to tackle the ceiling and woodwork in the kitchen.

CHAPTER 42

DAY 43 FRIDAY

E mma woke up when Maxie jumped up on the bed.

"I've done it again, haven't I girl? I've turned off the alarm." She slung her feet over the edge of the bed and grabbed her phone. It was eight o'clock.

"Not too bad, Maxie."

Emma let Maxie outside and went to organise their breakfasts. After eating a bowl of cereal, she took her coffee to the front veranda and sat on the front step beside Maxie, planning her attack.

"Ceiling first, I think, Maxie." The dog looked up and then followed Emma back inside to watch the day's work unfold.

The ceiling proved to be the most challenging surface in the kitchen. It was high and every bit as dirty as the walls, but Emma still managed to have it washed by lunchtime. Emma ate her meal while the ceiling dried and then started on the painting. By the time the children arrived on their way home from school, the first coat of the ceiling was complete, and she had cleaned up.

"Wow, Emma. This is so much better than when we did our first dinner party." Jess was very complimentary.

Tim agreed, "It's so much lighter in here! You're a whizz with the painting. You could do it for a job."

"Thanks, Tim, but I think I'll leave that to the professionals."

The three of them enjoyed a cold drink and some chocolate chip cookies that Emma had bought several days earlier and chatted about the upcoming dinner with her parents.

"What will we cook?" Tim asked.

They concentrated, thinking of possibilities.

"What about a barbeque?" Jess suggested.

"That'd be great. We love barbeques," Tim agreed.

"I don't have one."

The twins looked at Emma dumbfounded. "But everyone has a barbeque. Amy and Steven have one, Zoe and David have one, we have one. See, everyone."

Emma doubted that the netball team counted as 'everyone', but she knew a barbeque would be handy. She looked at the worried faces of her visitors and made a decision.

"You know I haven't given myself a housewarming present yet so I could buy myself a barbeque, couldn't I?"

The twins vigorously nodded. Emma wasn't sure they knew what a housewarming was, but that didn't matter; they understood she was buying a barbeque.

"So that's settled. I'll have to ask your mum where to buy the best sausages."

"We know that; it's Mr and Mrs Miller's in Winsthorpe. They make their own," Tim said. "That's where everybody buys them."

Emma smiled at the 'everybody' again but was willing to bet the twins were correct. They spent another few minutes discussing the preparations for the big night in a little over a week, and then the children headed home.

"Something else for my shopping list, Maxie. Speaking of shopping, I need to buy a new bed for Clive's old room. I can't see Mum and Dad huddled together on his old single." And she laughed at the image this conjured up.

CHAPTER 43

DAY 44 SATURDAY

Emma decided to head to the same Bendigo furniture shops that had supplied her earlier purchases. She was delighted when she found an attractive, reasonably priced queen-sized bed with matching side tables. The best thing was the items were in stock and could be delivered on the following Wednesday.

Emma then headed to the store that sold linen products and came away with all she needed for the new bed.

While she was in Bendigo, Emma bought some seafood for her dinner with Ben; she wanted to keep it simple so she could stay focused on what she had to say.

As she peeled the prawns back in her nearly completed kitchen, Emma realised she was nervous. How much should she tell Ben? Did she want to risk what might be between them by telling him the whole truth? Was it too soon to load all of this onto him? She really liked Ben and hoped he felt the same, but she also didn't want to spoil their friendship by oversharing. Her thoughts went backwards and forward as she worked. Eventually, a decision was made; she would tell him the whole truth.

Her path decided, Emma felt better as she set the dining room table and finished preparations for the meal.

Everything was ready when Ben knocked on her back door. Maxie danced around him in greeting as Ben placed a bottle of chilled wine on the kitchen table and kissed Emma's cheek.

His eyes swept the room. "It certainly looks much better in here. Not much to go now by the looks of it."

Emma was pleased with the praise. "Thanks for the wine. Are you able to open it? I thought we could sit out on the front veranda at least while we have a drink; it's such a lovely night."

Ben obliged, and they made their way to Emma's salvaged chairs. As he sat, Ben turned his chair so that he could look straight at Emma. "So what is it that you want to tell me?"

Emma took a sip of her wine and started.

"Everything that I told Libby is true, but I didn't tell her the whole story. It's true that Roy and I had been drifting, and we might have kept going like that for years before either of us had the courage to call it quits. Something happened that hurried the end along, and that's what I want to tell you."

"Are you sure you want to tell me?"

"You do need to know this before we decide to take things any further, but I'd appreciate it staying between us. No one else knows the whole story or needs to know. So here goes. What you need to understand is that Roy and I had decided early on that having children was not on our radar."

Ben kept his eyes firmly fixed on Emma.

"Then, about two years ago, I discovered I was pregnant. I guess I got careless. I was terrified at the start because I didn't know what I wanted to do. And then suddenly, I did know; I wanted to keep her. I fell more in love with her every day that she was growing inside me. When I was past ten weeks and had the results of all the tests, I knew she was healthy, and I knew I wanted her. So I told Roy I was pregnant. He was horrified and called me all sorts of names. He got even angrier when he realised I'd known for 6 weeks and hadn't said anything.'

Emma paused, looking down at her hands.

"He put a lot of pressure on me to have a termination, but I was determined to keep her. So he moved out, making it very clear I was on my own. I could have forgiven him for his reaction; after all, I was the one who'd broken trust, but his later behaviour.... unforgivable."

"So what happened?"

Emma continued talking as if he hadn't spoken.

"Everything was going well. I thought the baby was fine. I had done all of the recommended testing, and everything was positive. Once I had passed 16 weeks, I no longer felt ill, and I really started to enjoy being pregnant. I could sit for hours just touching my belly and chatting to her. Then, out of the blue, when I was twenty-four weeks, I went into labour. I'd had a sore back for a couple of days, but I never connected that to being in labour. I didn't think that was a possibility. I was home by myself, and it all happened very quickly. She was born within minutes of the contractions starting. My dear little girl never made a sound."

Ben reached out and took Emma's hand in his. Tears glistened in his eyes. "Oh, Emma, I'm so sorry. That must have been just awful to get through."

"I'm not through it, Ben. You just get better at living with it," she snapped, a hard edge to her voice.

Ben hesitated before asking, "Did you name her?"

"Yes, I called her Ruby after my grandmother, my mother's mum."

"That's a lovely name. How long were you alone after she was born?"

"I rang for an ambulance as soon as I could. In reality, the paramedics arrived quickly, but it seemed ages. There were two of them, a man and a woman. They were so kind and caring. They checked us both over and asked me if I realised what had happened to my baby. I said I did, but I was in shock. I just couldn't believe what had taken place in such a short space of time. One of them took Ruby and wrapped her in a blanket, and then she gave her back to me and asked if I would like photos taken. I am so glad I said yes because that's really all I have of her. They were so kind. I am forever grateful for the care those paramedics took of us."

"I am so sorry, Emma. I can't begin to imagine how sad and traumatic that must have been for you. Did you have a funeral for her?"

"Yes, just with Mum and Dad and me. My parents have been amazing through all of this. They retired to the Gold Coast a few years ago, but they were on the first plane out of there to be with me. They stayed for a couple of months until I thought I was well enough."

"Is that why you went on leave from school?"

"Yes. I did go back, but after a few days, I realised I wasn't able to give my best to the children. My colleagues were very supportive, though. I returned to the classroom at the beginning of the following year, but my heart just wasn't in it, so I applied for a year's unpaid leave and under the circumstances, they were happy for me to take it."

"You didn't mention your husband going to the funeral."

"It was the absolute end for me. When I rang to tell him I had lost the baby, he just said, 'Thank God for that.' I've never told anyone that, not even my parents."

The look of shock and disgust on Ben's face reflected her own feelings of revulsion for the man she once thought she'd loved.

"I started divorce proceedings as soon as I could. I haven't spoken to him since. Any communication has been through my lawyer."

Ben stepped towards Emma and wrapped his arms around her.

"I am so sorry for all that you have been through, Emma," he said into her hair.

Emma clung to Ben as tears streamed down her cheeks. They stayed like that until Maxie broke them apart, pushing her nose between them.

Emma gave an uncertain laugh. "Sorry, Maxie. Are you telling me it's dinner time?"

Ben gave Emma another hug, and they drew apart.

"I'd better feed this animal and then us." She made to go, but Ben grabbed her arm.

"Emma, why did you feel you needed to tell me?"

"You need to know that I am not getting involved with someone who doesn't want children. If that's you, then this goes nowhere. My experience with Ruby showed me how much I want to be a mother, and if you're not on board, then we will stay friends, and no more. I know this is very intense, given that we haven't even kissed, but I hope you now understand."

Ben reached out, took Emma in his arms and kissed her tenderly on the lips. "No going back now," he said.

CHAPTER 44

DAY 45 SUNDAY

Emma woke and looked across at the man sleeping beside her. She and Ben had talked for hours after dinner the previous night, and going to bed together seemed like the most natural thing to do. Their lovemaking had been gentle at first as they slowly explored each other's bodies, but desire had fired their passion until they were both deeply satisfied. They'd fallen asleep in each other's arms in the early hours of the morning.

Emma slid out of bed to let Maxie out and to feed her breakfast. When she returned to the bedroom, Ben was awake.

"Come back to bed, Emma. It's still quite early."

As she slid in beside him, Ben reached out for Emma, and they were soon entwined again in each other's bodies.

"I could get used to this," he whispered in her ear an hour later. "What a lovely way to start the day. But now I have work to do, and so do you; that kitchen isn't going to finish itself."

Ben then asked, "Is it okay if I take a shower?"

Emma grabbed a towel from the laundry and handed it to Ben before heading to the kitchen to make coffee.

"I'd better go and see to those sheep." Ben kissed Emma as he headed out the door. "See you later."

Emma took her coffee to the front veranda, sat on the chair and hugged herself, reliving the events of the past twenty-four hours.

Maxie cuddled up beside Emma, the two of them enjoying the warmth of the morning, not rushing. They sat together until Emma felt ready to start work.

"Come on, Maxie. It's time to get this kitchen finished."

Emma was just cleaning up her painting equipment when Ben arrived back at the house in the late afternoon.

He hugged Emma in a tight hold and then asked what he could do to help.

"I have a new bed coming on Wednesday for Mum and Dad, so I need to shift Clive's old bed. I thought it could go on the veranda to fill in a bit of space. It can act as a day bed and another spare bed."

After stripping the sheets and blankets from the mattress in Clive's room, Ben stood at one end and Emma at the other.

"If we tip the mattress onto the floor on its side, we should be able to slide it to the veranda quite easily," Emma suggested. With a decent shove from them both, it was soon on the floor.

Ben shuffled backwards dragging the mattress, with Emma pushing it, until they reached the veranda, where they rested it against the back wall.

"Let's hope we can get the bed apart; I think it'll be too awkward to move it otherwise." Emma set off to locate a ratchet set while Ben sprayed a lubricant on the bolts. With much straining and cursing, the bed head was finally separated from the base, and they were able to move it to the veranda and reassemble it.

"Let's get this mattress back on," said Ben, taking up his position at the end of the mattress again. Emma stretched her arms wide to push it the ninety degrees required to line it up alongside the bed frame.

As Emma scrambled to get a decent grip on the mattress, her left hand touched something unexpected.

"What on earth is that?"

"What's the problem?" Ben stopped his pushing.

"I think there's something in the mattress." Emma rubbed her hand over the area again. "It's crinkly feeling, like paper."

Together, they moved the mattress so it could fall upside down to the floor. "See, there."

Ben ran his hand over the area Emma indicated. "If you look closely, you can see the material has a cut in it, and someone's made rather a mess of stitching it back together," Ben said, eyes wide.

Emma dashed to the kitchen and returned with scissors in her hand. Falling to her knees, she located the slit and cut through the clumsy stitching. Ben pushed his hand through the opening she'd revealed and drew out a bunch of slightly yellowed pages.

"How very odd!" Emma remarked. "What are they?"

Ben ran his eyes quickly over the pages. "They look like bank statements. See what you think." Ben handed the sheets to Emma. She scrutinised the pages, her eyes running up and down the columns, her breathing becoming quicker as she deciphered more and more information.

Emma could not believe what she was seeing.

"Not only are they bank statements, there's a ridiculous amount of money here." Emma pointed to the figure at the bottom of the first page.

Ben let out a loud whistle. "That's a lot of money. Does it say whose account it is?"

"Yes, it's Clive's," Emma looked confused, "but I don't understand. Carson told me there was only enough money in Clive's account to pay for his funeral. Maybe he didn't know about this one."

Ben shook his head, also confused by this information. "Is there a date?"

Emma scanned the pages and then showed Ben the date of issue for the statement; it was a bit over three years earlier.

Ben pondered for a moment. "That could be around the time Clive was diagnosed with dementia, although I know he'd had problems for a long time before that. That's why I was leasing the land from him."

Emma considered the pages in her hand. "Why did Clive go to so much trouble to hide these sheets? If he'd been diagnosed with dementia, it could be there's nothing rational about it at all."

"That's true," Ben concurred, "and yet he was rational enough to cut a pocket in the underside of his mattress, hide the papers and sew the cut up."

"Maybe we should assume he knew what he was doing and analyse the entries; perhaps there was something in these pages that upset him in some way." Emma carried the pages to the kitchen table and organised them into page order. Ben followed.

Sitting side by side, they scanned the entries on the first page.

"There doesn't seem to be anything odd here. Clive appears to be making cash withdrawals. He probably preferred that to a credit card," Emma remarked when she reached the bottom of the page and prepared to check the second page.

Ben stopped her. "How much money do you think a ninety-something-year-old would need for expenses each week? Remember, he wasn't farming by this stage, so any withdrawals are just for personal spending."

Emma pondered, "Maybe a couple of hundred dollars at most unless he had bills to pay."

Pointing at one of the pages, Ben said, "Add up how much money left his account the first week in July then."

Emma paled as she realised the several listed amounts totalled more than one thousand dollars. "Oh, I see what you mean."

Emma grabbed some lined paper from a kitchen drawer and started recording the details for each week.

"Look, Ben, there are also transfers to another bank account."

As Emma listed the data, Ben was adding up each week's withdrawals. "Emma, the amounts coming out of the account are increasing. In the fourth week in July, ten thousand dollars went."

The statement was for the three months to the end of September. By the time they reached the last entry, the balance in the account was under two hundred and fifty thousand, down from a starting point close to three hundred and fifty thousand.

"What can he have done with the money?" Emma was stunned by their discoveries. "Surely he didn't spend one hundred thousand dollars on himself in just three months."

"Maybe his dementia was worse than we all thought at the time, and he was just giving the money away," Ben suggested.

"That's possible, and if it's true, well, it was his money; he could do whatever he wanted to do with it," Emma admitted. "But he went to a lot of trouble hiding these statements. He must have had a very good reason for doing that."

They sat in silence, both considering the implications of their find.

"I think," Ben finally began....

"That someone was stealing from him," Emma finished his sentence.

"But who? Was he being scammed? Older people can certainly be targets," Ben lamented.

"Again, I don't think that explains why he hid the pages. Surely, he would have just told Carson about it. Or the police?" Emma stopped, a wave of cold fear sweeping through her.

"Ben, this must be what the intruder was looking for."

Ben looked at her, considering Emma's suggestion. After a moment, he nodded his agreement. "That certainly makes sense. The dining room was targetted until we cleared it all out, and then their focus shifted to the shed, and when that was done, it was the stables."

"The losses we've discovered would give any thief plenty of reason to want to find these pages and destroy them. If Carson said there was almost no money left in Clive's account by the time he died, then another two hundred or so thousand has been taken between September three years ago and Clive's death," Emma was processing her thoughts.

"Probably more than that," Ben added. "Don't forget that he had income from our leasing arrangement."

Emma queried, "So what are we going to do now? We should speak to Carson, don't you think. After all, he was Clive's solicitor. He might know something?"

Ben hesitated. "I'm not sure that asking Carson is a good idea. What if he's the person who's taken the money?"

Emma glared at Ben. "I know you don't like him, but he's been nothing but helpful to me. Think of all the hours he's spent sorting papers for ..." Her voice trailed to a stop. "For me," she finished lamely.

After a moment, Emma frowned, thinking of Carson pushing her to sort the dining room papers out. The hours she'd spent painting while he insisted he didn't need her help. Did he find more documents that he just 'disappeared'?

Finally, she said, "Is there anyone else we can ask? Clive's bank manager? The police?"

Ben shook his head looking bewildered. "I don't know, but I do think we should make a copy of these papers in case anything happens to the originals. You have a printer, don't you? "

Emma led Ben back into Clive's bedroom and pointed to the printer set up on the desk in the corner of the room. Together, they scanned the documents and printed two copies.

"Come on, let's have a glass of wine while we think about our next move," suggested Emma. She carefully placed the copies and originals into one of the buffet drawers before pouring two glasses of wine, which she carried to the front veranda. Ben was standing next to one of the cane chairs as she came through the door. He reached out and took the wine from her, placing it on the coffee table. Then he put his arms around Emma and hugged her fiercely.

"I hope you're not too upset by what we found today."

Emma hugged Ben back and then drew his head down to hers to gently kiss his lips. The kiss didn't stay gentle for long; their passion escalated quickly, the wine quickly forgotten as they made their way to Emma's bedroom.

"I definitely like your idea of the next move, Emma," said Ben, kissing her ear.

Sometime later, they emerged from the bedroom, pushed out by Maxie, intent on being fed. "I have some steaks that you could cook while I make a salad if you feel like eating."

"Are you kidding? I'm starving; all that energy I've just expended!" Ben laughed and gave Emma a quick hug. "Just point me in the direction of the barbeque."

"One problem with the barbeque; I don't have one. I meant to buy one yesterday but forgot."

"Then into the pan they go." Ben had the steaks cooking in minutes.

"Have you told Libby about us?" Emma asked Ben later as they were eating their meal. "I don't want to say anything to her if you would prefer to keep this between ourselves."

"She guessed I'd stayed with you. Or, to be exact, she said she hoped that's where I was last night. She seemed pretty happy about it. And I don't mind who knows if you don't have a problem with other people knowing."

"Ben. I am happier right now than I have been for a very long time, but it's early days, and I'm not sure where this is going, so can we keep it to ourselves for now."

Ben stiffened, his disappointment at Emma's words obvious. "Just for the record, Emma, I don't sleep around. I haven't been with anyone for a very long time. I thought we had something special going on here, and I thought, or at least hoped, you felt the same."

Emma could see that she had hurt Ben and tried to explain her feelings. "I'm sorry, Ben. I do think we have something special, but I was terribly hurt by my ex-husband, as you know, and I just think I need time to adjust to being in a relationship again."

"That's fine, Emma. Let me know when that happens. Thanks for dinner." Ben stood, shoving his chair so hard it fell to the floor, and disappeared out the back door without another word.

"Oh, Maxie, I stuffed that up, didn't I?" The dog looked at the door and back at Emma as if to agree.

Furious with Emma for what she'd just said, Ben walked at a brisk pace in the direction of his home. "What do I have to do to show her I love her. I'm not a player. How can she think I am?"

CHAPTER 45

DAY 46 MONDAY

Emma had a restless night, her mind full of thoughts about Ben and also the bank statements. She was sitting on the veranda drinking her third cup of coffee for the day when Libby knocked on the back door and entered. Emma registered the scowl on Libby's face immediately.

Libby got straight to the point. "Ben doesn't know I'm here, but he came home last night looking like thunder. What's going on?"

Emma explained her comments that had led to Ben leaving the previous night.

"No wonder he's upset, Emma."

Tears spilt down Emma's cheeks. "I know I upset him. I think I love Ben, but I'm scared."

"So talk to him, explain how you feel, only do it much better than you did last night. Anyway, I'm off to work. Sort it out with him, Emma, please." Libby left after Emma nodded her agreement.

Emma decided a walk might help her thought process, so she grabbed Maxie's lead, and they headed off along the bridle path. The peaceful surroundings of the path helped Emma to focus on her two problems: Ben and the bank statements. Two hours later, she was back at her house with what she hoped was a solution to both issues.

She first messaged Ben with an invitation to dinner that night and issued an apology for upsetting him the previous night. Then she messaged Carson and asked him to come for drinks on Friday night to thank him for all of his help.

Ben responded first with a curt, "See you at 7."

Carson's reply was equally brief, "See you Friday."

By five o'clock, Emma had a cooked chicken in the fridge, along with a green salad and a cooling bottle of wine. She had rehearsed what she wanted to say to Ben many times and hoped she could make him understand.

Emma opened the bottle of wine at seven, expecting Ben to be punctual as always. She sat in the kitchen, monitoring her phone clock as the minutes ticked away without any sign of him. At half past seven, Emma opened the bottle of wine and poured herself a glass. At 7:45, she served herself dinner and sat at the table to eat, her misery growing with each passing moment. She pushed the food around the plate, sadness robbing her appetite. At a quarter past eight, Emma gave up the pretence of eating and stood up to return her food to the fridge. She poured another glass of wine and sat back at the table, tears sliding down her cheeks. Maxie rested her head on Emma's knee, sensing her beloved owner's distress.

Deep in thought, Emma jumped when there was a knock on the door. She grabbed a tissue and wiped her eyes before opening the back door. Ben stood there, uncertainty written across his face.

"I nearly didn't come, Emma, but then I thought about you waiting and worrying if I didn't front, so here I am."

Emma didn't say anything. She just turned and headed back to the kitchen. Emma handed Ben a glass of wine and sat down at the table. She didn't wait for Ben to sit before launching into her speech.

"I have spent hours and hours worrying that I had lost you before we had really even got started, and when you didn't arrive tonight, I thought that was it." Emma made no attempt to stop the tears that were sliding down her cheeks. "Ben, what I was trying to say last night, and I know I did a crap job of it, was that I think I'm falling in love with you but that I'm scared it will all go wrong. If it does, it will be much easier for me to stay in this community if the general population doesn't know about us."

Ben reached for Emma's hand and held it firmly. "Emma, hearing you say you think you love me makes me very happy because I think I love you too. I'm sorry I left so abruptly last night. All I could hear you saying was that you didn't want anyone to know. I think my ego was reacting, not my brain. If it does go wrong, you're right. Everyone would think worse of you, not me, whether that's right or not, because you are the newcomer. I don't think it will go wrong, but yes, I'm happy to keep it to ourselves for now."

Ben stood up and pulled Emma into his arms. Without speaking, they headed to Emma's bedroom, falling onto the bed, their arms wrapped around each other as they slowly undressed. This time, their lovemaking was slow and sensuous, each valuing what they thought they had lost.

CHAPTER 46

DAY 47 TUESDAY

It was early when Ben kissed Emma goodbye as he headed off to work, taking the original bank statements with him. They had decided the previous night that it was safer for the papers to be at Ben's house now.

"I'll see you tonight. Perhaps after netball training, we can eat that dinner we were supposed to have last night," Ben suggested.

Emma laughed and headed to the shower. Back on the veranda with her morning coffee, Emma reviewed her plans for the day. She still hadn't told Ben her idea for Carson.

"We were too busy for that," she blushed with pleasure as she patted Maxie. As the furniture for Clive's old bedroom was coming the next day, Emma decided on a trip to Bendigo to purchase a new rug to finish it off. By lunchtime, she had achieved her goal, so she set about giving Clive's room a final clean, including the window where a new blind and curtains now hung.

The room was finished and just waiting for the bed to complete its transformation when Ben returned with Libby and the children to collect Emma for training.

On arrival at the courts, David approached Emma immediately. He brought her up to date on the plans for the roof painting and installation of the cooling system.

"The painter will be at yours in the morning to make a start. He won't be painting tomorrow; he'll be doing the preparation, which will probably take him all day."

"Thanks for organising it, David. I hope it's not too hot tomorrow if he has to be on the roof all day."

"That's why he's coming tomorrow; it's meant to be overcast. There's a lot more work to get it prepped than in the actual painting. Expect him early."

Amy called them all onto the court to begin their practice drills, and there was no more time for conversations about her roof.

After practice, Libby dropped Emma and Ben back at Emma's door, leaning out the window as she prepared to back away.

"If you two want to keep this a secret, you'll have to do better than you did tonight. Mooning over each other is bound to give the game away," Libby laughed.

The twins in the backseat were on the alert instantly. "What secret? Who's got a secret? What's going on?"

They could still be heard as Libby reversed to the lane. As always, Maxie greeted Emma like she'd been left alone for a month instead of a couple of hours.

"Come on, Maxie, toilet stop, then your dinner."

Fifteen minutes later, a contented dog lay under the kitchen table, snoring gently as Ben and Emma finished the meal and wine from the previous night.

"That was still delicious. Thank you." Ben stood to clear the table and start on the dishes. Later, they headed out to the front veranda with their coffee. Settled on the raffia and cane chairs, Emma felt ready to share her plan for Carson.

"We have no way of knowing if Carson has any knowledge of the money that left Clive's account, and I would hate to accuse him if he knew nothing about it. So here's what I'm going to do. I have invited Carson for drinks here on Friday night."

Ben frowned.

"I told him it was to thank him for all the help he's given me," Emma continued.

"And then what?"

"I plan to show Carson the bank statements, not the originals but a copy. Guilty or not, I expect he will ask where I found the pages, given how many papers he's sorted for me over the weeks."

Ben nodded his agreement. "What will you tell him?"

"The truth. I'll tell him they were in Clive's mattress."

"Are you sure that's a good idea?"

"Just hear the rest of my plan. I'm going to tell him that what he's looking at is a copy and that the originals are back inside the mattress. They won't be, though, because they're already at your house. I'll put a copy into the mattress. If Carson is the intruder, I expect he will come here on Tuesday night when we are at training. Of course, we won't be at training; we'll be in the laundry. We can hide my car and Maxie in your stables so it looks like we've done what is usual on a Tuesday night. Now, if Carson doesn't turn up here, we know it's not him. "

"You think that would show he's innocent?"

"Yes, and if he is, he should react the same as we did when he sees the statements. He might also have some useful suggestions for finding out what has happened to the money."

"I think I like it," Ben didn't sound totally convinced. "What makes you so sure he'll come on Tuesday night if he's guilty?"

"All of the intrusions have occurred on a Tuesday or Thursday night. I have long thought that the intruder knew we were at netball."

"I'm not sure that you have thought enough about what happens if he is, in fact, the one who's taken the money. I reckon you should talk to Maria to see what she thinks."

"Fair enough. I can speak to her after the game on Thursday."

Ben stood up. "I'm going to head home now." Seeing the look of disappointment on Emma's face, Ben hugged her and said, "If we're keeping us a secret, I think I need to sleep in my own bed most nights because those twins are as effective as any bloodhound at sniffing things out."

A much happier Ben reluctantly left Emma to walk home.

"Thank goodness we worked it out. I guess I was a bit of an ass to just storm out last night; I should have stayed and listened to her." Then he thought about Emma's plan to test out Carson's involvement with the potentially misappropriated money. "I'm glad Emma's going to run her plan past Maria; she's bound to see the pitfalls and risks."

CHAPTER 47

Day 48 Wednesday

Darius arrived before seven, introducing himself to Emma before setting up his ladder and hose to begin cleaning the roof. She was conscious of him moving across the roof throughout the morning.

Around midday, the new bed and mattress were delivered by two helpful men, who carried the bed to Clive's old room and set it up. When they left, Emma dived into the laundry and collected the basket holding the new, freshly washed and dried linen and made up the bed. Later, she stood in the doorway admiring her achievements.

"Doesn't that look great, Maxie? I'm sure Mum and Dad will be very comfortable in here." The room bore no resemblance to that which had greeted her when she first arrived. In fact, the whole house was a different creature, one she knew she could live in for many years, alone or with Ben.

Maxie rubbed her head against Emma's leg.

"Are you waiting for a walk, girl?"

At the mention of a walk, Maxie started jumping around Emma in excitement.

"Come on then, let's go."

When they arrived home a couple of hours later, Darius's vehicle had gone, and the roof looked much better than it had done the day before. Emma assumed Darius would return in the next couple of days to continue the job.

CHAPTER 48

DAY 49 THURSDAY

Darius, in fact, arrived early the next morning to apply the first coat of paint. Emma thought she should follow his lead and finish painting the kitchen. Her Mum and Dad would be arriving in a week, and it had to be finished by then. Darius left before lunch, saying he'd be back on Monday for the final coat. Emma took a break from her painting to admire the new roof.

"It looks fantastic, Maxie, and it will look even better when the gutters are replaced."

After a quick lunch, Emma resumed painting. Two hours later, she stood up from the floor where she'd been painting the skirting boards.

"Maxie, that's it! I've finished. Everything inside the house is done." Emma couldn't contain herself, so she jumped around the kitchen in delight. Maxie had no idea why her owner was so excited, but she joined in anyway, leaping and barking her approval. Emma cleaned her brushes and prepared for the netball game.

The game was to be played in Winsthorpe, a home game. Emma drove herself as she wanted to arrive early to speak to Maria. The senior constable knew Emma was coming to catch up with her but didn't know the reason.

When Emma drove into the carpark, she could see Maria was already on the court shooting goals. She stopped on seeing Emma and waved a greeting.

"How about we sit here, and you tell me what's going on?" Maria indicated the courtside benches.

Emma sat down, gathering her thoughts. She hoped Maria didn't think her idea too fanciful; after all, Ben hadn't exactly been enthusiastic.

"Come on, Emma, out with it."

A copy of the bank statements was clutched in Emma's hand. As she started talking, Emma handed the sheets to Maria.

"What am I looking at?"

Emma began her explanation, detailing the intruder incidents, Carson's insistence that there was no money left in Clive's account after the funeral and his seemingly out-of-character helpfulness.

Maria listened, giving Emma her full attention. She then scanned the pages.

"So what do you want to do about it?" she said without looking up from the statement.

Emma outlined her plan to challenge Carson with the pages on Friday night.

"And what do you want me to do?" Maria looked steadily at Emma.

Now she'd repeated her plan out loud, Emma realised how naïve she sounded. As if Carson was suddenly going to admit he'd stolen the money from her great-uncle. He could say he was following Clive's instructions, that Clive had just given him the money, that Clive wanted to give the money to whoever, that he knew nothing about it at all.

"Well, I hoped you'd hide in the laundry with me and catch him if he broke into my house to get the sheets." Emma looked as doubtful as she felt.

There was silence.

Then Maria grinned. "He's a pompous little prick; I think I'd enjoy catching him out. But I'm not going to hide in the laundry, and neither are you," she said in a stern voice that left no room for argument. "We will wait in the shed until he comes back out of your house with the sheets in his hand. Then, I can arrest him for breaking and entering. And theft."

Relieved Maria didn't ridicule her entire idea, Emma clapped her hands. "Thank you!

The policewoman urged caution. "I'm not sure how far we will be able to go with an investigation into Carson possibly stealing money from Clive, but if we can convince a magistrate to approve a warrant to look into his financial situation, we might make some headway."

Emma nodded. "I usually leave for training at around five. If Carson's expecting me to be here, at training, I'd better appear to have left by then. You need to arrive around then, too, so you can be in place by 5:30pm at the latest. You should leave your car at Ben's and Libby's. I've spoken to Ben about my plan, so I'm sure he'll be happy for you to do that."

"I won't leave the car at theirs; if I need to make an arrest, I want the car to be right there, at your house. Any suggestions for where I can hide it closer?"

Emma thought for a moment and then said, "It would be out of sight around the side of the shed. It's a bit of a risk, I suppose, but he's unlikely to go looking around there when he knows the papers are in the house."

"I think that's a much better idea. Let's keep this between ourselves. Ben and Libby will need to know, of course. I'll see you at five on Tuesday, if not before."

Several cars pulled up in the carpark, and team members and opposition players made their way to the court.

Emma realised this team was the one she'd played against in her second game when she'd been soundly relegated to her back foot by her towering and nimble opposition player. She wanted to do better in this game but held little hope.

When the teams were on the court, Emma was lined up against a girl about the same height as herself.

"Where's the really tall guy that was your goal defence last time we played?" Emma asked.

"You mean Nick? He couldn't make it tonight."

Emma felt her shoulders relax at this very welcome news. The whistle blew at the start of the game, and Emma raced ahead of her opposition to receive the ball and score. This time, Emma's team was victorious, and they headed to the pub for a celebratory meal.

"If you're going ahead with this, I need to tell Libby. Otherwise, she'll wonder why three of us are not attending training and why one car and a dog are being hidden at the stables," Ben commented later when they were back at Emma's and Emma had relayed her conversation with Maria.

"You're right, of course," she hugged Ben. "Now, are you staying tonight?"

"I won't tonight, but I really want to stay for the next few nights until after Tuesday night. If he's guilty, I'm worried that Carson might try to retrieve the papers before Tuesday while you're here alone."

Emma nodded. "Perhaps you could just stay for an hour now, just to get in some practice for the weekend."

Ben laughed. "How do you suggest we fill in the next hour, then? Watch TV, play cards, look at the stars?"

"I have another suggestion." Emma grabbed Ben's hand and gently pulled him in the direction of her bedroom. He needed little encouragement.

CHAPTER 49

Day 50 Friday

O n Friday morning, Emma drove into Winsthorpe to purchase food and drinks for the weekend and for her meeting with Carson. She also visited the hardware store to inquire about barbeques, having promised the twins that she'd have one to use when the family came to dinner next. Emma was delighted to find a barbeque that she liked and returned home with the promised item. Emma planned to set it up on the front veranda and thought that perhaps she and Ben could do it while he stayed with her for the next few nights.

The thought of having Ben with her for the weekend made her tingle with anticipation. She loved how he made love to her.

Back at home, she dragged the two boxes for the barbeque to the front veranda and then set about making sure the house was clean and tidy for Carson's visit. She was just changing the sheets on her bed when there was a knock on the back door, and Libby breezed in.

"How's the preparation going for the trap?" Libby asked outright.

"So Ben's told you." It was a statement, not a question. "I have to admit to feeling rather anxious. I'm just about ready, but the closer it gets to the meeting, the more nervous I'm becoming."

"Well, you'd better get over that before Carson gets here, or he'll be wondering what's going on. You need to be sure to treat him the same as you always do," advised her friend.

"You're right, Libby. I'll be fine. I hope."

"Anything I can do to help?"

"Keep me company for a while. That'd be good. I was just changing the sheets in my bedroom. When I finish, could we have a coffee?"

"I'll set the coffee machine going while you do that." Libby headed for the kitchen, and Emma returned to the bedroom.

Ten minutes later, they were sitting on the front veranda, sipping their coffee and enjoying the warm afternoon.

"So, you and my brother… is it serious?" Libby was direct.

"I hope so, Libby."

"So why the secrecy?"

Emma explained her fear of the community taking sides, mostly against her, if the relationship soured.

"Fair enough. I can understand that. This is a small town, and you're the newcomer. But how long do you intend to keep up the pretence of just being friends? Tim and Jess already have their suspicions that something has changed."

"I guess time will solve that dilemma." Emma changed the subject. "Can I tell you my plans for this evening?"

Libby sighed, "Okay, we'll talk about something else. Tell me your plans."

When Emma finished, Libby stood up and hugged Emma.

"Here's hoping he takes the bait. Just be careful," Libby cautioned and then left.

Half an hour later, David messaged to say that the air cooling technician would install the ducts and vents on Monday morning, early and then complete the job first thing Wednesday morning, which would give the roof time to get dry after the second coat was applied on Monday. Hopefully, the weather will not get too hot for the planned work on those days. "And when I say they'll be at yours first thing, I mean you can expect him between 6:00 am and seven."

"Early start on Monday then, Maxie, but it'll be worth it. It will make a big difference, I'm sure." It was around half past four when Emma emerged from a refreshing and calming shower. Maxie followed her into the bedroom.

"You need to stay here; you know Carson is not your biggest fan, and you're not his." She set out the refreshments on the kitchen table and waited, telling herself to stay calm, to relax. Emma expected Carson to be on time, and he was. Fixing a welcoming smile on her face, she opened the door to greet him. He hesitated, on the verge of stepping out of his car.

"Hello Carson, thanks for coming." Seeing him scan the yard, she continued, "Don't worry. Maxie is locked in my bedroom."

A look of relief flashed across Carson's face. As always, he was immaculately dressed, even for a casual visit on a Friday night.

"Come on inside. I thought you'd like to see the house now that it's nearly finished, and I wanted to thank you for your part in getting it to this stage."

Emma ushered him inside, pointing out the changes she'd made as they walked through the house, apart from her bedroom.

"It looks terrific. You have certainly worked hard. I'm glad if anything I've done has made the job easier for you." Carson looked very impressed by what she had achieved.

It was easy to be honest and relaxed about this part of the conversation because it was true; Carson had been a great help to Emma.

"Would you like a drink? Wine, beer, tea, water?"

Carson nodded. "A glass of wine would be very pleasant, thank you."

"You go through to the front veranda, and I will get the drinks." Emma headed to the kitchen, where she poured the wine and then carried the drinks and the food back to the veranda.

Carson took his glass and clinked his against Emma's. "Cheers and congratulations. It looks terrific. Have you finished the shed and stables, too?"

"Yes, everything, although I still need to paint the outside weatherboards. I don't know if you've come across a man named Darius, but he's been restoring the roof. That will be finished on Monday, and then Steven, the plumber, will replace the guttering. Even more exciting is that I'm getting an evaporative cooler installed."

"I did notice the roof was painted; it looks just as fabulous as everything else, and a cooler is essential around here," Carson agreed.

"I also need to get the chimneys seen to. I imagine it will be cold here in winter, so I need to be sure I can use the fireplaces if I want to. I also need to investigate electric heating, but I reckon there is plenty of time for that," Emma laughed as she fanned the heat from her face; it was a very warm evening.

Carson smiled, "Definitely no need to rush."

They were quiet for a short time while they ate and drank.

Finally, Emma excused herself and headed to the dining room to collect a copy of Clive's bank statements. She could see her hand was shaking as she picked up the papers. "Don't ruin it now, Emma!" She took a deep breath and returned to the veranda, clutching the papers in her hand.

"Carson, can I show you something I found?" she said, holding the papers out to him.

"Sure." He took the papers. "What am I looking at?"

"Well, I think these are pages from Clive's bank statements. They show he had a very large sum in the account several years ago, which, throughout these pages and many transactions, was reduced by thousands."

Carson kept his head down, focused on the print in front of him so Emma couldn't gauge his reaction.

Finally, he lifted his head and spoke. He sounded as shocked as she had been on discovering the pages. "I don't understand? Where did all this money come from? Are you sure these are real? There wasn't anything like this in the account when he died. I told you there was only enough to pay for Clive's funeral." He was looking directly at Emma now. "Where on earth did you find these papers?"

Emma was confused by Carson's reaction. She had decided he was the most likely intruder, trying to find these papers or more like them. Now, she wasn't so sure; Carson seemed genuinely shocked by the contents of the documents. She thought quickly and decided to stick to her original plan, to tell the truth.

"Believe it or not, they were sewn into Clive's mattress!"

Carson's voice rose, "In his mattress! That's crazy."

"I bought a new bed for when my parents visit next weekend. Ben and I were moving Clive's old bed out to the back veranda; I'm going to use it as a day bed in there. I could hear rustling noises when I put my hand on the bottom of the mattress, and then I realised there was a slit in it that had been sewn up, rather badly at that. I cut it open and pulled the sheets out. Carson, I wondered if this was what the intruder was trying to find."

"What makes you say that?"

"I think papers were the target. When the papers were cleared from inside the house, the intrusions into the house stopped, same with the shed and then the stables."

"I guess that's possible. Your theory certainly makes sense. If that's the case, I'm glad I was able to expedite sorting the papers out," Carson remarked.

"Yes, I am very grateful for all you did."

"I wonder what the old bugger was up to?" Carson shook his head. "How can I help?"

"I thought you could take the sheets away and have a really good look at them. I was hoping that you'd be able to find out what happened to the money," Emma suggested, "or find out if it actually existed at all."

Carson nodded, "Certainly, I can do that. Have you shown the sheets to anyone else? I mean, has anyone offered an opinion about them?"

"No, I thought you were the best person to ask as you seem to have had the most to do with Clive, both professionally and personally, in the last months of his life."

"That's probably true. Now, I'll just finish this glass of wine and be on my way. Can I take these sheets with me?" When Emma nodded, Carson folded the pages and slipped them into his shirt pocket.

After collecting the remnants of their food and drinks, the two passed through the kitchen to leave what they held before making their way to Carson's vehicle. He opened the car's door and prepared to step in just as Emma said, "Don't worry if you lose any of it. I've still got the originals."

Carson eased into his seat. "Oh, okay. Where are the originals then?" he asked. "They must be in a clever place."

"Back in the mattress. If the intruder was after these pages, they didn't find them, so I reckon it's the safest place for them to be."

Carson laughed at her logic. But then said, "You're probably right." He shut his car door and backed away down the driveway. As she returned to the house, Emma felt her shoulders relax for the first time in a couple of hours. She opened her bedroom door to a very happy dog.

"Well, that's done, Maxie. Let's see what happens next."

Ben arrived several hours later.

"Sorry I'm late; the twins wanted the next instalment of their favourite book read to them." He kissed Emma and then asked, "How did your meeting with Carson go? Tell me all about it."

Emma poured them both a glass of wine and pulled the leftover snacks from the fridge. They sat at the kitchen table while Emma relayed her earlier conversation with Carson.

"So what do you think now? Is he the intruder? Did he have anything to say about the money in Clive's account?"

Emma pondered her response, and then she said, "To be honest, I don't know what to think. He seemed genuinely shocked by the amount of money in the account. He repeated what he'd told me weeks ago, that there was no money, apart from a few thousand, to pay for the funeral. He certainly didn't act guilty, although I'm not entirely certain what that would look like."

Ben sighed, "I guess we just have to see what happens on Tuesday night. He does know where the originals are now?"

"Yes, he does. I dropped that into the conversation just as he was leaving."

"And his reaction to that?"

"Nothing, he just said goodbye and backed down the driveway."

"So there's nothing else we can do tonight. Time for bed?"

"Yes, please."

Ben took her hand, and they headed to the bedroom.

CHAPTER 50

DAY 51 SATURDAY

Again, Ben slipped out of bed early; he wanted to be home before the twins were up. Eyeing the space left by Ben, Maxie shuffled onto the bed and lay down along the length of Emma's back.

"You cheeky animal!" Emma turned and ruffled the dog's ears for a moment before pushing her off and taking herself to the shower.

"I think I'll have to make a list of anything I need to do before Friday for Mum's and Dad's visit," Emma told Maxie while having her breakfast.

They wandered the house together, deciding if anything needed to be done or bought for the visit. With her short list completed, Emma decided to take Maxie for a walk.

As she trotted along the bridle path, Emma found herself thinking about the previous night's conversation with Carson.

"Is he that good an actor, Maxie?" she mused. "Could he really conjure up that much surprise when I showed him the papers? He seemed genuinely shocked." Replaying the conversation again and again in her head, she couldn't decide whether his reaction was real or concocted.

Back at home, Emma made a coffee and took it to the front veranda, Maxie at her side. "What if he's not the intruder, Maxie? Where does that leave us? And what if he is?" These and similar thoughts rolled around in Emma's head for much of the day.

When Ben arrived later that night, Emma shared her ruminations.

"To be honest, Ben, I'd be quite upset if Carson does out himself as the intruder. I know you and Libby are not his greatest fans, but he's only ever been pleasant and helpful to me."

"I think you're just going to have to wait and see what happens on Tuesday night," Ben reassured her. "Then you can decide what you want to do about it if it should turn out to be Carson."

Emma knew she had to be content with that and exercise patience.

CHAPTER 51

DAY 52 SUNDAY

Dressed very lightly, Ben and Emma were sitting out on the front veranda, enjoying an early breakfast before Ben headed home when they saw a vehicle heading up the laneway.

"That looks like Steven's work truck. He must be heading to mine," Ben looked perplexed for a moment until he sighed, "Oh shit! I just remembered that he messaged me yesterday to say he was coming this morning to look at a leaking tap in the stables."

Ben stood up to head to Emma's bedroom to dress when there was a sharp knock on the back door, followed immediately by Steven.

"I saw your truck in the driveway, Ben …." He stopped at the sight of his friend standing in the hall, only wearing underpants.

"Whoa! Now that's a sight I don't need to see again. Is there something going on that I don't know about?"

Emma, similarly dressed as Ben but with an added t-shirt, came inside from the veranda.

"Ok, so this is rather weird. I think I'll go out the door and come back in when you both have more clothes on." Grinning, Steven did just that.

Ben shrugged at Emma, "Oh well, so much for secrecy." They slipped into her bedroom, pulled on their shorts and footwear, and then invited Steven inside.

"So how long has this been going on, and why am I just finding out now? Does everyone else know? Wait 'til I speak to Zoe. She should have told me," Steven blustered.

"Don't get ahead of yourself, Steven." Ben put his arm around Steven's shoulders and guided him to a chair in the kitchen. "We haven't told anyone apart from Libby, and we want to keep it that way for now."

Emma nodded her agreement.

"Well, I'm really glad for you both. You make a great team. And I will keep it to myself."

"Would you like a cup of coffee?" Emma offered, trying to smooth Steven's obvious embarrassment.

"No thanks, I'd like to see to that tap, though."

Ben nodded, grabbed his wallet and keys, and headed out the back door with Steven when their phones pinged. Steven looked at the screen. "Have to go," he told Emma. "There's a fuel spill at Smithton."

"Do you think they need me?" Ben asked.

"No, I don't think so; the Smithton crew is already on site." His phone pinged again. "And so is the Winnabong crew. I'm not sure they actually need me either, but I'd better go. Sorry about that leaking tap. Another time." And he was gone.

There was a moment of silence. Then Emma and Ben looked at each other and burst out laughing.

"Did you see the look on his face?" Ben cried.

"He didn't know whether to be shocked or happy or embarrassed or what," Emma shrieked.

Maxie dashed out of the bedroom to see what all the noise was about.

"It's okay, Maxie, everything's all right."

The dog didn't look convinced until the noise abated. Ben ruffled the dog's head before hugging Emma and heading home.

"Well, that was entertaining, but I do hope Steven keeps his word," Emma thought as she headed for the shower.

CHAPTER 52

Day 53 Monday

Expecting the early arrival of her tradespeople, Emma was up at half past five. The evaporative cooler technicians arrived at 6:30, followed shortly after by Darius.

"Thanks for letting us start so early; it's a real help. It gets unbearably hot under a metal roof, even in moderate temperatures," said one of the technicians. "Now, where's the manhole?"

By mid-morning, the men were finished, with the technician telling Emma they'd be back at around the same time on Wednesday morning to finish the installation if that was alright.

Darius had invited Emma to admire the now-finished roof, which looked like new.

"That's fabulous. You've done an amazing job," Emma enthused as she accompanied Darius to his vehicle.

After he left, Emma drove to Winsthorpe to visit the hardware store; she wanted to buy shelving for the shed and the other few items that remained on her list.

Back at home, she spent what remained of the day erecting the shelving in the shed and organising the storage of her painting equipment. Emma knew the outside of the house would have to be painted at some stage, but she'd had enough of painting for now, and needing to wait for cooler weather was the perfect excuse to defer. When Ben arrived later that night, Emma showed him the results of the day's activities.

"The roof looks amazing, just like new. I might get Darius to repaint our roof, too." Ben was as impressed as Emma had been.

"Come and see my new shelves," Emma said excitedly, "although you can't see much of the shelves, they're covered in painting equipment."

"So the painting inside is done?" Ben asked.

When Emma nodded, Ben reached out and hugged her. "That's remarkable! I need to see what the house looks like now without painting gear lying around everywhere."

Laughing, Emma punched his arm, and they headed inside.

Later that night, as they lay in bed, Ben asked Emma, "Are you nervous about tomorrow?"

"I am, but I'm sure I need to do this."

The hug Ben gave Emma quickly turned into something more intimate.

CHAPTER 53

DAY 54 TUESDAY

Although still early, it was windy and already hot when Ben prepared to head home. "I'm glad no one has to be in or on the roof today. Hopefully, it'll be better tomorrow. Otherwise, you might need to wait for that cooler to be finished," he said as he kissed Emma. "I'll see you later on."

After she was dressed and had fed Maxie, Emma decided it was too hot to do anything outside, so she contented herself with vacuuming up the dust that the wind was driving in through the smallest gaps in the house. Between the wind and anticipation, Emma felt quite fractious when she drove out of her driveway with Maxie in the seat beside her several hours later. She parked her car around the back of Ben's house and walked quickly around to the stables with the dog at her side.

Ben was in there, organising a bucket of water to leave for Maxie. He looked up from the tap as they entered. "How are you feeling? Do you still want to do this?"

Emma nodded. "I think I have to find out. And in answer to your first question, I'm really nervous. I know Maria is going to be with us, but that doesn't stop the butterflies."

Ben gave Emma a comforting hug. "Come on, let's get going."

With Maxie secure in a stable, and after giving her one last pat, the two of them headed off down the lane towards Emma's. As they neared her driveway, a police vehicle crested the hill. Maria was behind the wheel, accompanied by another younger officer.

"Sorry, we're a bit later than I hoped. You head to the shed; we'll be with you in a minute after I hide the car. I'll make sure it's out of sight."

In the shed, Ben and Emma were arranging a barrier that could shield them should anyone come looking. They grabbed the bins and the few boxes of papers that were yet to be sent to recycling and moved them to the enclosed end of the shed. Maria and the young constable came in just as they finished setting up.

The policewoman gave her approval after she had crouched behind the temporary wall to check she had a clear view of the back of the house.

"This should work. He'd have to do some serious searching to find us here. Now, let's run through the plan once more. First of all, Emma, are you sure you want to do this?"

Despite the knots in her stomach, Emma gave a quick nod.

"So, Ben, Emma, and I are going to hide behind this barrier. Thien is going to wait out of sight around the back of the shed. We are going to let Carson access the house and the document. Then, when he comes out, I am going to make an arrest. If I need a backup, it will come from Thien. Do you understand?" she paused and stared hard at Emma and Ben. "No heroics from you two. Is that clear?"

Emma and Ben nodded. Emma had never seen their netball teammate in operational mode before; she was impressive.

Maria looked at her watch. 'Okay, everyone. It's time to take up positions. And Emma, don't be too disappointed if no one turns up. That is a possibility, you know that, don't you?"

Emma knew she'd be disappointed if that was the case, but she also knew she'd have to accept whatever happened.

Maria, Emma and Ben stood in silence behind the barricade. Standing, they could easily see over the top of it and had a clear view of the back of the house. They strained to listen for an approaching vehicle, but the noise of the wind gusting through the trees made it difficult. Tense, they stood side by side, waiting. Time dragged; nothing happened.

"What time is it?" Emma whispered to Ben. He pulled out his phone and checked.

"It's half past five."

"I think Maria may be right. I don't think he's coming." Emma felt deflated even though she'd known this was a possibility. "I guess I should be glad. It means Carson isn't the intruder."

"Just wait. Something could still happen," Ben encouraged Emma to be patient.

The wind suddenly dropped, and in the quiet, the chug-chugging sound of an approaching motorcycle could be heard coming up the lane. Emma gripped Ben's hand, and they ducked down, out of sight behind the barricade.

The motorcycle turned into Emma's driveway and slowly travelled the short distance to her back door. The rider, dressed in full leathers and a helmet despite the heat, alighted and sprinted to the door, knocking briskly. When no one answered, the rider returned to the motorcycle, grabbed the handlebars and quickly rolled the bike into the shed.

Emma's hand flew to her mouth to stop herself from crying out. Ben gripped her other hand even tighter. They waited. The sound of activity kept them crouched down. It was only when silence again returned that they allowed themselves to peek over the top of the barricade. The rider was standing at one of the louvre windows, wiggling a small panel of glass until it came free in his hand. Then, he started on another one. They ducked down again.

The intruder was gaining confidence and became careless about making noise. Those hiding could now easily identify the sound of more glass panes being removed. Then, the flywire was pushed into the enclosed veranda. This was followed by grunting noises, which the waiting group assumed was the rider climbing through the now glass-free window. Then there was silence. Maria slowly put her head above their barricade again and then motioned for the others to follow her lead. They stood and stretched their cramped legs. Crouching for so long had been difficult.

Maria moved as quickly as her stiff legs allowed and grabbed the key from the motorbike's ignition. She scurried back behind the barricade. "Understand that you two are here as witnesses. You are not here to get in my way," Maria whispered firmly. "Is that clear?"

Ben and Emma nodded their agreement. Emma was relieved; she wanted no part in Carson's undoing.

The wait for the intruder to reappear seemed endless.

"What is he doing in there? I just about had a signpost on the bed," Emma thought to herself, struggling to keep calm.

Minutes later, they spied a hand grabbing the window frame from inside the house. They ducked out of sight again. The intruder was holding papers in his hand as he sprinted across the driveway towards the motorbike.

A voice rang out. "Police! Get down on the ground! Put your hands behind your back."

Ben and Emma stood up. The rider lunged for his bike, jumped on the seat and reached to turn the ignition key. It wasn't there. The rider hesitated for just long enough for Maria to be joined by Thien. They wrestled the rider from the bike and handcuffed him.

"Right, let's get this off so we can see your face." Maria reached for the helmet.

As it was lifted up, a long black plait tumbled out. Emma drew in a sharp breath. "It's not Carson."

Maria gave Emma a quick glance and then asked the rider, "What's your name?" The rider remained silent, a mutinous look on her face. The senior constable proceeded to caution the woman, whose only reaction was to glare at those around her. The younger officer brought the police car to the front of the shed and helped the woman into the back seat before settling himself into the front passenger seat.

"Well, that was certainly a surprise!" Maria said. "Do you know who that woman is?"

Still shocked by the turn of events, a trembling Emma just mumbled a very quiet negative.

"What about you, Ben?"

"I don't think so. I can't believe it wasn't Carson. I was just so sure it was him." Ben was shaking his head.

"Why was that?" Maria wanted to know.

"Well, he's spent so much time here, helping out and didn't seem to want anything in return. It's seemed so unlike the Carson I remembered that I just thought he had to have an ulterior motive."

"He may still have a connection; we won't know until we've investigated further. Anyway, we'll get on our way to the station." Maria slipped into the driver's seat. "I'll let you know when we have further information." She started the car and headed for the highway.

Ben watched the car disappear down the lane and then turned to Emma. "Are you okay?"

Tears were sliding down Emma's cheeks. Ben crossed the floor and folded her into a tight hug. "Why are you so upset, Emma?"

"I'm not really sure. I think partly it's relief that Carson wasn't the thief. If he had been, it would mean I'd forever question my ability to judge people's character. And hopefully, this person's arrest means the intrusions are over forever."

"Come on, let's go inside. We had better check she didn't damage anything," Ben urged Emma forward.

Inside the house, they soon saw there was really nothing to worry about other than the torn mattress material. The woman had obviously just grabbed the papers and left.

Ben hugged Emma and said, "Let's go collect Maxie; she won't be happy locked in the stables." Ben grabbed Emma's hand, and they jogged up the lane to his house. As soon as Emma entered the stable block, she heard Maxie crying for her. The dog leapt at the sight of Emma and ran circles around her for minutes before settling down.

"Come on, Maxie, we're going home. It's dinner time!" Emma put the very relieved and happy dog into her car, and the three of them drove back to Emma's.

"You feed Maxie, and I'll refit the louvre panes," Emma suggested to Ben.

Emma was still working on the window when Libby turned into the driveway and pulled up opposite Emma. The children tumbled out of the car, demanding to know where Maxie was.

"She's inside, just finishing her dinner," Emma smiled at the twins.

"Everything okay?" Libby asked as she stepped out of her car. "Did your plan work? Was it Carson?"

"Everything is okay. The plan worked perfectly, but no, it wasn't Carson."

Libby looked stunned. "So who was it?"

"We actually don't know. It was a woman, but none of us knew her. Maria has arrested her and escorted her to the police station."

"Wow! That is a surprise. Look, I haven't said anything to the twins about it, so let's keep it that way. I said you and Ben had to do something to get ready for your parents, and that's why you didn't come to training tonight."

Emma nodded in agreement, and they walked inside to join the children, Ben and Maxie.

CHAPTER 54

DAY 55 WEDNESDAY

Anxious to complete the installation of the evaporative air cooler before it got too hot, the technicians arrived at 6:30 a.m. There was already a hot north wind blowing up the hill, dancing through the gum trees and carrying dust from the paddocks into the house. By nine o'clock, the work was finished.

The lead technician knocked on the back door of the house and invited Emma to see what they had done. Stepping outside, Emma could easily see the large unit now installed on the roof.

"Now you know how these things work?" he asked.

Emma nodded, "Yes, I had one in my last house."

"Great, well, just make sure you have lots of windows open, or you'll end up with puddles on the floor. Have you got flywires? You don't want to be issuing invitations to mossies." He handed her the controller and told her the storage pocket for it was fixed to the kitchen wall. Emma thanked them and headed inside, out of the hot wind.

Before starting the cooler, Emma moved around the house, opening only windows that faced away from the wind and had fly wires in working order. She opened all the louvre windows along the back wall, and the cooling breeze from the air cooler quickly forced the heat out.

After making herself a coffee, Emma sat in the kitchen, relishing the cooling breeze that now flowed through the house and thought about the previous evening's events. While she had yet to find out the connection between Clive, Carson and the person arrested, it did seem likely that her intruder was no longer a threat and that she could now look forward to her parents' arrival without that hanging over her.

CHAPTER 55

DAY 57 FRIDAY

Thursday night's game had been played in Winnabong; it was a tough match. The home team had ten players to rotate, and Winsthorpe only eight, so the away team members were very tired when the umpire's whistle signalled the final quarter was over. Emma had declined the invitation to dine with her teammates and had gladly returned home to Maxie and her bed.

When the alarm went off, Emma wanted to just stay in bed, but her parents were expected around lunchtime, so she and Maxie were up early. She had done all the necessary food shopping the previous day, before the game. She only needed to put the final touches to the guest room and make a dessert for dinner. She was keeping it simple today: sandwiches for lunch, cold meat and salad for dinner, followed by a homemade ice cream cake. On Saturday night, she had invited Ben, Libby, and the twins to join them. The children were again involved in the preparation and serving of the salads accompanying the barbeque. At the children's request, Emma was making a chocolate ripple cake this morning for dessert the following night. She'd also make a pavlova, her father's favourite, on Saturday.

With the dessert made and a plate of sandwiches in the fridge, Emma decided she could take a break. She took her coffee outside, sat on her reclaimed chair on the front veranda, and admired the view that she had grown to love.

Emma closed her eyes and relaxed to the sounds of the bush that surrounded her. Sometime later, she woke with a start. She reached out to pick up her coffee and, feeling the cold cup, realised she'd been asleep for longer than a quick nap.

Stretching as she stood, Emma checked the time and was astonished to see that two hours had passed since she'd come outside; her parents would be arriving at any minute.

After a quick trip to the toilet and to the bathroom to splash her face with cold water, Emma was ready.

Five minutes later, she heard a vehicle travelling slowly up the laneway as if not sure of its destination. She hurried to the back door and stepped outside just as the car pulled up in her driveway. The driver emerged from the vehicle and was wrapped in a tight hug by Emma.

"Oh, Mum, it's so good to see you." And tears ran down Emma's face. Her mother, Meredith, grabbed Emma's shoulders and gently pushed her away.

"I'm really glad to see you, too, sweetheart, but I didn't expect tears. What's the matter?"

"Sorry, I didn't mean to cry." She turned to her father as he reached her side and hugged him, too. "Come on, let's get your bags and go inside."

Her father struggled with the unfamiliar hire car's boot release, but eventually, they were all inside, and the luggage was stowed in what was now the guest room.

"I'll give you the guided tour later, but you must be ready for a cool drink and lunch. The bathroom and toilet are down there," she said, pointing at the door of the bathroom. "I'll take our lunch out to the front veranda. See you outside in a few minutes."

Emma dragged a kitchen chair outside and then set the sandwiches up on the little table with glasses and a jug of chilled water. Her parents joined her and took a seat in her reclaimed chairs.

Meredith surveyed the scene. "What a fabulous view. I bet you sit out here often."

"I do. It's fantastic except when there's a hot northerly wind blowing. What do you think of my chairs? I found them and the coffee table in amongst the rubbish in the shed."

"Rubbish? What do you mean?" her father, William, asked, concern apparent in his tone.

"Well," Emma paused and then launched into a description of the state of the house and the surrounding outbuildings while they ate the sandwiches.

When she finished her story, Meredith was aghast. "Why didn't you tell us? We could've come sooner and given you a hand?"

"That's exactly why I didn't tell you. And it's not like I haven't had help. My neighbours up the road have been great, and so has the lawyer who administered Uncle Clive's estate. Anyway, if you've finished eating, I can show you around."

Emma collected the remnants of their lunch and then led her parents to the lounge room. William and Meredith admired the fresh paint, the fireplace, the furniture and the new window furnishings before Emma led them across the hall to her bedroom.

"These two rooms," she said, pointing at the lounge room and her bedroom, "weren't too bad in terms of rubbish, but they did need cleaning and painting. Same with the hall."

After admiring Emma's work, they followed her further down the hall until she stopped to open the doors of the dining room and guest room.

"Now, these two rooms were a different matter altogether. Here, let me show you photos of the 'before' in these two rooms." And she took her phone from her back pocket.

"You're kidding!" exclaimed William. "How could there be so much paper in one space, and look at that bedroom! Unbelievable!"

"Oh, Emma! That's dreadful. How long did it take to clean it all up?" Meredith was appalled by the mess depicted in the photos.

"My neighbours and the lawyer I told you about, Carson, were a great help. The poor recycling bin is full to the brim every time I put it out for collection, and there are still boxes of papers in the shed awaiting disposal. And then there were the two huge skips that I filled with rubbish from the shed and stables."

"What did you think when you first arrived?" Meredith was stunned by what she'd seen in the photos.

"Well, I was tempted to send the moving van back to Melbourne with me right behind it, but I didn't, even though the men from the van wanted me to."

"Well, it's simply amazing what you've achieved," said her father, running his hand over the freshly painted woodwork of the dining room door. "Did you do all the painting yourself?"

"Most of it. I've actually painted inside the whole house; it really needed it. I won't say it wasn't without its challenges, especially the kitchen, but it's done now."

"You must have inherited the painting and decorating gene from me," joked William, his wife rolling her eyes.

The tour of the house continued with Emma showing the 'before' photos of each room as her parents admired the finished product.

"Do you feel like a walk?" invited Emma. "The tour won't be complete until I take you to my shearing shed." Her parents looked at each other and then filed out the door, following Emma and Maxie, who was not to be left behind.

"Are they your sheep?" An astonished William asked when he spotted the sheep wandering around the paddock behind the stables.

Laughing at his expression, Emma reassured him, "My land, Ben's sheep." And she went on to explain the arrangement made between Ben and Uncle Clive some years previously. They inspected the shearing shed and shearers' quarters before heading back to the stables. As the group approached the house, the twins could be seen jogging up the driveway.

"Who are they?" Meredith asked.

"Come and meet my lovely neighbours," Emma waved a greeting at the children. "The school bus drops them on the highway at the end of the lane."

Jess and Tim waited by the back door for Emma and her parents to catch up to them.

"Hello, I'm Tim," and he extended his right hand to shake theirs. "I guess you are Emma's Mum and Dad."

Jess followed his example.

Meredith smiled at the twins. "It's lovely to meet you. I believe we're having dinner together tomorrow night."

"Yes," said Jess, "and we're preparing the salads and serving the meal."

"I look forward to that very much," William said as he continued on his way inside the house. "Sorry, can't stop. I should have put my hat on."

"Do you want us to do anything before tomorrow night? That's why we called in," Jess turned to Emma.

"Well, you could set the table now if you like; you know what to do. There'll be seven of us."

The twins dashed inside, dropping their school bags just inside the back door. By the time Emma and her mother arrived at the dining room door, the children were already busy setting out cutlery and plates.

"How many courses?" Tim demanded. Emma told them and then left the children to get on with it.

"Well, they seem to know what they're doing." Meredith was impressed. Emma told her about the dinner party the children and she had hosted when the dining room was first ready to be used.

"How about a cup of tea?" Emma switched on the kettle and set out three mugs. She called to the twins, "Would you like a cold drink?"

"Yes, please," they answered in unison.

Emma sliced the cake that she'd made the day before and set everything out on the kitchen table.

"Oh yum!" Jess pulled out a chair with one hand and grabbed a piece of cake with the other. "Double yum, Emma. This is delicious."

Tim swooped in and grabbed a piece for himself before swallowing his drink in one long gulp.

"The table is set. You'll have to have your dinner here in the kitchen; otherwise, you'll mess everything up." And then, embarrassed by his blunt instruction, Tim blushed and looked at the ground.

Emma smiled. "No problem, Tim. We won't eat in there tonight. Thanks for setting it up, you two."

Tim looked relieved that he hadn't offended Emma.

"Are you going to look at what we've done?" Jess asked.

"Certainly," said Emma as she followed the twins into the dining room. She stood at the door of the room, admiring the neatly set-out cutlery and bread and butter plates.

"Well done, that looks great," and she hugged them both. "Now, could you be here at around six o'clock tomorrow evening? That will give us plenty of time to make the salads. Tell Ben and your mum to come at seven."

The twins hugged her back and said goodbye to William and Meredith, grabbing their school bags on their way out the door.

When Emma returned to the kitchen, her mother remarked, "What lovely, confident children they are."

Emma then explained the children's situation to her mother.

"That's very sad for them, but they're obviously very fortunate to have their uncle take so much interest in them."

"Yes, Ben's one of the good ones."

Emma was refilling the kettle and didn't see the look that passed between her parents.

William and Meredith were tired after having flown from the Gold Coast and then driving up from the airport, so the three of them had dinner early. Her father retired to bed soon after.

"I'll be with you shortly," Meredith called after William as he headed to their room.

"Would you like a cup of tea, Mum?" Sure that her mother would agree, Emma was already setting out cups.

Tea made, Emma joined her mother at the kitchen table. Meredith took her daughter's hand in hers.

"Now, why did you cry when we arrived? And don't just tell me it was because you were glad to see us."

Tears again slid down Emma's cheeks as she told her mother the entire story about the break-ins, what her friends had done to help put a stop to them and the final outcome of the arrest of the anonymous woman. Her mother managed to look shocked, defiant and indignant all at the same time.

"What did the police do?" her mother demanded.

"Well, after the first obvious break-in, they sent crime scene officers who took fingerprint samples, but the person wasn't in their system, so that didn't go very far. The policewoman who plays on my netball team was fabulous, and it was her and her colleague who arrested the woman for stealing papers from the house. That was only on Tuesday."

"But what was the woman looking for? It sounds like she broke in several times, at least?"

Emma then explained the money that had been taken from Uncle Clive's account and the evidence that she and Ben had found tucked inside Clive's mattress.

"So, do you think this person stole money from Clive?"

"It seems very likely. The police are still investigating, and we haven't heard anything since the arrest."

"And this has been going on the whole time you've been here? Why on earth didn't you tell us?"

"I thought I could sort it out myself, and I did, with help from my friends. And I didn't want you rushing down here to rescue me."

Meredith was silent for a moment.

"You said you have friends here. Tell me about them."

"Well, you already know about Ben, Libby, and the twins. They have been fabulous. You'll meet Ben and Libby tomorrow night. And then there are the people in the netball team. They are such fun. There's also Carson, the lawyer who administered Uncle Clive's estate. He's been very helpful, too. He's spent hours here sorting papers for me. You really can't imagine how bad the place was when I arrived. The 'before' photos don't really do justice to the mess."

Meredith smiled at her daughter. "I am so glad that you've made friends and have established a new life for yourself, Emma. Maxie seems happy, too." She reached under the table to stroke the dog's head.

"She is. She loves walks along the bridle path and up to Libby's and Ben's. Right now, I think I need sleep. I'll just take Maxie out for a pit stop and head to bed. Give me a yell if you need anything. Good night, Mum."

CHAPTER 56

DAY 58 SATURDAY

As always, Emma was up early, but she was surprised to find her mother sitting on the front veranda with coffee in hand.

"Couldn't you sleep, Mum?"

"Your father was snoring, so I left him to it."

"I'm sorry you had a disturbed night. You could sleep on Clive's old bed on the back veranda if you need to, or there's the sofa in the lounge room. Is Dad alright? He's been rather quiet since you arrived."

"Just getting older, I'm afraid. He's definitely not as active as he was."

Emma nodded. "You seem as bright as ever. Would you like to come for a walk with me and Maxie after we've had breakfast? I'd like to take you to the bridle path if you want to come."

Her mother was as enchanted by what they encountered on the bridle path as Emma had been on her visits there. Kookaburras laughed in the trees, and magpies warbled at each other. It was cooler near the river and in the shade cast by the giant trees. The lemon-scented gums released a beautiful, lemony fragrance into the air.

"It's a beautiful place, Emma," Meredith sighed with contentment.

"I'm so glad you like it. It's a wonderful place to ride or walk."

"You've been riding, as in a horse?" Emma's mother was astonished. "You haven't done that in years."

"And my backside definitely lets me know!" The women laughed. "Come on, Mum, we'd better start back, or Dad will send out a search party."

They had just returned from the walk and were standing in front of the shed, with Emma pointing out what she had achieved in there when a police car turned into the driveway.

Maria climbed out of the car and went to stand in the shade cast by the shed. She introduced herself to Meredith and then turned to Emma.

"Any news?" asked Emma.

"I do have some interesting information for you about the woman I arrested on Tuesday. It seems she is Carson's personal assistant."

Emma's shoulders slumped. "Oh, so he was involved."

"We're not sure yet. He says not. In fact, he appeared devastated when I spoke to him yesterday afternoon. We're still looking into the circumstances. I will let you know as soon as we have more information. Gotta go. I'm interviewing Carson again this morning."

Maria climbed back into the car and reversed back to the lane.

"That doesn't sound like it solves anything, or am I wrong?" Meredith looked at her daughter.

"No, you're right." Emma sighed. "Come on, Mum, let's get a coffee."

They drank their coffee on the front veranda with William, who had not long been up.

"We're planning a trip to Winsthorpe to see what your local town is like. If there's a café, we'll have lunch there. Is there a café in Winsthorpe?" Her father seemed to think the local town was without services.

"Of course there is. It's not that small," Emma was indignant.

"We might buy some flowers and take them to Clive's grave, too. You've been to his grave, I seem to remember," Meredith looked at Emma for confirmation.

She nodded and then said, "The café is good, and the bakery sells delicious pies and chocolate eclairs. But don't eat too much; remember, we have visitors coming for dinner."

Having sent her parents off with instructions to reach their planned destinations, Emma headed to the kitchen to begin work on her speciality dessert, pavlova. She knew her Dad, in particular, loved the famous fruit and cream-topped meringue.

It was after four o'clock when her parents returned from their day out, carrying a beautiful bunch of flowers.

"I bought some for you too, Emma." Meredith handed the flowers to her daughter.

"You were right about lunch," said William, patting his stomach. "The café served delicious food. We decided to follow your advice and had afternoon tea of chocolate eclairs. You were right about them, too."

"What did I say about eating too much today?" Emma's face was a picture of mock horror.

"I'm going to have a sit down to prepare for my next meal," her father said, laughing.

"I'm going to join him," said Meredith, pausing at the bedroom door, "And we found the grave. It was sad about his little sister dying so young."

Everything that could be prepared for the dinner party without stepping on the twins' territory was done, so Emma took the opportunity to drink a restorative cup of tea while sitting at the kitchen table.

Just before six, the twins bounced in the door. "We're here. What will we do first?"

"Why don't you check that the table is still set the right way and take these flowers to put on the mantelpiece and the small one is for the table." Emma indicated the two vases sitting on the sink. They were filled with the brightly coloured blooms that Meredith had bought.

Five minutes later, they called Emma to see their work.

"That looks great! I'm sure our guests will be most impressed." The twins smiled at Emma's enthusiastic praise.

"What do you want us to do now?" Jessie was ready for the next task.

Emma explained what she needed them to do to ready the salads, and they immediately set to work.

At ten to seven, everything was done, so Emma went to change while the twins admired their handiwork over a glass of lemonade.

Promptly at seven o'clock, a knock at the back door announced the arrival of Ben and Libby. Emma's parents emerged from their bedroom at the same time as the twins ushered their mother and uncle into the dining room.

Jess commanded the guests to be quiet while she performed the introductions.

"Meredith and William, this is my mum, Libby, and my Uncle Ben."

Greetings were exchanged between the adults.

"Is this your marvellous work?" Ben asked, indicating the beautifully set table.

"Yes,'" the twins smiled proudly.

"That looks fabulous," said William. "I wouldn't know where to start; there's so many pieces."

"Emma helped us because she set out an example for us to follow the first time we did it," said Tim.

"Clever Emma," muttered Meredith, at which time the host entered the dining room. Emma looked particularly attractive in her clinging red dress and with her hair falling in soft waves around her face. Ben smiled at her and then offered to organise everyone's drinks. The two of them headed to the kitchen; Emma grabbed the glasses, and Ben reached into the fridge for the bottle of sparkling wine that he'd brought.

"Have you told your parents about us?" Ben murmured as he poured the chilled, bubbling wine into the glasses.

"No, I haven't had the opportunity." Emma glimpsed the disappointment on Ben's face. "And besides, I wasn't sure that I should say something without talking to you. After all, we are keeping it a secret from everyone else."

"Fair enough. How about we go for a ride in the morning and talk about it then."

"Great idea. Now, let's get the drinks into the dining room before the others come looking for us."

Ben planted a quick kiss on Emma's cheek before collecting three of the now full glasses while Emma brought the rest.

"Jess, Tim, can you grab the antipasto plate out of the fridge? Pour yourselves another glass of soft drink while you're there." The twins were quickly on their feet and, within minutes, were back at the table with the food and their drinks.

The conversation flowed freely. Emma's parents were keen to learn more about local farming, and Jessie and Tim confidently contributed comments about sheep and horses. After about thirty minutes, the twins and Emma left the table to organise the barbeque.

"I'm going to heat the barbeque," Emma explained to them. "Do you remember what I told you about the salads?" The twins nodded and headed to the kitchen. Emma went out the front door to the veranda and set the barbeque going.

Ben appeared a few minutes later, carrying the tray of steaks and the barbeque tools.

"Come on, Emma, this is man's work." Seeing the look on Emma's face, he laughed and said. "No, I'm joking, but I really enjoy cooking on a barbeque if you'll let me."

"Go for it. I'll see what the children are doing to the salads." And she disappeared inside.

Twenty minutes later, everyone was helping themselves with the food that was laid out on the table. There were three different salads and four different sauces, which included Libby's homemade tomato chutney to have with the meat. The meal was finished off with Emma's pavlova and the children requested chocolate ripple cake.

"Mmm," her father sighed, rubbing his stomach," I haven't had such a beautiful pav since you moved out of home." Seeing the scowl directed at him by his wife, he added. "Of course, your mother makes a beauty too."

"Good save, Dad. Now, who would like coffee or tea to finish up with?"

She had no takers, and shortly afterwards, Ben, Libby and the twins headed home.

"See you in the morning, Emma. Make it eight, if that's okay; it's going to be a hot one tomorrow," Ben called out as he climbed into Libby's vehicle.

Helped by her parents, the dishes were quickly washed, dried and stored, with special care taken of Clive's rosebud-adorned plates, and the dining table cleared of any debris.

"We like your friends very much, Emma," said her mother as they parted ways at their bedroom doors.

Emma smiled as she climbed into bed. "We like them too, Maxie, don't we?"

CHAPTER 57

DAY 59 SUNDAY

It was already quite hot when Emma arrived at the stables.

"Is it too hot to ride?" Emma didn't want to go if it was.

"We'll go along the bridle path, and there's plenty of shade there. There's no hot wind blowing either, so I'm sure it'll be fine," Ben reassured her. The horses were already saddled, so they set off down the hill straight away.

Ben had been right about the bridle path. It was cool in the shade of the giant gums, and the riders kept up a slow but steady pace. They stopped at the point where Libby had first taken Emma and slid from their horses.

Ben took Emma's hand and led her to a rock large enough for them to both sit on.

"Okay, Emma, let's talk," Ben went straight to the point. "Where do we stand, Emma? Are you ready to commit to us, to tell your parents and the twins and the whole netball team that we are an item or not?"

"Wow, Ben! You don't beat around the bush." Emma was somewhat surprised by Ben's forthright questions. She paused before answering.

"Ben, I think I'm in love with you." Ben's eyes held hers. "But, do you remember what I said about wanting a baby, and if you didn't, then we were going nowhere?"

Ben nodded, "I do want a child, maybe even more than one, and with you." He leaned into Emma and kissed her deeply.

"We need to take the horses back. I am not going to make love to you lying on the tree roots and leaf litter here," he growled.

Back at the stables, Ben and Emma washed and groomed the horses before returning them to their boxes.

"Our turn?" Emma asked as she removed her tee shirt and jeans. Ben followed her lead, and they lay down together on the straw of an empty horse box. They made love slowly, enjoying every part of each other and laughing when pieces of straw stabbed into their bare skin.

"I love you, Ben," Emma whispered to Ben.

"I love you too," Ben mumbled as he nodded off to sleep.

"Not the most romantic declaration, Ben," Emma smiled to herself.

She woke up with a start twenty minutes later. What had woken her? She listened, and for a moment, all she could hear was the quiet movement of the horses. Then, a deep rumbling rattled the wooden structure of the stables.

"Thunder. Of course." Another crack followed.

"Sounds close." Emma turned to wake Ben when she realised she could smell smoke, which was always a worry at this time of year when the paddocks were browning, and the undergrowth in the forest was drying out.

"Ben, wake up! I can smell smoke," Emma shook his shoulder. Ben's fire brigade pager was now going off; she hadn't even realised he had it with him. Ben was alert quickly, and the pinging of the pager immediately brought him fully awake. He grabbed his jeans, retrieved the pager and read the message.

"There's a bushfire about twenty kilometres from here, near Saffron. It's moving slowly at this stage, but I need to get to the fire station."

Emma's phone sounded. There was a "Watch and Act' message from Emergency Services Victoria.

"Emma, I think you should ring your parents and tell them to get to the sports complex in Winsthorpe. It's a safe place, and others will be heading there too. If they take Maxie, you can take the horses and the farm dogs. Use my ute. Get your parents to drop your car up here before they head to town. Then I'll have transport."

"Do you think you're overreacting, Ben?" Emma was taken aback by Ben's sense of urgency.

"Ever been through a bushfire, Emma?" he looked at her intensely.

"No," she admitted, "but I have seen it on the news."

"Well, you don't want to. This way, I know you're all safe. I'll ring Libby in a moment. Tell them to stay in Bendigo. They left early for a sports carnival in Bendigo."

"What are you going to do?"

"First, I'm going to turn on the sprinklers for the roof and garden. It's run by a diesel generator, so even if the power goes out, the house and any garden next to it will still be getting wet. I'm sure your uncle had the same system, so ask your dad or mum to check it. It's probably in the laundry. I'll keep my best dog, Buster, with me to help round up the sheep. I'm going to move them all to the other side of the hill, behind the house. There's not much feed on that paddock to fuel a fire, and there's a dam at the bottom of it. I'll head to the fire station after I've done that." Ben and Emma had been dressing while they talked. Now, they were both ready to move.

"Do you need my help to attach the horse float to the ute?" Seeing Emma nod, Ben moved quickly to connect the two. That done, he turned to Emma, and she walked into a tight embrace.

"Be careful. I love you," he mumbled into her hair.

"You too, Ben." Emma nodded and waved at Ben as he drove away on his quad bike. She phoned her mother to pass on Ben's instructions.

"Do you remember seeing the sports complex when you were in town yesterday? That's where you have to go."

"Will you be alright, Emma? Towing that float?" Meredith, Emma knew, was concerned for her daughter's safety.

"I have to be. I'll see you in a while. Love you, Mum."

Emma set off to bring the horses out, one at a time, from their boxes and led them onto the float. The younger horse was quite flighty; Emma didn't know if she was less used to being on a float or if the smoke was spooking her, but eventually, both horses were safely on board. Just as she was about to load the farm dogs, William arrived in her car.

"Leave the keys in the ignition, Dad. Then Ben can use it. How did you go with the generator?"

"No good, there wasn't any diesel in it." He looked worried.

"That's my fault. Can't change that now." Emma's shoulders slumped in disappointment.

Her mother pulled up in her car, and her father made for the passenger door. Emma followed, leaned into the back seat and hugged Maxie.

"Look after her, Mum."

"Take care, Emma," Meredith called.

"You too," and she blew a kiss towards her parents as they headed back down the driveway. Emma moved to the back door of the dual cab, opened it, and crossed her fingers that the dogs would run from their kennels to the ute; she didn't have time to chase around after them if they ran off. She held her breath as she opened their cages. They dashed across to the vehicle and sat up, looking very pleased to have the luxury of travelling inside the cab instead of sitting on the tray. Relieved, Emma shut the doors and climbed into the driver's seat.

The smell of smoke had grown stronger while she was seeing to the animals, so Emma didn't hesitate to get moving. Unused as she was to the vehicle and to the weight of two heavy, moving animals in the float, Emma's progress down the driveway and lane was slow. When she reached the highway, Emma turned cautiously and drove at low speed for some time, but she accelerated as she gained confidence. The smoke cut visibility, so she wasn't tempted at any time to travel too fast.

Reaching the town limits' speed sign was an enormous relief, and she was even more pleased to arrive at the sports complex. Stopping at the entrance to the oval, she scanned the scene in front of her to locate the floats. Through the light, smoky haze, she spied a possible parking spot and proceeded to drive across the oval to reach it. The wind was now blowing hot, pushing smoke and the smell of burning bush across their sanctuary. At least, Emma hoped it would prove to be a safe place for herself and all the others who had arrived at the complex.

Relieved to have transported her charges without incident, Emma sat in the car momentarily, planning her next move. Her door handle was seized by a strong hand and wrenched open, startling Emma.

A woman was standing beside Emma, saying, "You seemed to have managed the float okay. Well done."

Seeing the confusion on Emma's face, the woman said, "I'm Margaret Hudson, Amy's mum. We met at the Op Shop. Remember Clive's clothes. She asked me to keep an eye out for you."

"Oh! Of course. I'm sorry I didn't recognise you straight away. In answer to your question, it was a bit scary at first, but I got more confident as I went along. The horses seem reasonably settled, but it's too hot in the float, so I'm going to get them out. And the dogs, too. "

"Good idea; I'll help you. We'll make use of whatever shade we can find."

With Margaret's help, Emma spent the next hour tending to the needs of the animals in her care. Fortunately, even in her haste to leave, she had thought to pack food for the dogs and horses. When the animals were unloaded and tethered to the vehicle or float, Margaret directed Emma to the water tanks so she could provide them with fresh water. She congratulated herself on having the forethought to bring bowls and buckets, so once she found the water tank, this proved an easy task.

"Thank you, Margaret. Your help has been amazing. I don't think I'd have managed without you."

Margaret smiled, "I think you would have, but I'm glad to help. Now I need to get back to my crew."

With the animals settled, Emma had nothing to keep her mind from thinking about the enormity of this terrible event. She suddenly thought of Libby and the children and realised that Ben might not have been in touch. Wanting to preserve her phone battery, Emma decided to send a text message. "I have dogs and horses at the Winsthorpe oval with me. Ben shifted the sheep to the back paddock before going to CFA. Hope you're safe in Bendigo."

A reply came through immediately. "We're all good. Stay safe. Keep me updated when you can. Xxx."

More and more people and animals were arriving at the oval. Emma could see dogs on leads, cats and birds in cages and even a bowl of goldfish. A tear slid down Emma's cheek as she thought about what could be lost to the bush fire, especially the native animals that didn't have a safe haven to flee to. And, of course, she was scared for Ben and all the other firefighters. What had been a few tears rolling down her cheeks became a sobbing, overwhelming emotion. Her head was on her knees when someone tapped her shoulder.

Emma looked up, rubbing her hand across her face. "Mum, Dad, where did you come from? Oh! And you've got Buster and Maxie."

Emma pushed herself up from the ground and, in quick succession, hugged her dog, her mother and her father. She knew better than to hug Buster, but he was too excited at being reunited with his mates to worry about the humans.

"How have you got Buster? Have you seen Ben? Is he okay?"

Her father nodded, "We're parked near the entrance, so Ben found us easily. He handed Buster over and then headed straight to the fire station."

"I'm so glad to see you," and Emma felt more tears forming.

"You managed the float alright then?" William asked.

"Yes. I wasn't too confident to start with, but I got the hang of it pretty quickly. The animals are fine now; Margaret Hudson helped me get them settled next to the float. She's the mother of one of my netball team members, and I met her when I took Clive's clothes to the Op shop. Margaret's really kind and knew just what to do; I think she's done all this before. Thanks for what you two did this morning, too." Emma hugged her father again. "I'm sorry this has happened. I hope it doesn't spoil your holiday."

Meredith scoffed," Oh, Emma, we were Victorians for more than sixty years. I think we know a thing or two about bushfires. Unfortunately, Victoria's had more than its fair share. Now, are you hungry? I saw the club rooms have been set up to make and distribute food. Will I get us something?"

Seeing their agreement. Meredith headed in the direction of the clubrooms, returning half an hour later with sandwiches and bottled water.

"I'm sorry I was so long, but there's a lot of people looking for food."

"No problem, Mum. Thanks for queueing, but I don't think I can eat anything right now."

All afternoon and evening, the evacuees listened to the sound of water bombers flying in to refill from the nearby lake before heading back to the firefront. Smoke hovered over everything, and occasional pockets of ash dropped around the evacuees. Meredith kept her car radio tuned to the ABC to get updates on the fire. In the early afternoon, the news wasn't good; the fire was being pushed along by the ever-present north winds. But by evening, it appeared that the firefighters were gaining the upper hand, helped by the failure of the predicted gusty wind change to eventuate.

Around ten o'clock, Emma, Meredith and William decided to try to sleep after a final update from the radio station. Her parents returned to their car, taking Maxie with them while Emma lay down on the ground next to the float, making sure the farm dogs and horses knew of her presence. Other people followed her example, but they all knew that sleep was unlikely as they wondered about their homes, animals, and properties. As Emma tried to find a comfortable position on the grass, thoughts of Ben flooded her mind; she just hoped he was safe.

CHAPTER 58

DAY 60 MONDAY

At first light, most of the evacuees were up, having given up their attempts to sleep and were seeing to their animals. Very few had had any meaningful sleep as fear and smoke kept them on high alert.

The dogs were eager for food, and Emma obliged them before feeding the horses. Just as she finished these tasks, her mother arrived with Maxie, seeking food for him. Emma greeted them both with a hug.

"Did you get any sleep, Mum? And what have you done with Dad?"

"The answer to the first question is not much. That car wasn't designed for two older people and one big dog to camp in. Maxie insisted on sleeping up against me, but I couldn't shift her." Meredith reached out to pat the dog with affection despite her complaint. "Your father went to find some food, but I think I see him coming now."

William arrived with packets of sandwiches, a paper plate holding scones loaded with jam and cream, and bottled water.

"These scones are delicious," said William as he crammed a second scone into his mouth.

Emma ate with unexpected enthusiasm; she hadn't realised how hungry she was until she started eating.

"I really needed that sugar boost," she said, licking the last of the jam from her fingers.

"I listened to the radio for an update before I came over here. The firefighters seem to be getting the upper hand," Meredith reported the latest information.

"That's good news." Emma felt some relief, but she still worried about Ben and all her netball friends, who were all involved in the battle in one role or another.

As the morning wore on, the smoke thinned, giving hope to the people gathered at the oval. By early afternoon, the news came through that the fire was officially under control. The evacuees were advised to remain at the oval for another night to be sure that it was safe for them to return to their homes and farms.

There was a far more positive atmosphere in the camp that night as it was generally accepted that the 'firies' had saved the day again. Nevertheless, another restless night followed; sleep was as difficult to come by as it had been the previous night.

CHAPTER 59

DAY 61 TUESDAY

In the late morning, a cheer went up around the oval when the evacuees were told it was safe to return home; the fire had been stopped before it encroached on the Winsthorpe area. They were also advised to monitor the radio and phones for any updates in case the situation changed for the worse. It was still hot and smoky, but remarkably, the winds had died away to almost nothing. Just as Emma finished messaging Libby to tell her they were allowed home, her parents arrived with Maxie in tow.

"Are you going to head back now, Emma? Do you need help loading the horses?" William stood next to Libby's mare, stroking her neck.

"Please, just stay until I have them on board. I should be right, but it'd be good to know you're there if I need you."

Emma approached the older, more docile horse first, untied her lead rein from the float and led her to the back end of the float. The horse trotted up the ramp without incident. Again, it was the younger horse that caused some concern, at first refusing to enter the float. Still, Emma's calming words settled her, and she eventually cooperated. Buster included, the dogs were next; they were happy to jump up onto the back seat again.

"I hope you don't expect this treatment from Ben." She grinned as the dogs either lay on the seat or poked their heads out of the partially opened back windows. After packing up the buckets and bowls she'd brought with her,

Emma messaged Ben to say she was leaving the oval.

"Mum, Dad, please take Maxie with you. I'll walk back from Ben's after I've taken care of this lot." She pointed at the vehicles beside her. "Let's get going."

It was slow exiting the oval as many of the evacuees were ready to leave at the same time, but eventually, they were on the road home. Meredith and William followed Emma's animal entourage as far as her driveway while Emma continued on to Ben's and Libby's stables. The dogs were let out first and were coaxed into their kennels with large handfuls of biscuits. Their water bowls were filled before Emma headed to the float to let the horses out. She decided it was better to lock the horses back into the stables; if they had to evacuate again, it would be quicker to get them from there rather than the paddock. Emma made sure they had food and water before securing the stable doors.

Leaving Ben's vehicle attached to the float in case she needed to get the horses out in a hurry, it was six o'clock by the time Emma was ready to walk back to her house.

Making her way down the laneway, Emma was delighted to see Libby's car heading towards her. The children hung out the windows, shouting their excitement.

"We saw the helicopter. It's huge. It was scooping water for the fire. Did you see it?"

"Yes, I saw it." Emma was too tired to match the excitement of the children.

"You alright, Emma?" Libby had stopped beside her friend.

"Desperate for a good night's sleep. That grass on the oval's not as soft as it looks." Relief behind the giggle she and Libby shared. Emma explained what she'd done with the dogs and horses.

"Thanks for looking after them. What happened to the sheep? Did Ben manage to get them away?" Libby obviously hadn't spoken to Ben either.

"He was planning to use his bike and Buster to herd them over the top of the hill into the paddock on the other side, the one with little feed on it. I'm sorry, but I forgot to check them this morning." Emma looked guiltily at Libby.

"No problem, I'll see to them now. You haven't heard from Ben today?"

"I haven't heard from him since we were here, planning the evacuation of the animals." Emma looked at Libby. "You don't think we've got anything to worry about, do you?"

"No, he's probably just mopping up spot fires. He'll message one of us soon, for sure." Libby didn't look as confident as she was trying to sound. "Now, get home and have a shower."

"Is that a polite way of saying I smell?" laughed Emma.

"Well…"

"Okay, I'm off. Do let me know if you hear from Ben. Oh, and I'm telling my parents that Ben and I are together. We made the decision to go public on Sunday morning before the fire started."

"What's that mean? Go public?" The ever-sharp-eared twins were eager to know what was going on. Libby reached through her open window to squeeze Emma's hand.

"That's great. I'm so pleased."

The twins persisted, "What are you talking about? What don't we know?" Libby rolled her eyes at Emma, waved and continued up the hill towards the house while Emma headed down the hill to her own.

By the time she arrived home, her parents had both showered and changed. They were sitting at the kitchen table, drinking coffee and eating toast, and Maxie was close by.

"Got some of that for me?" Emma hugged her mum and then squatted down to cuddle her beloved dog.

Several slices of Vegemite toast later, Emma felt ready for a shower, but before that, she wanted to tell her parents about her and Ben's budding relationship. Although Emma didn't expect any negativity from her parents, she was nevertheless nervous about making the relationship official. Taking a deep breath, Emma just spat it out.

"Mum, Dad, you met Ben on Saturday night. I hope you like him because we're in a relationship."

Her parents said nothing for a moment and then looked at each other before bursting out laughing.

"Why are you laughing? You don't like him; you do like him?" Emma was very confused by their reaction.

Her parents continued to laugh for some time before her mother eventually managed to say, "Of course we like him. And it was obvious you were together. We just had a bet on how long it'd be before you confessed. If you want to keep things a secret, I suggest you be more discreet about the number of toothbrushes on your bathroom sink."

Emma blushed.

"Oh, come on, Emma, don't be embarrassed. You're not exactly a baby." Meredith smiled at her daughter's rosy cheeks. "We couldn't be more delighted; he seems like a lovely man. He's obviously devoted to his sister and the twins and to you."

William was smiling at his daughter, "Is he home yet?"

"No, I haven't heard from him since Sunday morning. I'm sure he's fine; he's just too busy to make contact. Anyway, I'm off to have that shower. I hope you didn't hog all the hot water."

It felt good to get the smell of smoke out of her hair, if only for a little while, as smoke still drifted around the hillside. Back in her bedroom, Emma dressed in clean clothes and bundled up the dirty clothes to take to the laundry. Just as she set the machine going, her phone rang.

Expecting it to be Ben, Emma snatched it up but was disappointed to see that the caller I.D. showed it was Libby.

"Hi Libby, I thought you were going to be Ben." Emma couldn't keep the disappointment out of her voice. "Heh! I've had that shower, and I'm glad to say I don't smell anymore. I can't say the same for my clothes, but they're…"

"Emma, stop. You need to listen to me," Libby's voice was sharp. "Ben's been taken to hospital in Bendigo. His truck was hit by a falling tree limb."

Emma felt the blood surge away from her head; she slumped into the chair by the back door. "How is he? He's not going to die, is he?" Emma howled with the fear of losing this man she'd come to love.

"That's all I know. If your parents can look after the twins, I'll drive the two of us to Bendigo. Keep it together, Emma, for both our sakes. We just need to get to the hospital," Libby's voice was firm.

Emma was now quiet; Libby's words had stopped her cries. Meredith and William were at her side, and Meredith took Emma's phone to speak to Libby.

"Of course, bring the children here. We'll take care of them," Meredith assured Libby. "We'll see you in a couple of minutes." She returned Emma's phone, pushed Emma into a chair so she could slip shoes on her bare feet and then ushered her out the back door to await Libby.

The children were crying when they stumbled out of Libby's vehicle. William took their hands and escorted them inside while Meredith helped Emma into the front passenger seat.

"Ring us when you have news, Emma. Give our love to Ben." Meredith headed back inside the house to be with the children, and Libby reversed down the driveway to the lane.

"Give our love to Ben? What was that about?" Libby looked at Emma as she turned the car towards the highway.

"I just told Mum and Dad that Ben and I are a couple. They were delighted and said it was obvious, especially as Ben has a toothbrush in my bathroom," Emma managed a small smile.

"I'm so glad that you told them and that they were happy about it, Emma." Neither of them expressed the thought that the commitment might be short-lived.

There was little conversation during the rest of the journey to the hospital, and each of them was too busy with their own fears and worries.

At the hospital, they sprinted to the main desk and asked about Ben's location. The receptionist typed an inquiry into his computer.

"He's still in the Emergency Department. If you go through those doors there," the young man said, indicating the double doors to the right of the reception desk, "you'll be able to wait for more news of him there."

Emma and Libby thanked him before hurrying through the doors, which took them into the Emergency Department. A nurse greeted them and showed them to the Relatives' Room.

"Someone will come back to you with news as soon as they can."

Libby and Emma thanked the nurse as she quietly closed the door to the room. Three people dressed in dirty CFA uniforms sat on chairs lined up along the wall, staring at the floor. They struggled to their feet as the anxious women entered.

"Libby, Emma, we were with him," It was Steven, their friend and captain of their local CFA brigade. He looked haggard and grey as if the day's experiences had added years to his age.

Zoe stepped forward and wrapped her arms around Libby. "We're so sorry, Libby."

David left his seat to stand beside them.

"What happened?" Libby, voice trembling, looked at her friends for answers. Emma stood with Libby, the two women holding each other's hands, waiting for information.

"We were out of the truck, hosing down small spot fires, and Ben went back to move the truck forward. That's when it happened when he'd just climbed back into the truck. This huge branch came down. Thank God it didn't hit the top of the cabin, but it landed across the front of the truck, trapping Ben inside. We couldn't move the branch because it had wedged in the metal, and we couldn't move the truck, so we had to wait for help. He was conscious the whole time, talking to us, and even told a couple of jokes. Pretty bad ones at that," he recounted grimly, his face reflecting the agony of waiting for help. "The State Emergency Services were fast on the scene, and the paramedics close behind. The SES crew got him out as quickly as they could, but it took a while because part of the branch had pierced the truck just in front of the windscreen, and it went through his right leg, too. That's why we couldn't move him," Steven stopped when he saw the looks on Emma's and Libby's faces. "I'm sorry, I'm babbling, I know. I think we're all in shock."

"Do you know how he is?" Emma was desperate to find out.

"We're hoping to hear something soon."

Over the next two hours, those waiting for news milled around the room, sometimes sitting, sometimes walking, and sometimes just standing. There was little talking, and any conversation was whispered.

Finally, the doors opened, and a doctor appeared. The waiting group stood as one, their faces reflecting the fear they felt for their loved one.

"Who's Libby?" asked the doctor.

Libby stepped forward, pulling Emma with her.

"He's a very lucky man. Most of the injuries are scratches and scrapes, but the wound to his leg will require surgery. There's no break in the bone, but there are little splinters right through the area where the branch entered. The surgery will focus on cleaning the wound out completely and then stitching it. Ben will probably need a drainage tube in case of any infection. He won't be going home until we're sure the healing is well on its way."

Emma had been listening to every word the doctor was saying. "So he's not going to die? He'll be alright?"

The doctor smiled. "No, he's not going to die, and he will be alright as long as he follows our instructions and doesn't try to do too much too soon."

There was a collective sigh of relief, and all five were soon smiling.

Emma turned to Libby and hugged her tightly, tears rolling down both their cheeks. Libby called out to the departing back of the doctor, "When can we see him?"

"He's on his way to surgery right now, so when he comes out, and no, I don't know how long that will be because it depends on whether they find more or less damage than expected."

"Thank you so much, doctor." Libby made her way to a chair and sat down. "Oh, Emma, that's great news. You'd better ring your Mum and Dad, and I'll ring the twins."

Steven approached Libby. "Now we know he's going to be okay, is it all right with you if we go home. We haven't had any sleep for I don't know how long."

"Of course, Steven, you must be exhausted. Thank you for looking after him today."

"You'll let me know when you have news?"

"I'll message you, Steven. Now go home." Libby all but herded him and the others from the room.

The Relatives' Room was very quiet when only Emma and Libby remained. They took advantage of it to make calls to Meredith and the children.

Emma could hear the twins in the background, shouting with excitement as she spoke to her mother.

Meredith was delighted at the news. "That's really great. You must be so relieved. Are you going to wait for Ben to come out of surgery?"

"Yes, we both are, so the twins can sleep in my room if we're not home by their bedtime."

Phone calls finished, Libby and Emma sank down onto the chairs.

"Oh, Libby, I thought I was going to lose him," Emma sobbed.

"You and me both. I couldn't cope with losing someone that I love again."

Emma gasped. "Oh, Libby, I'm sorry, I hadn't thought of that." They hugged each other tightly.

After a few moments, Libby pulled back, "Besides, I quite fancy you as my sister-in-law." They hugged again.

Emma stood up. "I'm hungry. You stay here, and I'll see what I can find." She was out the door before Libby could say anything and was back almost as quickly, carrying two cans of lime soda, a bag of crisps and a large block of chocolate.

Libby eyed the chocolate. "No half measures with the chocolate, I see. You're a girl after my own heart," and she broke a large chunk from the block which was in her mouth in moments. "Hmmm! Heavenly," Libby sighed contentedly.

"What was your husband like, Libby?" The women hadn't spoken much about him.

In between eating chocolate and sipping on the soda, Libby spoke with great affection of the man she had loved since meeting at university, both studying nursing, and the life they'd led in Melbourne, how thrilled they were when Libby discovered she was pregnant and then the shock of finding out their one baby was two.

"He loved our children to bits. They were heartbroken when he died. It was possibly harder for them than for me; my adult mind understood what had happened, but not so much for them. Ben is fabulous with the twins; he's not their father but definitely a pretty good substitute."

"It must still be hard for you all," Emma squeezed her friend's hand.

"It is, but you and Ben getting together is a real positive for me and the twins. Jess and Tim think you're wonderful, and Mum and Dad will adore you. They'd just about given up on Ben ever finding a partner, male or female. They wouldn't mind which. They just want him to be happy, and he's certainly happy with you." Libby took Emma in a firm embrace.

The two women continued chatting about various people in their circle and about the situation with Carson. Just before midnight, the door of the room opened, and a doctor entered. She was older than the first one and taller, with her greying hair bundled into a loose bun at the back of her head. She looked tired but spoke gently to Libby.

"The surgery went very well. The wound is now clean and has been stitched. Ben is currently in the recovery room but will be taken to a ward shortly. You can see him there for a few minutes but no longer; it's been a long day for you all."

"Thank you so much," Libby and Emma both responded. The doctor nodded her acknowledgement and exited the room. The women slumped onto their seats.

A short while later, a nurse appeared at the door. "If you would like to see Ben, you can follow me now," he said, "but I'm sure you've been told to only stay a short while."

Emma and Libby nodded and followed the nurse along several corridors to Ben's room. The nurse opened the door with another reminder to only stay a few minutes. The women crossed the floor, approaching the bed with trepidation, not wanting to wake Ben if he was actually asleep. Ben's hands were on top of the bed cover, so each gently took a hand. Emma leaned down to kiss the hand she held. Ben opened his eyes and mouthed, "Love you," before falling back to sleep.

"Come on, Libby, we should go. We know he's safe, and that's the most important thing."

Libby kissed her brother's forehead and then walked out of the room,

Emma's hand in hers. "It's too late to collect the twins now, so you can sleep in Ben's room tonight," Libby suggested.

Emma nodded her agreement, too tired to speak.

Back at the car, Libby instructed Emma to stay awake for the drive home. "Two pairs of eyes are better than one when it comes to spotting kangaroos on the side of the road. I really don't want to hit one tonight, and they could be sillier than usual because of the fire."

"I'll stay awake, and I'll keep watch, don't worry about that," Emma reassured Libby.

They arrived home without incident and were in bed in record time. Sleep, however, was elusive; both women fuelled by adrenalin flowing through their systems.

CHAPTER 60

DAY 62 WEDNESDAY

Voices coming from the kitchen woke Emma from the deep sleep she'd finally fallen into in the early hours of the morning. She staggered out of bed and headed in the direction of the noise. Her parents, the twins, and Libby were sitting at the table, eating breakfast.

"Hello, everyone," muttered Emma. "Is there any coffee for me?"

Her father poured her a cup and made more toast for them all.

"Thanks, Dad, I need this. Have you rung the hospital this morning, Libby?"

"Yes, and the news is good. We can see Ben this afternoon, and if all goes well, he'll be home on Friday."

Gleeful, Emma clapped her hands together. "That's wonderful, Libby."

"And I've spoken to Steven, too. It seems the fire is well and truly under control, and rain is expected later today, so if we get enough of it, the fire could be extinguished altogether."

"That's great news, Libby. It was certainly worrying there for a while. Now, what time will we visit Ben?" As expected, Emma was set on seeing Ben as soon as she could.

After some discussion amongst the group, it was decided that it might be too much for all six of them to land on Ben at the same time.

"What do you suggest, Libby?" Emma was very keen to see Ben as soon as possible but wanted to know what her friend thought.

"Why don't I take the twins with me first? They are desperate to see their Uncle Ben, aren't you?" The twins vigorously nodded their agreement. Libby said she'd take them first, and Emma and her parents could go later.

Emma found it difficult to focus on any task while she waited for her turn to see Ben, but then the time finally arrived for them to head to the hospital.

"I'll drive, Emma," Meredith's voice was firm. "You've had an exhausting few days."

"Thanks, Mum, but let's get going." Emma wasn't going to argue the point; she just wanted to see Ben.

Emma and her parents arrived at the hospital as Libby and the twins were leaving.

"He'll be very happy to see you, Emma," Libby called out as they passed each other in the car park.

Ben was awake and sitting up in bed when his next set of visitors arrived. He held his hand out towards Emma as she approached the bed. The lingering kiss they exchanged left no doubt in Emma's mind or her parents that Ben was delighted to see her.

"Three visitors might tire you out, Ben. We'll go for coffee now; let you two have some time alone." Her mother was discretion itself.

"You go," said William. "I want to see how Ben's doing."

"You can, after we've had our coffee, now come on." Meredith wasn't taking no for an answer.

Ben and Emma smiled at each other.

"As subtle as a sledgehammer, my mother," grinned Emma.

"Oh, Emma, I'm so glad to see you. I know the animals are fine; Libby gave me an update on them. But are you?"

"I am now. I was so afraid that I'd lost you before we'd even got started." She leaned over the bed to hug Ben.

"Ouch!" he grimaced. "Sorry, but I'm sore all over."

"Were you scared when you were trapped in the truck?"

"Only because I didn't know how badly I was hurt. I had my crew with me, and I knew they'd take care of me."

"They certainly did look after you. I expect they'll be in to see you later today." Emma held Ben's hand as they continued to talk about the fire. "I was so impressed by the way the whole community swung into action; it was like a well-oiled machine with everyone knowing their role, from the firefighters to the volunteers conjuring up food."

"That's what living in a small community is all about, Emma, and I hope you're going to stay here long enough to find that out."

"I'm staying." Emma bent to kiss Ben again just as her parents returned with their coffees.

"We're so glad you're doing well, Ben. We look forward to getting to know you better when you're up and about again, especially as you seem to have taken a liking to our daughter." William's eyes twinkled with delight.

Ben grinned, "I like her, alright."

They chatted for a little longer before Ben started to tire. His visitors said their goodbyes and left him to rest.

Mindful that Libby was now responsible for the farm, Emma rang her when she arrived home to ask if she needed any help with the sheep.

Libby was grateful for the offer. "If you could help me get some feed to them, that'd be great. Come up around five if that suits."

Not only did Emma help feed the sheep, she saw to the horses and the farm dogs.

"I'll come back tomorrow to help with the animals again if you like," Emma told Libby as she prepared to head home.

"Thanks, I'd appreciate that. The sheep should be fine now for a couple of days," Libby hugged Emma her thanks. "We'll make a farmer out of you before you know it."

"See you tomorrow," Emma called, laughing, as she headed off towards her house.

CHAPTER 61

Day 63 Thursday

Emma had a restless night, her sleep disturbed by dreams of Ben trapped in the truck, speared to the seat and unable to escape. By six o'clock, all thoughts of sleep had left her, and she headed to the kitchen to brew coffee. Mug in hand, Emma stepped out onto the veranda. Despite it only being just light, Emma found her mother sitting out on the cane and raffia chair, drinking a glass of water.

"What are you doing, Mum? It's barely six o'clock."

"I couldn't sleep. I kept thinking about how lucky Ben was to have sustained the few injuries he has; it could have been much worse."

"You and me both, Mum." Emma extended her hand to hold her mother's, and they sat in silence, bringing comfort to each other through physical contact.

William found them still sitting together an hour later. Disturbed from her revelry, Emma headed off to help Libby with the animals before her friend needed to leave for work.

The farm dogs greeted Emma like old friends; the time spent together at the oval seemed to have forged something of a bond. Even the horses seemed glad to see her. When her tasks were finished, Emma headed home to shower and get ready to visit Ben in the hospital.

When she arrived in his room, it was to find all of the netball team, except

Libby, standing around his bed. They all greeted Emma warmly, but she only had eyes for Ben.

"Okay," she thought, "we said we were going public. No time like the present." Emma stepped through the group, put her hand out to take Ben's hand, and planted a long and definite kiss on his lips. She stood and looked around the group.

"Something we should know?" asked Paolo, grinning.

"Yep," Ben smiled, "we are officially an item." Clapping and cheering greeted this announcement, followed by various comments.

"Great news."

"Thought there were sparks between you two."

"I saw that coming!"

More banter followed before the group departed, with promises to be back to see Ben soon, either in the hospital or at home.

"No game tonight, Emma. The opposition team was impacted by the fires as well, so both teams agreed to postpone," called out Amy as she closed the door to Ben's room.

"Now that Amy knows, the whole of Winsthorpe will soon be informed, and probably half of Bendigo. That was quite a statement." Ben hugged Emma's hand to his chest.

Emma sat with Ben for some time, catching up with him about the welfare of his beloved dogs, the horses, and the sheep. Neither the fire nor the incident that saw him land in hospital was mentioned.

An hour after she arrived, Emma could see that Ben was tiring.

"You look like you're ready for a sleep. I'll go now. Libby is bringing the twins in after school, so you'll need to be prepared for that." Emma kissed him. "I'll see you tomorrow."

At home, Emma was determined to make sure that the diesel-fired pump would be ready if there were another fire. She had ignored it, sitting in the laundry, not actually knowing what it was. This time, she and many others had been lucky, but there'd be a next time without a doubt.

CHAPTER 62

DAY 64 FRIDAY

Sometime after arriving home from tending to the horses and dogs, Emma's phone rang. It was Libby to say that Ben was being discharged from the hospital that morning and asked if Emma wanted to accompany her to collect him.

"I have to work later; if you could stay with him until I get back, that would be great. It's only a short shift; I wasn't supposed to be working at all, but someone has called in sick."

"I am very happy to stay with Ben, Libby."

"I expected that's what you'd say, but I had to ask." Emma could hear the amusement in Libby's voice. Then Libby continued, "Could we take your car? I think it'd be easier for Ben to get into than either of our four-wheel drives."

"Of course. What time should I pick you up?"

Arrangements were made, and Emma changed out of her work clothes and into a neat blue shirt and black shorts before driving to collect Libby.

At the hospital, they found Ben sitting in a chair beside his bed, bag packed, anxious to head home.

"The nurse has just gone to collect my antibiotics, and then we can go." Ben's left leg was jiggling up and down, his restlessness obvious.

Emma bent down and kissed Ben on the mouth. "We'll be home soon, be patient."

The nurse appeared with the tablets, gave final instructions about wound care and sternly reminded Ben that he needed to rest to allow his leg to heal. He was manoeuvred into a wheelchair, and the group headed to the car.

"I think it'd be better if you sat in the back seat behind the driver. That way, you're not putting weight through your injured right leg to get into the car," the nurse advised. So they travelled home with Libby and Emma in the front seat and Ben, making himself as comfortable as possible, in the rear seat.

Back at the farm, Ben used the crutches lent him by the hospital to access the house and then his bedroom, finally slumping onto the bed. Libby and Emma lifted his legs from the floor and swung them around so he could lie on his side, injured leg on top.

"I'm sorry, Ben. I have to go to work, but I'll be home by four. Emma's going to stay with you until then." There was no time for Ben to respond as Libby was already walking out the back door.

"Can I get you anything, Ben?" Emma stood beside Ben's bed. She could see what the effort of travelling home had cost him.

"Get into bed with me, please, Emma, I need you."

"I don't think your leg has recovered enough for that, Ben," Emma attempted to laugh.

"No, I don't want sex; I just want to be held." Emma could hear the misery in Ben's voice. She quickly removed her shoes and climbed onto the bed, lying along Ben's back. She curled her right arm over his rib cage and hugged him. His hand covered hers, and they lay like that for several minutes before Emma became aware that Ben was shaking.

Emma spoke to Ben's back, "What is it, Ben? How can I help?"

As an answer, Ben just squeezed her hand tighter before a great sob escaped his mouth.

"Ben, what is it? Tell me, please." She held him as tight as she dared, not wanting to hurt him. Slowly, the sobs abated. Ben raised Emma's hand to his lips, sighed deeply and started talking. "I was so scared when I was trapped inside the truck, Emma. All I could think of was me dying and you being left alone again. I love you so much, Emma, and I thought I'd never get the chance to build a life with you. I can't tell you how relieved I was when the SES blokes got me free, and I knew I wasn't about to bleed out or get trapped in the cabin if the fire flared up again."

Emma leaned over Ben's shoulder and kissed his cheek. "I was frightened I'd lost you too, Ben. But you're safe now, thanks to those wonderful people who have looked after you. We have our chance now, Ben. Let's not waste it."

"This isn't the most romantic setting, Emma, but will you marry me when Mum and Dad come home in May?"

In answer, Emma slipped off the bed and hurried around to the opposite side. She knelt down on the floor and kissed Ben on the mouth.

"That's a yes, Ben."

Libby returned home at the expected time and headed straight to Ben's room. Opening the door, she smiled when she saw them both sleeping, with Emma curled around Ben.

"You've got yourself a good one there, Ben," she whispered before backing out of the room and heading to the kitchen to eat a very late lunch.

Half an hour later, Emma emerged from Ben's room and found Libby in the kitchen drinking coffee. The two women hugged.

"I hope you're both feeling better for that sleep, Emma, but," Libby continued, "I'm very glad you're up. I didn't want to have to explain to the twins what you were doing in bed with their uncle." They both laughed.

"It feels good to be happy after the drama of the past week. I'm going home now, but Ben asked if you could go in and see him before the twins arrive home. I'll check on the dogs and horses on my way out."

Curious to know what Ben wanted to see her before the twins came in the door, Libby went straight to his room. He was sitting up in bed, looking very pleased with himself.

"Okay. Spill! What's going on?" demanded Libby.

"Emma and I are getting married when Mum and Dad get home." Ben couldn't keep the excitement out of his voice.

Libby looked delighted but then cautioned her brother, "You haven't known each other very long, a little more than two months. Is it too early for such a commitment?"

Ben looked crestfallen. "I thought you'd be happy."

"I am. I think Emma's wonderful, but I'm only saying what others will likely think or even say, including Mum and Dad. Do they even know she exists?"

Ben frowned. "You're right. I'd better introduce her to them. I'll organise a FaceTime call. Libby, we're not teenagers; we've both been disappointed in the past, but we can see a strong future for us. Apart from us having known each other for only a couple of months, what do you think?"

"Ben, I think you are a great match, and I'm sure you'll be very happy together. Is this engagement for public consumption? Given the netballers have only just found out you're together, this may come as a shock!"

Ben considered this. "You're right, as usual. I'll speak to Emma about it." That was as far as he got in his thoughts as the twins came dashing in the door and flung themselves at the bed.

"Watch out for Uncle Ben's leg," cautioned Libby, but it was too late. Ben yelped, and the children leapt off the bed like it was on fire.

"Sorry, sorry," they both cried out.

"That's okay. It's so good to be home with you. Now tell me all about the sports carnival."

Back at home, Emma sailed in through the back door, relief and happiness bubbling out of her in equal measures.

"Mum, Dad, where are you?"

Her parents had been sitting on the front veranda with Maxie curled at William's feet.

"We're out here. What is it? Is Ben alright?" Anxiety pitched Meredith's voice higher.

"He's fine, Mum. Don't worry. I'm just happy that everything's worked out. Come on, let's go for a walk."

CHAPTER 63

DAY 65 SATURDAY

Before feeding the farm dogs, Emma called in to see Ben. She was surprised to find him sitting at the kitchen table eating breakfast.

"Does this mean your leg is feeling more comfortable today?" Emma kissed Ben.

"Yes. Definitely less sore. Thank goodness," Ben smiled in relief and then asked, "Have you told anyone about our engagement?"

"No, I haven't. I didn't know if you asked under the influence of the anaesthetic or maybe the emotions of a near-death experience."

"It wasn't the drugs, Emma. If I'm honest, the experience in the truck reminded me that life is precious and there's no point in wasting time waiting to see if you or I have habits that annoy each other. I don't care if you leave the lid off the toothpaste or put the toilet paper on the roller the wrong way around. The big picture is that I love you and want to spend my life with you. Libby thinks we'll cop some flak for getting engaged after such a short time, but that's other people's problem, not ours."

Emma leaned into Ben, and they exchanged a deep kiss. Ben groaned. "I wish we could take this further, but my leg won't let it." Then he laughed. "You should have seen the look on the twins' faces when they landed on the bed yesterday, and I yelped. They were terrified they'd done something terrible."

Emma didn't look so amused. "I hope they didn't do any damage." Then she glanced at the kitchen clock. "Those poor dogs will be wondering what's happened to their food this morning."

"I'll come too."

When Emma looked doubtful, Ben said, "I haven't seen them since the fires." Emma handed Ben his crutches, and, with small steps, they arrived at the kennels. Four excited dogs jumped and twirled in circles at the joy of seeing Ben.

"Have they been out for a run?" Ben asked.

"No, I was afraid they might not come back," Emma admitted.

"I'll let them out two at a time. When they settle back down, they can have their food." Ben directed Emma to open Buster's gate and then Spider's. The two ran off into the next paddock, thrilled to be running free. The other two dogs whined their resentment while they waited. After fifteen minutes, Ben whistled, and Buster and Spider returned immediately. The other dogs then had their turn. Emma fed the horses while they waited for the dogs to calm down after their exercise. Then, with all the animals taken care of, Ben and Emma slowly returned inside.

"You know it's only two weeks until Christmas, Ben. What do you think of having a Christmas cum engagement party on Christmas Eve? That's a Saturday. It gives us plenty of time to tell families and friends our news."

"I love the idea. Do you want to have it here?" Ben indicated the courtyard near the swimming pool.

"No, it can be part housewarming as well. So at mine. I have other plans for your family's courtyard next year."

A couple of hours later, the party was mostly organised, apart from inviting their guests.

CHAPTER 64

DAY 66 SUNDAY

When Emma arrived the next morning, Ben greeted her with a request to help him move the sheep. Seeing the look of disbelief on Emma's face, Ben reassured her, "The dogs will do all the work."

"They'd better," she grumbled. "Why can't Libby help you?"

"She's taken the kids into Bendigo."

Spider and Buster were duly released from their kennels and leapt onto the tray of the ute, their excitement at being back at work obvious. Ben sat behind Emma in the back passenger seat, following the nurse's advice. She drove the ute up the lane to the paddock over the hill where the sheep had been since the fire. Although Ben had managed to get into the ute, Emma wasn't about to let him out in the paddock.

"You can direct the dogs from in here, or I'll take you back to the house," she ordered. "Now, what do you want me to do?"

Ben pointed out the two gates he needed open, so Emma drove the ute through the two paddocks, opening each gate as she went. Back at the first paddock, Ben ordered the dogs to get behind the sheep and herd them into the new paddock. The dogs carried out his orders exactly, and the sheep were soon in their new home with access to the second paddock when they wanted to move on.

"These paddocks," Ben said, indicating the two where the sheep now resided, "have more feed on them than the one they've been on for the past week." Ben was happy with the smooth transition and called the dogs back to the vehicle.

At the house, the other dogs were given a run before being fed.

Getting in and out of the vehicle and being out of bed had tired Ben, so he elected to return to his bed where he could elevate his leg. When he was settled, Ben asked Emma if she'd heard anything from Maria about the break-in.

"I'll give her a ring when I get home. It's ten days since the arrest, so hopefully, she'll have news," Emma decided. "I'll see you later. My poor dog thinks I've deserted her. It's lucky Mum and Dad are here, or she'd really be upset."

On arriving home, Emma was met by a very excited dog. She gave her parents an update on Ben and then grabbed the dog's lead.

"Come on, you poor thing. Let's go for a walk."

Later in the day, Emma phoned Maria at the station, but she wasn't available.

"I guess I just have to wait until she's ready to speak to me," she told her parents and then Ben.

CHAPTER 65

Day 67 Monday

When she went inside to see Ben after attending to the animals, Ben asked Emma if she could drive him into Bendigo.

"Are you sure that's a good idea?" Emma chided. She knew that the activity of the previous day had really tired Ben.

"There's something I need to do," he explained. They set off in Emma's car, and Ben again was in the back seat. With him directing Emma where to go, they arrived at one of the busiest streets in the centre of the city.

"Park over there, Emma." Ben directed Emma to a space next to the footpath.

Emma reversed the car into the bay and then helped Ben out.

"Where are we going? I don't want you to be on that leg for too long."

"We're going in there." Ben was pointing at the jewellery store that was just in front of them. "If we're engaged, Emma, we need an engagement ring."

"Oh, Ben, that's not necessary. I've done this before; I don't need all the fancy trimmings."

"So have I, but I want you to have something to show our commitment."

The salesperson asked what Emma might like.

"Simple, nothing ornate." Emma was definite. Soon, she had a tray of rings in front of her. The one that best fitted that description was quickly chosen, and

Ben slid it onto her ring finger. It was a white diamond solitaire set in white gold.

"You have great taste," cooed the salesperson, "but I think that's a little too big. We can make one the right size or take a little out of this one."

Although disappointed that they couldn't leave with the chosen ring, they settled for it being resized as that was the quickest solution.

"It'll be ready in a couple of weeks," the salesperson told them.

"Well, that gives us time to introduce you to my parents and tell yours," said Ben as he settled into the rear seat of the car for the trip home.

"And the twins. I wonder what they'll say."

Ben looked embarrassed as he muttered, "They know."

"What do you mean 'they know'? Why did you tell them? We were going to tell them together," Emma said, unable to hide her disappointment.

Shamefaced, Ben admitted that the twins had sensed something was going on and had wheedled the news out of him.

"You know they are like bloodhounds when they think people know something they don't."

Resigned to having missed out on seeing the children's reaction first-hand, Emma asked, "So what did they say? Were they happy?"

"Tim said, 'That means we can do dinner parties at Emma's all the time,' and Jess said, 'I'm getting an aunty. I've always wanted an aunty.' So I think that means they're both happy for us."

"Well, that means three members of your family are pleased for us. Only two to go. Come on, we're home. Let's get you inside."

Emma helped Ben settle into his bed and left him resting with a cold drink in one hand and the television remote control in the other.

CHAPTER 66

DAY 68 TUESDAY

Emma drove Ben to the hospital in Bendigo to have his wound checked. He had been following all of his doctor's instructions to the letter, albeit with a few personal interpretations. He wanted to be back at work as soon as possible.

"Ben, I'm going to ask you to return on Friday. If you're still going this well, it might be your final check-up," the doctor said after she inspected the wound.

Back in the car, Ben asked Emma if they could go back to her house; he felt like a change of scenery, he said. Emma called her mother to let her know that she should expect Ben's visit, and they set off. A batch of scones was just leaving the oven as Ben made his way into the kitchen, crutches easing his progress.

"Mmm, they smell delicious," said Ben, sniffing the air appreciatively. He settled on the chair Emma had pulled away from the table and greeted William and Meredith. When they were all at the table, provided with cups of tea and scones spread with jam and cream, Ben turned to Emma's parents.

"I've asked Emma to marry me in May when my parents return from their travels. I hope you're okay with that." Emma looked shocked that Ben had been so blunt, but her parents just nodded.

William was practical. "Are you both sure? You have only just got together, and now you're planning to get married."

"Mum, Dad, I was with Roy for years before we married, and that didn't guarantee success, did it?" Emma hoped her parents would understand. "And Ben knows all about what happened with him, and he knows about Ruby. He knows what I want, and he shares my vision for the future."

"I really love Emma, William and Meredith, and I can't wait to get started on our life together."

Emma's parents looked at each other and smiled.

"Then congratulations to you both," said Meredith. "We've only known you for a short time, but you seem very well-suited. Have you told your parents?"

"No, but I sent them a message to set up a time when they could FaceTime with us, and they'll meet Emma then."

William frowned. "So they haven't met Emma yet, but you're going to tell them you're engaged? How do you think they'll take that?"

"William, my parents trust that I know what I'm doing. I'm sure they will welcome the news just like you have."

Feeling his opinion had been rebuffed, William just shrugged. "Let's have a cup of tea to celebrate." And they clinked cups together to toast the happy news.

CHAPTER 67

DAY 69 WEDNESDAY

Despite his confident speech to William the previous day, it was with some trepidation that Ben sat at his kitchen table with Emma by his side to FaceTime his parents.

"Hi Mum, hi Dad," he began as they came on screen.

"How's your leg coming along. Are you able to work yet?" That was Ben's father, Conor.

"Not yet, but I have an appointment on Friday at the hospital, and hopefully, I will get the all-clear then. How's the weather there?"

Emma rolled her eyes at Ben's mundane question. He took the hint.

"Mum, Dad, I have someone here that I want you to meet. I've told you about her before; she's our new neighbour. I know Libby and the kids have told you about them hosting dinner at her place, and she's joined the netball team. Emma's not just our neighbour; she's someone who's become very important to me." His parents were now all attention.

Ben held the camera so that Emma's face filled the screen.

"Hello, Mr and Mrs Arnold. I'm Emma. I'm your new neighbour." Emma made her voice bright and friendly.

"Please call me Conor, Emma," Mr Arnold followed Emma's example. "Nice to meet you."

"Hello Emma, please call me Olivia," said Mrs Arnold, not sounding quite as enthusiastic as Emma or her husband. "I expect you had quite a mess to contend with."

"I certainly did, but with a lot of elbow grease and paint and helpful neighbours, the house and sheds now look great."

"We'll have to see it when we get back. I look forward to that." Mrs Arnold looked like she wanted to ask more, but Mr Arnold jumped in.

"Ben said you were important to him. Why's that?"

Emma now knew where Ben got his directness from.

Ben grabbed the phone. "She's important to me, and she's going to be important to you, too, because we plan to get married when you get home."

His parents were silent. After a long moment, Conor asked," How long have you known each other?"

"About two months." Emma read the disappointment on Ben's face at the muted response from his parents; he'd been so certain they'd welcome her into the family. She, too, was disappointed but not surprised.

Mrs Arnold spoke in a gentle tone, "Emma, we'd like to speak to Ben by himself if that's okay. It's been good to meet you, but we'll say goodbye now."

Emma nodded, left the kitchen, and walked home, her eyes filled with tears.

Her parents knew immediately that the call had not gone well.

"I thought you would come as a shock to them. After all, you've never met his parents, and Ben tells them he wants to marry you. Any parent would be taken aback. Just let them get used to the idea, Emma, and I'm sure it'll be okay in the end." Her father's words brought some comfort.

Later, Ben phoned and apologised for his parents' response to their news.

"But it's my fault, not theirs; I should have taken more notice of what Libby and your parents were saying. I'm sorry."

"Dad said we just have to let them get used to the idea, and I think he's right. We were just so excited that we expected them to be the same. We were both a little too naïve."

"It'll be alright, Emma. I know it will." She didn't know if he was reassuring her or himself.

CHAPTER 68

DAY 70 THURSDAY

L ibby called in on her way back from taking the twins to the school bus.

"Are you okay? Ben told me about my parents' lack of enthusiasm. I rang them myself later and told them about our friendship and how much the twins adore you."

"Giving me a character reference, were you?" Emma asked with a wry grin.

"It was just a shock for them, Emma. Ben's been single for so long that I think they gave up thinking he'd ever find a partner. And worse, they really liked his last girlfriend until she did the dirty on him. So please don't blame them for reserving judgment. They only want what's best for him."

"I appreciate that. I think Ben misjudged the situation; he should have just introduced me as his girlfriend and left it at that, but we can't change what's happened."

"Please go and see Ben; he's feeling bad about it all."

"I'll head up soon. Have to feed my canine friends anyway."

Libby had left for work when Emma arrived to do her morning chores. She went into Ben after seeing to the animals. He was sitting up in bed reading a book, sadness marking his face. Emma sat down on the edge of the bed and took hold of Ben's hand.

"It'll be okay, Ben. Just give them time."

"I love you, Emma." And he pulled Emma into a tight hug. "I so need my leg to be better." He grinned at her.

"We'll see what the doctor says tomorrow."

After a final kiss, Emma stood up. "Wish us luck for the game tonight."

"Be great to finish up with a win. Last game before Christmas," commented Ben.

"I'm sure the twins will keep you informed of the outcome," grinned Emma, and she headed out the door.

As she walked home, Emma checked her phone messages to see that her parents were on their way to Winsthorpe to have lunch at the café. They planned to stay in the town until it was time for her netball game, and they'd come and watch.

Emma groaned, "Really, Mum and Dad? I'm not in high school!"

Several hours later, when Emma arrived at the courts, it was to find they only had seven players; Ben was obviously out, and Maria was on duty. She groaned again.

"I'm going to be wrecked!"

"We can do this, guys," Amy urged. Her fellow team members rolled their eyes but took up their on-court positions.

With the twins, Meredith and William, cheering from the sidelines, the team did actually win. The opposition also had only seven players, and one of them had strapping on both ankles and his left shoulder. After the game, no one felt like adjourning to the pub for a celebratory dinner; they were all too exhausted.

CHAPTER 69

DAY 71 FRIDAY

Finally able to slip into the front passenger seat unaided, Ben was excited to be travelling to the hospital with Emma for what he hoped would be his final check. His optimism was rewarded when the doctor said his wound was well on the way to being healed and that he didn't need to return.

"Now, this doesn't mean you can do whatever you want; you still need to be careful," the doctor warned Ben.

As Emma drove them home, her phone rang. Her car's monitor showed the caller to be Maria, so Emma pressed the 'accept' button on the steering wheel.

"Hi Maria, how are you?"

"I'm good. Can I come and see you this afternoon at, say, three o'clock?"

Ben and Emma looked at each other.

"I want to update you on the break-ins and the missing money," she said when Emma asked what she wanted to discuss.

"Yes, please come. We'll be there." For the remainder of the drive home, they speculated on what Maria could tell them.

Promptly at three o'clock, Emma heard the police car coming down her driveway. Maria and Thien were soon seated at the kitchen table, drinking tea and eating biscuits with Ben and Emma's parents, who were all making small talk with their guests.

Growing impatient with the chatter, Emma interrupted the conversation. "So what have you found out?"

The group fell silent. Maria looked at Emma and began with an apology. "I'm sorry it's taken me so long to update you on what we now know about the break-ins, but dealing with the fire was our priority."

Emma nodded her acknowledgement, and Maria resumed speaking, her audience listening intently.

"First of all, the woman we arrested on your driveway is named Bettina Barry. She's Carson's personal assistant, and she worked for Carson's father before that. In fact, she's been with their company for over twenty years."

Emma shook her head in disgust. "So he was involved!"

"The bastard!" Ben made his feelings plain.

"Let's hear the rest of what Maria has to say before finding him guilty," reasoned William.

"A couple of years before your Uncle Clive was diagnosed with dementia," Maria continued, "he realised he was becoming forgetful and was finding it difficult to keep track of everything, so he authorised Carson to have Power of Attorney over his financial assets."

Emma seethed, "So that's how he did it!"

"Emma." Her father's stern voice stopped her from saying anything further.

"It seems Carson carried out his responsibilities assiduously for two or three years, paying Clive's bills, providing him with cash if he wanted it and so on," Maria stated. "Then Carson's father died unexpectedly, and Carson was left to run the entire business himself. He was suddenly a very busy man, so busy that he involved his father's P.A., now his, in administering a number of portfolios, one of those being Clive's finances. In the beginning, he took the time to oversee what Bettina was doing, but he trusted her and ended up signing whatever cheques she put in front of him. Clive insisted on only having a cheque account, which made it very easy for her."

"Made it easy for her to do what exactly?" asked Meredith.

"To steal from Clive," Maria declared. "Unfortunately, Carson wasn't aware of two things about Bettina. First, she had been his father's lover for most of the time she'd worked at the company and was devastated by her lover's death. The other thing he didn't know was that she had a gambling problem. While Carson's father was alive, Bettina was happy with just a little flutter on the horses or the pokies, but after he died, she became very lonely. She started going to the pokies, just for company, a few nights a week at her local pub, but over time it became every night. Her gambling losses soon mounted up."

"Poor Bettina," sympathised Meredith.

"You feel sorry for her, Mum? How can you? She broke into my house, she frightened me, she stole from Clive?" Emma was indignant to think her mother had any pity for the intruder.

"Think about her for a moment, Emma. She lost her lover of twenty years, and no one could know. She couldn't show her feelings to anyone; no sympathy for her from friends and acquaintances. She must have been very lonely, and loneliness can have a dire impact on mental health."

"I'm not sure I can feel sorry for her," muttered Emma.

"Can I continue Emma? There's still more to tell, "Maria asked.

When Emma nodded, Maria resumed. "When Carson delegated the responsibility of Clive's finances to Bettina, she saw this as compensation for the loss of her lover. She understood why she hadn't been mentioned in the will in that capacity, but in her mind, she'd given twenty years to the company and to him and deserved some recognition for that, at least. So she started writing cheques made out to 'cash', cheques that she 'liberated' for her own use and to cover her losses. There was no fancy car or holidays. It was all spent on gambling. This went unchecked until Clive died, and Carson had to prepare the financial statements for probate. When Carson looked at the final month's bank statement, he was staggered; he remembered how much money approximately had been in the account when he had first started administering it and could not believe how low the balance now was."

"So what did he do? Did he confront her or just come up with some cosy plan to take some for himself," Emma demanded.

Maria shook her head and continued, "Before he confronted Bettina, he wanted to audit the statements. He located most of them in the office files, but obviously, he couldn't find them all. The pages he did have made it clear in his mind what had happened to the money. Carson approached Bettina for an explanation, and he informed her that he was going to take the matter to the police. Bettina threatened to tell the authorities that they'd been in it together and that Carson had told her what to do. This in itself would not have stopped him from informing the police, but Bettina kindly explained to Carson that he had as much to lose as her if it came out that his lack of supervision and his abrogation of responsibility to his client were responsible. Who would want to employ a solicitor with such a cavalier attitude?"

"That's blackmail!" William exclaimed.

"Still feeling sorry for her, Mum?" Emma asked bitterly.

"Carson realised she was right, but then he started worrying about those few missing pages of the bank statements. He couldn't locate them at the office, so he concluded they must be somewhere at Clive's. If they were, he needed to find them. Of course, he had informed you at this stage that you'd inherited the house. What he absolutely didn't expect was that you'd move in a week after he told you. He thought he had weeks, at least, in which to search for the missing papers. But you arrived, and he was terrified that you'd find them. And when you did, you'd want to know where the money was. So he and Bettina came up with a plan; he would search as many stacks of paper as he could, legitimately in the guise of 'helping' you, and Bettina would search when you were out. Of course, Carson told Bettina about you being out on Tuesday and Thursday nights for netball, and it was he who told her the location of the missing papers."

There was silence when Maria stopped talking.

Finally, Emma spoke, her voice trembling. "Thank you for telling us, Maria. In one way, I'm glad that Carson wasn't the thief, but I'm so disappointed that he failed to fulfil his responsibility to my uncle. It also upsets me that he didn't stop to think about how frightened I was by the break-ins. If it hadn't been for Ben and Libby, I probably would have given up and moved out."

"Maybe that's what he was hoping you'd do so he could keep looking without your interference," Maria said quietly. "I should warn you that it's likely they will be bailed when they appear in court. It will be a condition that they not come to your property."

Emma nodded, a tear running down her cheek. "I'm glad it's over. Thank you again for letting me know. And thank you for your diligent investigations."

Emma and Ben followed Maria and Thien to their car and then watched as they reversed down the drive.

"Are you okay, Emma?" Ben took her hand.

Emma hesitated for a moment, then looked at Ben and smiled." If you balance the good things against the bad things that have happened since I arrived, the 'good' wins hands down. So, yes, I am okay, in fact, much better than okay."

Ben grabbed Emma's other hand. "You know it's only nine days 'til Christmas. And even less time to our party. Now we have yet another reason to celebrate; no more uninvited guests!"

Emma smiled the relief she felt, grabbed Ben's hands, and they headed back inside the house.

CHAPTER 70

DAY 72 SATURDAY

By the end of the day, the party plans were finalised, invites issued, and the twins organised to help with the catering, which, of course, they were desperate to do. Ben was still using his crutches to get around, on the advice of the doctor. Still, he was more mobile, getting in and out of the car with greater ease and being able to sit in the front passenger seat. He thought he'd be able to resume working the farm independently at the end of the following week, with everything being well.

Ben had formulated a plan to help his parents get to know Emma better and shared his thoughts with her while they ate lunch together on her front veranda.

"I want us to talk to them every second day if they are within phone network range. Just talking to them, like about the party, only we'll say it's a Christmas party."

When Emma looked doubtful, he said, "It doesn't have to be for long, but I think it's the only way to win them over. And after a few conversations, we can introduce your parents."

Emma looked at him and took a deep breath. "You're right," said with determination. "Let's do it now."

Ben's parents answered on the first ring.

"Ben, is Emma with you?" his mother asked, hesitation in her voice.

Nervous of what might follow, Emma moved into camera range.

"Hi, Emma. We want to apologise to you. We were very surprised by Ben's news last time we spoke and, on reflection, I don't think we were very polite. We're both sorry. Ben, Libby and the twins have been busy telling us what a wonderful person you are and how much you mean to them all. We should have just trusted that Ben would only want to marry someone marvellous, and that seems to be you. Welcome to the family, Emma."

Tears formed in Emma's eyes. "Thank you, Conor, thank you, Olivia. That means so much to me, to us both. I'm really glad you're okay with it, and I can't wait to meet you in person."

"So tell us what you've been up to in the past couple of days. How's the leg, Ben?"

The conversation finished around fifteen minutes later. Ben and Emma smiled at each other and embraced.

"Did you know about their change in attitude?" Emma asked.

"Not really, but I know Libby and the twins have been working hard on our behalf."

"We owe those children a substantial treat!" Emma laughed.

They had been sitting on Emma's front veranda for the phone call, and now they ventured inside.

Seeing the smiles on Ben's and Emma's faces, William asked, "Were you talking to your parents, Ben? I hope the smiling faces mean it went much better than last time."

"It certainly did. Now we are definitely calling this party an engagement party!" Ben declared.

CHAPTER 71

Day 79 Saturday

The previous week had flown past amid party preparations and regular phone calls to Ben's parents. Now, it was the evening of the party. The weather was perfect, warm and clear, and of course, the new evaporative cooler was taking care of any excess heat. Purple and green adornments, which were Jess's and Tim's favourite colours, were everywhere. Their summer holidays had begun several days earlier, giving the twins ample opportunity to cycle to Emma's house at least twice a day with suggestions for food and decorations. Balloons and streamers of the chosen colours hung from every possible surface in the lounge, dining room and hall. Purple flowers sat in green vases on the mantle pieces, streamers hung over the back door, and the cupcakes the children had made with Emma were also iced in purple and green. Meredith had baked and decorated a beautiful engagement cake, which was currently hidden in Clive's old fridge, Emma having relented on her determination to throw it away. It was now a sparklingly clean fridge residing in the corner of the shed, a corner clear of all rubbish and debris. Meredith and Emma also made sponges, sandwiches, and, of course, pavlova and chocolate ripple cake. William had collected mini pies, sausage rolls and spring rolls from the Winsthorpe bakery earlier in the day; they were in the oven waiting to be heated.

As the start time for the party approached, Tim and Jess, wearing their new party clothes, were busy setting bowls of savoury dips and plates of crackers and chips around the dining room table; there was definitely no shortage of food. William and Meredith worked with the children, enjoying their company tremendously.

In her bedroom, Emma was partway through getting changed into her new shimmering, peacock-green dress that rippled when she walked. Looking at herself in the full-length mirror propped against the wall, Emma was admiring the effect when Ben walked into the room.

"Do I really have to wear this shirt? Purple just isn't me!" Ben scowled at his reflection as he came up to stand beside her.

"Tim and Jess will be very disappointed if you don't. They specially selected that one just for you when they went shopping with Libby."

"Remind me to do something nasty to my dear sister." His face cleared when Emma twirled in front of him. "Anyway, you look amazing. Here, I have something for you." He held out a small blue velvet box that he'd been carrying in his hand.

"Is that my ring?" Emma gasped in delight.

"Yes, Libby collected it this morning."

Ben took the ring from the box, grabbed Emma's left hand and slid it onto her finger.

"That feels better," she said as she jiggled the ring, assessing its size. "It's really beautiful. Thank you, Ben. I love you and can't wait to be married to you."

"I can't wait until my leg is one hundred per cent," he growled. They kissed again.

"Come on, Ben, our guests will be arriving, but first, take a photo of the ring to send to your parents."

He did, and they replied with a heart emoji.

"It's all good, Emma. They're happy for us."

"How lucky am I that my great uncle left me this house. I would never have met you otherwise." Emma looked up to the heavens. "Thank you, Uncle Clive, for my legacy." She took Ben's arm as they left the room to meet their guests.

Their friends arrived close together, some carrying even more food to contribute to the feast. Margaret Hudson was amongst the guests, as were all the members of the netball team. Emma's parents were introduced to anyone they hadn't met, and then Emma led a tour of the house for those who had yet to view its finished state.

"You've done an amazing job," Paolo commented. "It looks terrific."

Others expressed similar positive sentiments. Emma was glowing as she encouraged everyone to gather in the dining room and to ensure they had a drink ready to join her in a toast. "I want to thank you all for coming tonight and for your compliments about the house. It was hard work, but the job was made easier with the help I got from so many of you. I've felt very welcome since I first moved here, and I'm so glad Amy asked me to join our netball team. Your friendship is very important to me." She smiled at the people in front of her. "And," she joked, "so are your trade skills. Thanks to Steven and David, I now have a fully functioning roof and evaporative cooler; just waiting on that guttering, Steven."

He laughed at the dig, "Hint taken, Emma."

"And Maria, thank you for helping me to deal with my uninvited visitor." Emma had kept her left hand hidden throughout this first part of the evening.

"Now, help yourselves to food; the twins are our waiters for this evening and will bring food around shortly. Drinks are in the laundry; please help yourselves if you haven't already." Surprised no toast had been proposed, the group began to drift towards the food laid out on the beautiful dining table when Emma called them to stop.

"One last thing," Ben joined Emma as she held up her left hand, displaying the beautiful ring, "we're engaged." Libby, Meredith, William and the twins clapped with gleeful enthusiasm; it was no surprise to them. The other guests remained silent.

Dismayed, Ben grabbed Emma's right hand and squeezed it. After a moment's hesitation, David stepped forward to grasp Ben's hand and hug Emma.

"It's about time someone took Ben off the shelf."

"After finding you two in your underwear, I'm not surprised," Steven laughed as he came forward to congratulate the couple. His wife wasn't so amused that her husband hadn't shared this detail, so she slapped his arm playfully.

"Why didn't you tell me?"

"I made a solemn commitment to not spill the beans," Steven spoke airily, smug that he'd finally known something that Amy hadn't.

Then Maria and Paolo added their congratulations.

"You didn't need to thank me for dealing with your 'visitor' problem, you know. All part of the service. Anyway, excellent news," Maria said as she hugged Emma.

Finished remonstrating with Steven, Amy swooped on Emma.

"Looks like we've got a permanent member of the netball team. Oh, and if you want to work next year, there's a family leave position going for the first two terms if you're interested," Amy bubbled with her usual enthusiasm.

The only reticent team member was Zoe. When the twins brought plates of sausage rolls and sandwiches around, Ben sought her out. He found her standing on the front veranda, looking out across the paddock.

"Are you alright, Zoe?"

"How long have you been together, Ben?" Zoe asked bluntly.

"Not long, Zoe, but it just seems right. Please be happy for me."

"It's hard to get my head around it. We only found out you were together after your accident, and now you're telling us you're engaged! I hope you're planning a long engagement." Disapproval was evident in every syllable Zoe uttered.

"No, we're not," admitted Ben. "The plan is to get married at the end of May."

"What! This coming May!" Zoe was incredulous." Ben, we've been mates for a very long time. I don't want to see you hurt like you were before."

"Zoe, that's ancient history; I was only twenty-two. If you are my great mate, please respect our decision," Ben spoke through thin lips. "Do you actually have any objection, other than we haven't known each other for long?"

Zoe shook her head.

"You like Emma, don't you?"

"Yes, I do," Zoe acknowledged.

"Well, so do I. I love her, and we're getting married." Ben was emphatic.

Zoe shrugged her shoulders," Okay, Ben. You've made yourself clear." And with that, she headed back into the party.

Ben stood on the veranda for a little longer, calming his thoughts before he, too, returned inside. The guests were standing around the dining table enjoying the food when Ben stepped back into the room. Seeing the look on his face, Emma excused herself from the conversation between David and Steven about the merits of a particular brand of evaporative cooler and drew Ben out of the room.

"I take it Zoe isn't very happy about our engagement. Any particular reason?"

"Only the obvious one."

Emma hugged Ben, "Five out of six netballers ain't bad," she quipped, hoping to ease the tension.

Ben felt himself relax. "You're right. And she's got time to come around before the wedding."

"It took your Mum and Dad only a few days. And she's got five months."

Later, when the party was over, and Ben and Emma lay side by side in bed, Emma returned to his conversation with Zoe.

"What's the real reason Zoe is against us marrying?" Emma wanted to be sure there wasn't more to it.

Ben took a deep breath. "When April broke up with me. I was a mess. I couldn't believe she didn't share my ambitions. We'd talked about her coming here to live with me, and she never said she wouldn't. In fairness, when I really thought about it, she never said she would, either. I was so besotted I didn't notice that she didn't share my enthusiasm for us coming here to take over the farm. When April rejected my proposal, Zoe was an incredible support; I was depressed for quite some time. She drove me to counselling appointments and was always available for a chat, no matter what time of day or night. She's just worried that'll happen again and that I won't be able to cope," he told her honestly.

Emma hugged Ben tightly, "Thank you for sharing that with me, but she has nothing to worry about. I love you, and I want to marry you."

"Show me," he whispered."

And she did.

CHAPTER 72

DAY 440 (EPILOGUE)

It was nearly Christmas again, and it was almost twelve months since Emma and Ben announced their engagement to some very surprised people.

As planned, she and Ben had married at the end of May, three weeks after his parents arrived home from their travels around Australia. It hadn't taken long for Conor and Olivia to become very fond of Emma, and they were thrilled for the two of them. The ceremony had taken place in the late afternoon in the courtyard of Ben's family home, under the arbour. Across its roof structure, the vine leaves, dressed in their autumn colours, spread golden light over the couple as they exchanged vows. The twins, their only attendants, looked especially smart in their new clothes. Tim's suit was of a similar colour and style to Ben's, and Jess's simple white dress was tied at the waist with a blue sash, which was the same colour as Ben's and Tim's ties. Emma had worn a full-length egg-shell blue silk dress which fell in soft folds from her shoulders, and she carried a posy of white roses. The guests cheered when the ceremony was over, thrilled that their friends had found each other. Even Zoe had come to accept the relationship over time; the longer she spent in the couple's company, the more her concerns fell away.

It had been cool by the time food was ready to be served, so the guests moved inside the house to enjoy the feast and listen to the speeches. The retelling of Ben's younger antics caused much amusement. The children had, of course, insisted on helping with the catering despite the half-hearted objections from the professionals. The guest numbers were quite small, but they included all of the people who were important to Emma and Ben.

Before his parents arrived home, Ben continued to live part-time at Emma's and part-time at his family home, thus supporting all the people he loved most. The bushfire of the previous December had been the only fire of the summer in their area. Still, Emma, helped by Ben, made sure she was better prepared should another bushfire event occur.

Maria had kept Emma and Ben informed of the progress of the cases against Carson and Bettina. They had both pleaded guilty to their charges. Bettina's arrest was a catalyst to her seeking help, and with Carson's financial support, she'd booked into a residential rehabilitation centre. It hadn't been an easy process for her, but she had succeeded in managing her addiction and was a regular at support meetings.

Although Carson had no conviction recorded against him, he decided to move away from the area as too many people knew what he'd done. He was too embarrassed to continue living locally. Before he was able to do that, he had many hours of community service to carry out and there were even more for Bettina. Carson had rung Emma a number of times after his arrest, but she hadn't felt ready to speak to him. She had relented recently and listened to him apologising.

"I'm so sorry, Emma. I know you must be disappointed in my behaviour. I want you to know it wasn't just about finding the papers. I actually enjoyed helping you. And to be fair to your Uncle Clive, I must admit some of the mess you encountered when you first arrived was my fault because I was so desperate to find the papers that I didn't worry about the mess I made."

Emma had thanked him for the apology but said nothing to absolve him of his guilt. She had no intention of making it easy for him.

Now, Emma was standing in the doorway of what had been Clive's bedroom, leaning down to fondle Maxie's ears. The dog looked up at her with adoring eyes. She didn't yet know that her life and everyone else's were set to change dramatically in two months.

Ben came up behind Emma and put his arms around her belly. "That's getting harder to do," he whispered.

Clive's room had undergone another transformation; it now featured two cradles, two change tables, two wardrobes stuffed full of clothes for a boy and a girl, and various toys. The walls had been lovingly painted again, this time in a pale green colour and then decorated with different motifs. They moved the new bed that Emma had bought to the end of the back veranda and erected screens to create a room for when Emma's parents came to stay. Clive's old bed was gone for good.

Emma had been very anxious early in her pregnancy, concerned that it would go the way of her first, but she knew her twins were healthy. Having reached the end of the seventh month, she felt less worry and a lot more joy.

Jess and Tim were overjoyed at the thought of another set of twins in the family. They said they were going to show them all the ropes.

Holding Ben's hand, she spoke into the room. "Thank you, Uncle Clive, for leaving me your house. I can't be certain of your motivation, but I'll be forever grateful for your legacy; it has changed my life forever."

The End

ACKNOWLEDGEMENTS

I thank Rod Grigson for his two roles in seeing this book through to publication. In 2021, I was fortunate to complete two creative writing courses Rod developed and taught locally. Both courses helped considerably in developing my writing skills. When I finished my novel, Rod took on the role of editor and publisher, for which I am very grateful.

I also want to thank my husband and sister as my 'first step' editors. Their feedback and patience (they read several different drafts) were invaluable.

ABOUT THE AUTHOR

Jane is a retired teacher who has always been passionate about reading and writing. Although she lives in outer Melbourne suburbia, Jane has a love of the Victorian countryside, having spent many school holidays on her aunts' and uncles' farms. Maxie, the dog in the story, is fictional, but Jane is definitely a 'dog' person, having grown up with dogs and owning one or two of them all her adult life. Bendigo is a real country city in central Victoria, but all the other towns mentioned are the creations of Jane's imagination.

www.ingramcontent.com/pod-product-compliance
Lightning Source LLC
Chambersburg PA
CBHW030645020726
47493CB00006B/1884